– Coming Soon –

THE ARCHON'S LEGACY: BOOK 2

THE ARCHON'S
LEGACY

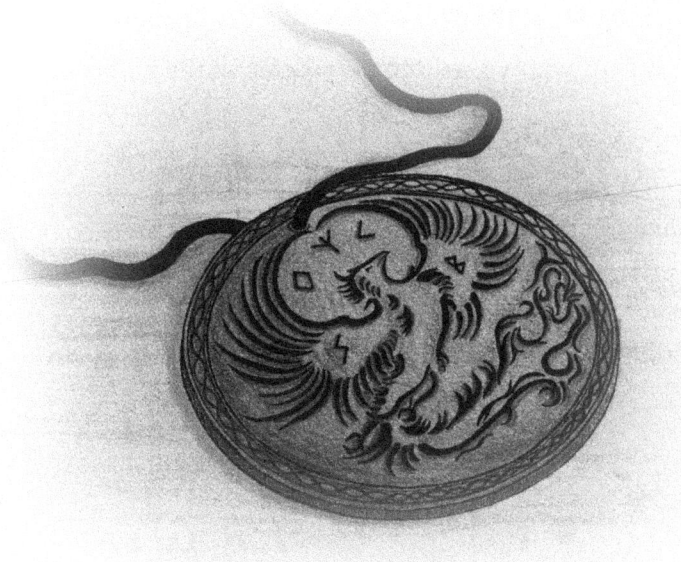

BY

GREG SCHWARTZ

ILLUSTRATIONS BY JENNIFER CARTER

Printed and Distributed in Charleston, South Carolina,
United States of America by CreateSpace,
a DBA of On-Demand Publishing, LLC.
First Paperback Edition, 2012

LCCN: 2011962400
ISBN-13: 978-1-4679-5660-4
ISBN-10: 1-4679-5660-0

Designed by Greg Schwartz

This, my first completed work, is dedicated to:

J - *Who taught me what life is about,*

R - *Who taught me to live without fear,*

H - *Who taught me to never stop dreaming,*

Al - *Who taught me that not getting what you want is sometimes a wonderful stroke of luck,*

Am - *Who taught me to be strong,*

- and -

S - *Who taught me to believe in myself.*

~CONTENTS~

Chapter One: An Average Beginning

Joshua Cooper was an ordinary young man. He was seventeen years old, very average in height, and perhaps slightly skinny. His dark, somewhat messy brown hair and blue eyes got him compliments from girls time to time at Salisbury High School, where his marks were generally quite good.

Salisbury—a city in well-to-do Wiltshire County in southern England—held around fifty thousand people, a number small enough so that most of the students knew each other quite well. Despite this, Joshua was just another teenager who blended in at school—neither bullied nor ridiculed, but not surrounded by adoring peers either.

At home he minded his own business; he did his chores, his schoolwork, and watched television in his free time. It was a constant struggle to drown out the sounds of his parents' incessant arguing, and it was because of the arguing that he seldom stayed around for dinner at his house, usually grabbing meals at one of the local pubs or a friend's house instead.

It was an unseasonably warm Friday for March in southern England, and the weather in Salisbury was no exception. A loud bell attached to the outer brick of the high school rang to signal the end of the academic day. Joshua unbuttoned his collar as he passed through the doors with the other students, grateful to taste the fresh air. He glanced over at a group of troublemakers who had obviously been there since long before classes ended playing cards on the grass nearby.

"All blue!" a particularly heavy boy with a mop of red hair exclaimed with a grin, turning his cards face up and scooping the coins in the middle. "Oy Joshie!" he added, spotting Joshua. "Fancy a hand or two?"

"No thanks," he replied, waving them off.

"Suit yourself," the boy said with a dismissive nod, and turned back to the cards.

He watched as other students flocked by him—some to the buses, others to duteous parents waiting in cars—all eager to return home so they could enjoy their two days of freedom before the dreaded Monday rolled around again.

Joshua had never enjoyed the walk home from school, for his house was directly on the other side of a less than respectable part of town, and he would have to go a great distance out of his way if he wanted to bypass it.

He refused to let his mind wander as he walked determinedly down an alley, drowning out the sounds of dogs barking and horns blaring. He briefly caught part of a conversation that two homeless men sitting against a brick wall were having—"…wireless said there's going to be a storm tonight…"—before continuing on.

Josh left the alley and turned down the cross-street, the buildings becoming less decrepit and the pavement not as cracked as he made his way toward the center of town. His mother had asked him to pick up some items at the store on his way home—a locally owned shop with large windows in the front that had NEIGHBORHOOD APOTHECARY and CIGARETTES AND LOTTO painted on them. As he entered, the shopkeeper—a wrinkled and balding, yet hospitable old man named Ned Cindley—welcomed him warmly.

"Hello there, young Mr. Cooper," he said with a smile. "What can I get for you today?"

"Milk, butter, and cheese," he replied. "Thanks."

"Oh, not at all," said Ned, walking to the refrigerator behind the counter and gathering up the items for Josh. "There's nothing else I can get for you?"

"Nope," replied Josh, pulling out a few pounds. He briefly turned to his left and looked at an old door that had a DO NOT ENTER sign on it, as it did every time he'd been in the store.

"Are you sure?" The old man smiled again, breaking Josh's reverie.

"You could tell me what's in there," he said nodding at the door and returning the smile.

"Now what would be the fun in that?" Ned laughed. "As I'm sure I've told you many times."

"A Mars bar, then," said Josh with a chuckle.

"That's the spirit," said Ned, grinning and bagging the items as Josh handed him a few notes. "There's going to be a big storm tonight."

"I heard," replied Josh, pocketing his change and picking up the bag.

"You should stay in," advised Ned. "Don't go partying like the rest of those kids."

"You know I don't," replied Josh easily. "I'll see you around."

"You too, Joshua." Ned glanced sideways at the young man for a bit before returning to his work.

Josh left the store and stepped out onto the sidewalk as the winds started to pick up around him. He looked up and saw that the once clean, blue sky had now been covered with dark clouds, threatening to spill their contents onto the world.

He quickened his pace so as not to get caught in the rain and noticed that the streets were unusually empty as he made his way home. He put it out of his mind, though, and began to think of other things, such as school and conversations he'd had with classmates. As he walked along, a dog chained to a nearby post began barking madly as if possessed, startling Josh. He turned, expecting to see a stray cat—or at the very least another dog competing for territory—but saw nothing. Indeed, the hound was barking at the air, as if there was something that only it could see. He stopped for a moment and considered trying to help the animal but was worried that it would turn on him and thought better of it.

He arrived at his house a few minutes later. It wasn't the nicest house in the world; it was on a crowded block where the walks were dirty and unkempt, and not all the street lights worked. The white paint on the exterior was peeling here and there, and the wooden porch was rotting a little, but it was home. Josh opened the door and stepped inside, kicking his shoes off as he did so. His mother liked the hardwood floors to remain clean.

"I'm home," he called out, hanging his jacket on the peg next to the door.

"Welcome home," greeted his mother, kissing him on the cheek as she walked by with some laundry under her arm. She was slightly shorter than Josh, with straight brown hair and matching eyes. "Homework?"

"Yeah, I'll be in my room," he said as his mother took the groceries with her free hand.

"Dinner's at six!" she called to him as he bounded up the stairs.

"Okay," he replied, stepping into his room and closing the door.

His room definitely looked as if a teenage boy lived there. A bed sat along the left wall with a pile of clothes massing at the foot of it. Books and movies were scattered about in various places, mostly clumped together on a small shelf above the heap of garments. There was a television on a table past the foot of the bed so that it could be watched while one was lying down. A desk was placed near his door with assorted papers strewn about on it, above which a poster for the Manchester United football club hung.

Josh sat down heavily on the chair at his desk and leaned back, looking up at the ceiling. He could hear the wind whistling outside his window, the view from which was obscured by an ill-placed tree. He glanced over, but there were no raindrops on the glass yet. Sitting up, he grabbed his book bag and pulled out a chemistry text, pushing all other thoughts out of his mind.

A few hours later his mother called for dinner, and Josh—his eyes growing weary from the pages of small type he'd been staring at—hastened downstairs, thankful for the temporary reprieve. He arrived in the dining room to find his father grumbling about the day's take at work.

"Bloody wankers keep trying to drive up the price…" Josh's father was a tall, athletic-looking man, with a strong jaw and dark brown hair; he'd played rugby in college but had blown out his left knee in a scrum and had a limp ever since. He currently worked in an upper-management position at a local department store, but it was easy to tell that he loathed his job and wished for his sport days back.

"Don't swear at the table," said Josh's mother, bringing a steaming steak and kidney pie into the dining room.

"I'll say whatever I want in my own damn house," he grumbled.

"Could you two not start for once?" asked Josh tiredly.

"Yes, sorry dear," his mother said, sitting down at the table quickly.

"How was school?" asked his father, shoveling a forkful of pie into his mouth.

"Same as always," said Josh, serving himself.

"How about that girl…wasn't her name Tricia?" inquired his mother. Josh raised an eyebrow at her.

"She was my lab partner *last year*," he replied, pushing his food around on his plate with his fork. "We're not friends."

"Oh, she seemed nice enough."

"She was horrid," said Josh flatly. "She spent most of our study time doing her nails."

"Now, that is no way to talk about your classmates—"

"Annie, leave him alone about it," said Josh's father, sighing. "If she was making him do all the work then he's right in calling her a bint." Josh looked up at his father who discreetly sent him a small wink.

"And how would *you* know what your son wants, Jacob, you're never home as it is."

"You know what," said Josh, standing and picking up his plate. "I think I'll eat upstairs."

"Oh see, now you've driven him off," said Jacob, annoyed.

"*I've* driven him off?" yelled Annie. "Well, let me tell you something Jacob Cooper…"

Josh reached his room and shut the door to block out the sounds of the argument. He finished the rest of his dinner in silence while reading his textbook, and by the time he was done the sun had completely fallen. The book was barely closed when the crash of a dish sounded from the floor below, followed by the furious footsteps of his parents coming up the stairs. He heard the door to their room slam a moment later.

Josh pinched the bridge of his nose and sighed, one of the first major arguments his parents had invading his memory.

"What the hell is wrong with you?" screeched Annie, staring at the overturned coffee table and spilt beer on the floor of the living room. Jacob had been watching a football match and when the team he'd been supporting scored, he stood up so fast that his knees hit the table and knocked it over, along with everything that was sitting on it.

"Could you not yell at me while I'm in pain?" he groaned, rubbing his bad knee.

"Oh sure, you're not the one who's going to have to clean this up!"

"Damn it, Annie, can't you be a bit more flexible for once in your miserable life?" he yelled, furious at having to defend himself while hurting.

"I should just take Joshua and leave," she spat, stalking out. "Maybe then you'd learn to take care of yourself and your belongings."

It was after that argument that Josh had started leaving on occasion—he had no desire to be a bargaining chip in his parents' fights.

An idea suddenly came to him, and he grabbed his mobile phone and dialed quickly, hoping his friend would pick up.

"Hello?"

"Hey, Dan, it's Josh," he said quickly.

"Oh hey, what's going on?"

"I know this is short notice, but do you think I could stay at your place for a night or two?"

"Um, we're actually spending the weekend in France visiting my sister's family," replied Dan. "They just got a house in Saint-Malo."

"Oh… look, my parents are at it again. Do you know anyone who could help me out?"

"Well, I guess you could come here if you want."

"Er…would that be okay?" asked Josh. "I don't want to get you in trouble."

"Nah, it'll be fine. You'll just have to find some way to get here."

"Yeah…I don't know how I'd manage that."

"Look, Saint-Malo's just across the channel. Hop a bus to Southampton and take a ferry. Give me a call when you dock and we'll come grab you."

"All right," said Josh with a sigh. He was somewhat skeptical about spending the weekend in France, but the desire to get away from his parents' arguing won out. "I owe you.

"No worries," said Dan warmly.

"I'll see you soon."

"See ya."

Josh hung up the phone and looked at his watch. It was a little after seven, and although he didn't know how late the ferries ran, he did know they wouldn't run if there was a lightning storm. The rain still hadn't started, so he quickly grabbed his backpack and peeked out the door, the sounds of his parents' raised voices coming from their room and wafting down the hall.

Tiptoeing down the stairs, he made his way into the kitchen and quickly scribbled a note explaining where he'd be and left it on the table, glancing at the shattered ceramic plate sitting on the floor nearby. Taking one last look upstairs, he grabbed his jacket, opened the front door, and stepped outside. Josh closed it quietly behind him, although privately he didn't think there was much need for discretion; his parents likely wouldn't hear the door over their argument.

Looking down the still empty lane, he hurried toward the center of town where he could find a bus. He arrived at a stop a few minutes later and sat down in the alcove, staring at a crack in the cobblestone. The flickering pale light of the streetlamp cast an ethereal glow over the corner, as tiny droplets of rain began to fall, splattering on the glass above his head.

As the minutes passed, an old man with a cane went limping by, muttering something about, "the bloody weather." He'd come and gone with plenty of time in between before the drone of a bus engine permeated the erratic beat of the drizzle, and two great headlights appeared around the corner. A green sign glowed brightly above the windshield, the letters spelling out the destination of Southampton.

"Just you, boy?" asked the driver, a wrinkle-faced elderly chap wearing a green cap and matching vest, once the bus halted and the doors had opened.

"That's right."

"Bit late to be traveling by yourself, isn't it?"

"I'm just trying to get to a friend's house," said Josh honestly. "My parents are having a row and I don't want to be there."

"All right, climb aboard, then," said the driver.

"How much do I owe you?" asked Josh, stepping onto the bus.

"Two fifty," said the driver, handing him a ticket.

"Thanks," said Josh with a grateful nod, giving him the money. He took a seat toward the back and leaned against the window. The gentle rumble of the bus was a good sedative, and it wasn't too long before he faded into an uneasy sleep.

"Joshua, come and help do the dishes," his mother said sternly.

The six-year-old slid off his chair at the table and toddled into the kitchen.

"How come I have to do chores?" he asked inquisitively as he climbed onto a stepstool in front of the sink. "None of my classmates have to."

"It's good for you to get into the habit early in life," his mother replied.

"Joshua, want to come watch the football match with your dad?" his father asked cheerfully, poking his head into the kitchen.

"Yeah!" he exclaimed, hopping down.

"Finish your chores," chastised his mother. "Then you can go watch."

"Annie, he's six," protested Jacob. "Does he really need to do housework now?"

"It's more productive than watching men on the telly," she replied shortly.

Josh's father stalked off, grumbling.

"Why are chores so important?" he asked.

"Because in a family, everyone needs to contribute and help," his mother replied, "or it all falls apart."

"Kay…"

The bus went over a large bump and woke him. He blinked and tried to push the dream he'd been having out of his head; he disliked reminiscing about any time his parents argued, but as with most things that one tries much too hard to not think about, it remained firmly planted in his mind.

"We're here, son," said the driver, pulling up to a station. "You must be tired."

"Yeah." Josh wiped at the slight drool that had accumulated at the corner of his mouth as he got up. "Can you tell me how to get to the port?"

"You're at it."

"Thanks." He nodded gratefully.

"Anytime. Be careful out there."

"I will."

Josh stepped off the bus into what was now a steady rain, and quickly ducked into the doorstep of a nearby apartment building. He watched a few cars pass by before deciding that the rain wasn't going to let up. Lifting the collar of his jacket up over his head, he jogged down the pier to the ferry station.

He paused for a moment under the awning to shake the water off himself before opening the door to the dull jingle of an old bell. The station was empty save for a very peculiar-looking woman sitting behind the counter reading a magazine. She looked to be in her late-fifties, and was wearing at least a dozen ornate rings on both her hands that clinked whenever she turned a page. She also had enough eye shadow on that one might've thought she'd just been in a fistfight. Josh thought she looked rather like a raccoon.

"Can I help you?" she asked, not looking up.

"I need a ticket to Saint-Malo, please," said Josh, rummaging through his pockets for some quid.

"We don't service the mainland," she replied.

"You...you don't?" asked Josh, taken aback.

"No, the nearest ferry to Saint-Malo is in Portsmouth."

"But that's at least another twenty-five miles from here," said Josh worriedly.

"That's not my problem, now, is it?" she asked, peering over the top of the magazine at him.

Josh didn't say anything. He was too disappointed to reply. Instead he headed back outside, deciding it would be better to grab a bus back home than spend the night wandering the streets of a city he didn't know too well.

He walked over to the bus stop and looked at the schedule that was pinned up on the side of the Plexiglas shelter. The next bus wasn't due for another hour and a half. Looking around, Josh was about to sit down on the bench when he spotted a flickering sign reading MCCLEARY'S PUB AND GRILL.

He decided he could use a little more to eat and covered up, stepping back out into the rain and jogging down the street. Upon reaching the bulky wooden door, he heaved it open and hurried inside.

The pub had a musty smell to it. Dimly lit lamps above the bar were visible through a fog of tobacco smoke—almost all the patrons were smoking in one form or another. All the tables were occupied, so Josh walked up to an empty stool at the wooden counter and sat down.

"You're kinda young to be in here," said the barkeep, polishing a glass.

"I'm just looking for something to eat," said Josh. "I won't be any trouble."

"All right," he said, reaching under the bar and grabbing a menu. "Here."

"Thanks."

"You look a little lost," said the man sitting on Josh's left. "What's a lad like yourself doing in a pub like this?"

Josh looked up and saw that the man was rather large; he had a scruffy gray beard and a thick accent. His face looked as if he'd seen much more than one should in a lifetime. He was wearing an old, beaten button-down shirt, and a large, yellow raincoat was draped over his shoulders. "Bad luck," Josh replied. "If you can call it that."

"I understand completely," said the man.

"Decided on what you want?" asked the barkeep.

"Fish and chips, please?" asked Josh politely. "And a water?"

"Coming right up."

"How about you?" Josh asked the stranger, deciding to make conversation. "Why are you here?"

"I got nowhere better to be," he said, picking at the food on his plate.

"You don't have a family?" asked Josh.

"Nah…my wife passed away a long time ago."

"Sorry…" said Josh sheepishly.

"It's all right, you couldn't have known."

"Still, though, I shouldn't assume things. After all, the Yanks say that assuming makes an ass out of you and me."

The man laughed. "They teach you that in school?"

"Mrs. Harmon, my fifth-grade teacher," said Josh with a chuckle. The barkeep placed a glass of water in front of him. "Thanks."

"Your meal will be right up," replied the bartender, nodding.

"Schools," said the stranger, taking a long pull from his lager. "I never went to University. The sea's been my home for nearly thirty years now."

"You're a fisherman?" asked Josh curiously.

"Tha's right," replied the man, wiping his mouth on his sleeve and turning to face Josh properly. "Name's Thomas Patrey."

"Josh Cooper," he replied, shaking the man's extended hand.

"Where're you from?"

"Salisbury."

"So what are you really doing out here, then? Southampton isn't the closest place in the world to Salisbury."

"My…my parents fight every day. I was trying to get to my friend in Saint-Malo—he said I could stay there for the weekend. Thanks," he added as his food was placed in front of him.

"Enjoy," said the barkeep with a smile.

"Yeah, there aren't any ferries outta here anymore," said Tom as Josh dove into his meal.

"I wonder why tha' ifs," commented Josh through a mouthful of food.

"I couldn't tell you," he replied, draining his stein. "But I'll tell ya what," he added, looking at his watch. "If you want, I'll ferry you over there."

"Tonight?" asked Josh, swallowing another mouthful. "Isn't it dangerous in this weather?"

"Maybe for someone who doesn't know what they're doing," he answered with a shrug.

Josh thought about this for a few moments. Every bit of common sense he possessed advised against the move, but for some reason, this man didn't seem like the malicious type.

"You'd really get me over there? You don't mind?"

"Normally, I wouldn't offer, but you seem like you could use a break," said Tom. "I've been there myself."

"I really appreciate it," said Josh gratefully.

"We should get going, though. I don't fancy being out on the water too late at night…or too early in the morning."

"Right," he agreed, waving over the barkeep. "Can I have a box for this?"

"Sure," the man replied, pulling out a Styrofoam container and placing it on the bar in front of Josh.

"How much do I owe you?"

"Just fish and chips? That'll be four fifty."

"Here's five," said Josh, placing a five-pound note on the bar, and scooping the rest of his meal into the box.

"Thanks, have yourself a good night," said the man.

"You too."

"Let's go, then," said Tom, feeding his arms into the sleeves of his yellow coat and straightening it over his shoulders. He opened the door of the pub, and Josh pulled the collar of his jacket up as they stepped outside into the rain. They set off down the road, walking briskly so as to not get drenched. "We're lucky my boat's close…this weather is a bloody pain in the arse."

"Yeah," he agreed. They hurried to the docks, and Tom led them over to a large gray ship, floating about peacefully in the water despite the rain.

"The *Iron Princess*," said Tom proudly. "Been my boat for almost twenty years."

"She's big," Josh replied, squinting up at the mast. It had to be at least thirty feet tall.

"Let's get in the cabin and out of this mess," he said, unraveling the mooring line from the iron peg on the dock. They hurried inside and up to the bridge, where Tom took off his coat and threw it on a nearby chair.

"You sure we'll be all right?" asked Josh, shaking himself dry.

"Course," replied Tom. "I've sailed in storms far worse than this." He pressed the igniter and the engines rumbled to life.

"Do you need me to do anything?" asked Josh.

"Nope, I can handle her myself," said Tom, steering the ship out of port.

"You don't fish alone, do you?"

"Nah, but my crew and I just came back from a two-week-long trip out to the ocean, so they're all enjoying their days off."

"You catch anything real big?" asked Josh.

"Nothing for the record books," he answered, pushing the throttle up, "but it was a good haul."

"Can't see a thing out there," said Josh, looking out the windows.

"Not much to see," said Tom. "Here." He flipped a switch to his left, and a massive flood lamp from high up on the mast flickered to life and shone a pale yellow light out over the choppy waters.

A large wave hit the boat and tilted the floor, sending Josh into the far wall on the left.

"Careful lad!" exclaimed Tom, coming over and picking him up off the floor. "Gotta get you some sea legs."

"Yeah…I wasn't expecting that," said Josh, shaking himself off.

"Always hold on to something," advised Tom. "I don't want you to get hurt."

"Right." Josh carefully grabbed onto the underside of one of the control panels, making sure to get a firm grip before letting his mind wander again. Lighting forked against the black sky in the far distance, briefly illuminating the water for a split second. "It's actually kind of pretty," he commented.

"The lightning?" asked Tom. "You should see it way out on the ocean—makes the whole sea light up like a flashbulb."

"What's it like out there?" asked Josh. "The middle of the ocean?"

"Usually it's nothing special," replied Tom as the ship went over another wave. Josh hung on and kept his balance. "But anything can happen."

"Like what?"

"I've seen a wave fifty feet high, a whale just as long, and some other stuff you wouldn't even consider believing if I told you about."

"Go on, tell me," urged Josh, eager to hear more.

"Well, about twenty five years ago—"

Whatever story Tom was about to impart to Joshua was cut off, for a massive bolt of blue and white lightning cracked into the sea not a hundred feet in front of them. The accompanying clap of thunder shook the whole ship and knocked both of them to the ground as the water roared up with fury in response to the assault from above.

"Bloody weather!" cursed Tom, straightening himself behind the helm. "You don't see that every day."

"Is everything all right?" asked Josh, grabbing onto a pipe along the wall and pulling himself to a standing base.

His question was answered for him as he looked out over the black water. The light from the mast illuminated a spot in front of the ship where the water disappeared from sight, the currents forming a spiraling funnel into the depths of the ocean.

"Tom?" he asked, a tinge of panic in his voice. When there was no response, he turned to see the older fisherman standing rooted in place, his eyes narrow and calculating, mumbling something under his breath. "What is that?"

"Nothing good," he muttered, not offering any other information.

"Um…what…what are we going to do?" The ship was drawing ever closer to the edge, and although Josh wasn't a mariner, he felt pretty sure that once one got caught in a vortex, you weren't getting out.

"We're not going to be able to go around it," muttered Tom again. "Look." He pointed out the side windows of the bridge, and Josh could see large waves crashing down on either side—waves large enough to overturn the ship if they tried to navigate them.

"Can you get us through this?" asked Josh as another bolt of lightning hit nearby, sending him to the deck. Tom, however, stayed standing this time, focused and driven as he revved the throttle to squeeze every bit of power out of the churning engines.

"Depends on what you mean by 'through,'" he replied, as the ship reached the precipice of the swirling waters. "If you mean across and out the other side, no."

Josh looked up at him from the floor of the bridge as waves crashed into the windows and distorted the view out into the night, while drops of water fell from the ceiling onto their heads.

"But there's another way."

Tom ripped open the top few buttons of his shirt and grabbed what looked like a small crystal hanging on a chain around his neck. Josh scrambled to his feet and watched in confusion as Tom began chanting at a high speed, a pale light beginning to glow from the nadir of the funnel. Josh looked around and saw little spots of light had appeared all around them—both in and outside of the ship—like tiny shards of diamond illuminating the night sky.

"Hang on to something, lad—we're about to go for a ride."

Josh barely had time to look back at Tom to ask what he was talking about, when the ship plunged headfirst into the light, and everything went black.

Chapter Two: A World of Wonder

"Do you think he's alive?"

"He dun look alive."

"Move over."

Warm, gentle hands touched Josh's forehead and he slowly felt his strength returning. Opening his eyes, he saw three people gathered around him, though his vision was blurry he and couldn't make them out very well.

"Good," a female voice said, and the hands left his skin. "I'm going to make some tea, make sure he rests."

"Where...who—" began Josh, but was cut off.

"Ye heard the girl, get sum rest," another voice said. "We'll explain everything later."

And Josh did just that.

When he came to, he was alone. The room was fairly dark, but a soft light was coming in from the edges of what he assumed was a covered window. Swinging his feet over the edge, he realized his shoes were gone, and that the floor was, in fact, dirt. He also wasn't wearing his clothes but something rather like pajamas.

"Where am I?" asked Josh quietly. At that moment, the door opened and a middle-aged man wearing what looked like a straw hat and a pair of blue overalls entered. He was fairly tall and well built, and carried himself with a sense of pride.

"Oh good, yer up," he said. His voice was scratchy but not harsh, and he had the presence of a man who'd seen a lot of troubles but knew how to take them in stride. "Lie back down, I'll bring ye sum tea." And he left without another word.

Despite his apprehension, Josh did as he was told, partially because the bed was so comfortable.

It didn't take long for the man to return, carrying a tray with a pot of steaming water and two mugs. He sat down in a chair next to the bed and handed one of them to Josh, who looked on as the man set the tray on the floor. He noted that there were some crushed herbs in the bottom of his mug.

"Watch yerself, it's hot," he said, pouring some water from the pot. The water turned a pleasant golden color and began to emanate a glorious scent of apples and cinnamon. "Drink up."

Josh took a tentative sip and made a face as he swallowed.

"I'm afraid it doesn't taste as good as it smells." The man smiled as Josh coughed. "But it'll do wonders for yer health."

"What is it?" he asked, taking another distasteful sip.

"Mandrogal root," the man said.

"Um…sorry?"

"Dun worry about it," said the man with a laugh. "Jus' drink."

"I don't mean to be rude," said Josh, "but who are you?"

"Me name's Wester," he replied simply, pouring water into the second mug. "Who're ye?"

"Joshua Cooper. Where am I?"

"You're in the village of Kendrall," said a young woman, coming into the room. She had a gentle voice, sparkling blue eyes, and flowing brown hair that fell to her lower back. She was wearing a plain blue dress and had the same aura of pride and resolution that the older man did.

"Ah," said the man, standing up. "This is Arya, my daughter. Ye can thank her cuz she's tha one that saved yer life."

"Father," she blushed, slightly embarrassed. Josh hid his grin behind his mug.

"I have to tend to the fields," said Wester, standing up. "She'll take care of ye."

"Thanks," said Josh with a nod. Wester left, squeezing his daughter's shoulder on the way out.

"How are you feeling?" she asked, sitting next to him on the bed.

"Pretty good," he replied, holding up the mug of tea. "Don't care much for this stuff, though."

"No one does," she agreed. "I wish I could find a way to make it taste better, but it's not that simple."

"You made this?" he asked, raising an eyebrow. Arya nodded. "Er…sorry."

"Not at all," she laughingly replied. "I've had to drink it myself a few times, so I know what it's like." Josh grimaced as he drank the last few dregs. "Have another." She smiled as she handed him the second mug.

"Ugh," groaned Josh, accepting it.

"You need it," she said as he took a sip. "I'm a bit surprised you lived, actually."

"Was I that bad?"

"Yes…one of my father's friends found you washed up on the bank of the Tiras River and brought you back here, not a minute too soon either."

"The what river?" asked Josh. "What is this place?"

"You're not the first person to wash up on our shores," said Arya gently. "You're a long way from home."

"This isn't France?" he asked stupidly.

I've never heard of France," she replied sympathetically. "You're in a place called Lumenaria."

"Say what?" asked Josh, blinking. Arya held out her hand.

"You'll understand better if you follow me." Josh took her hand and stood up, wobbling slightly for the first few steps. "Easy now," she said, leading him out of the bedroom. He found himself in a larger room with a table and some wooden stools. A small counter was against the back wall, over which various pots and pans hung. In the corner there was a brick oven and a small fire with a large black pot hanging above it. He could see some stairs leading up to the next floor and a large grandfather clock standing next to them. Looking around, Josh realized that he wasn't in a house but a wooden cottage. Golden light was flooding in from an open door leading outside, casting a very bright and warm glow over them. "This way."

She led him to the entrance and Josh's mouth fell open at what he saw.

A lush green landscape lay before them. Meadows and farmland stretched all the way to great mountains rising in the distance. A nearby road led to a cluster of buildings with a small forest on one side. The village looked to be about a mile away, and far beyond that sat a great castle. The most notable feature of the new environment, though, was the shimmering specks of light scattered about the air; the same tiny sparkles that Josh had seen right before the *Iron Princess* went into the maelstrom.

"Lumenaria," said Arya again with a smile, gesturing with her arm. "Wait until you see it at night."

"Did you find anyone else with me?" asked Josh, his mind momentarily wandering toward Tom. "Or a backpack, anything else?"

"No, just you and the clothes you were wearing," she said, confused. "Why?"

"Nothing," muttered Josh, hoping at least that wherever the fisherman was, he was all right. "Speaking of which, where are my clothes?"

"Drying on the line out back. We had to get you out of them or you'd have caught your death from cold."

"Thanks, then, I guess."

A nearby sparkle caught his eye and he held out his hand to catch it. Upon closer inspection he saw that it was actually a tiny grain of illuminated dust.

"What is it?" he asked, looking at Arya as it floated out of his palm.

"Essence," she answered, looking out at the landscape. "Life, for lack of a better term."

"I don't understand."

"Here," she said, holding her arm out in front of her. "I'll show you."

A small breeze picked up and Josh saw some of the nearby particles of Essence slowly move toward them. Silver light glowed softly from Arya's outstretched palm as the air began to materialize.

"What are you—"

"Shh," she hushed. "Wait for a second."

The shining spots of light began to spin around and converge, and a moment later there was a silver figurine of a horse sitting in her hand, the shimming Essence engrained into it like glitter.

"Here," said Arya with a smile as she handed it to Josh. "A present."

"Thanks," he said in awe, taking it. It felt soft and malleable, opposed to metallic. Despite that, it was quite sturdy, and the detail was so entrancing that when Arya coughed he jumped. "How'd you do that?"

"Most everyone here can," she replied. "It takes practice, but we can all manipulate the environment when we need to."

"Can I?" he asked, looking at the horse with intrigue.

"Maybe," she said, encouragingly. "There's actually someone we can see who could help you with that, but he lives a long way from here."

"I see."

"Don't tell my father I made that for you," she added sheepishly, nodding at the horse in Josh's palm. "We're not supposed to use Essence unless we have to."

"How come?"

"It's not limitless," she replied. "It does regenerate over time, but it's still not good to waste it."

"This place," he said, staring out at the landscape. "You weren't kidding that I'm a long way from home, were you?"

"I wasn't," said Arya with an apologetic look. A sudden wave of estrangement hit Josh, and he turned away from her, putting a hand against the door frame.

"I think I need to lie down," he said, stumbling back toward the first room.

"Are you all right?" asked Arya concernedly, following him.

"I just need some rest," he lied, climbing into the bed.

Arya hesitated for a moment before nodding. "I'll be out in the field behind the cottage if you need anything."

"Thanks."

"If it makes you feel better, I haven't heard of anyone who was *stuck* here," she said softly. There was a tinge of sadness in her voice. "Everyone always finds a way home." And she closed the door behind her as she left.

Joshua lay in the bed for what seemed like an eternity. Her parting words had left him feeling melancholic inside—he loved his family and didn't hate school or his friends, but the strange world he was currently a part of seemed much more friendly and mystical than Salisbury ever had. He wanted to stay, but at the same time he wanted everyone back home to know he was safe. For all he knew they could be worried sick and have Scotland Yard looking for him.

He looked at the horse Arya had made again—it awed him, the way those little spots of light just melded into the body of the animal and gave it an ethereal shine. It also calmed him a little—Arya didn't seem like a bad person, and he owed his life to her, along with her father and whoever his friend was.

Deciding that the best plan of action would be to repay her and her father as best he could, then try to find a way home, he stood and made to apologize for his abrupt exit earlier.

He emerged from the room to see Wester sitting at the table with a plate of food in front of him and Arya standing at the fire cooking something.

"Are you feeling any better?" she asked.

"A bit," said Josh, rubbing the back of his neck. "Sorry for running out on you like that…I was just shocked."

"Eh, yer not the first," said Wester warmly. He had his hat off, revealing a scraggly mane of silver hair that was matted down on top of his head. "It's a pretty place though, innit?"

"It is," agreed Josh.

"Want some food, lad?"

"Yeah, actually, I'm starving," he replied as Wester pulled out a chair for him. "Thank you."

"Not at all." Arya placed a plate in front of Josh with a single roll on it, although the roll was quite big. "Try it," continued Wester. "It's quite good." Josh took a bite and was surprised to find a sweet, creamy filling inside.

"It's delicious," he said. "What is it?"

"Special family recipe," winked Arya. "It's a bit tricky to make, but I've had a lot of practice."

"Well ifs grate," Josh managed to say, his mouth full.

"Much better than the tea, eh?" joked Wester, nudging Joshua as he finished his own dinner. "I'll be out with Isaac. Take care of everything, will ye, Ari?"

"Of course, Father," she said with a nod as he got up and pecked her on the cheek before heading out. "Isaac is the man who found you," she added once Wester had gone. "He and my father go out drinking from time to time."

"Not too much, I hope," said Josh, briefly thinking about how his own father had come home stumbling over his own feet once. Arya walked to the table, took her father's dishes, and placed them in a stone basin that was filled with water.

"I have to take care of him every once in a while," she said, the corners of her mouth turning up slightly. "But I would never fault him for it."

"How come?"

"He's been like that ever since my mother was killed," she replied softly.

"I'm…I'm sorry," said Josh, looking away.

"It's all right," said Arya, straightening up. "It was a long time ago…and you couldn't have known in any case."

"How'd it happen, if you don't mind me asking?" he asked, finishing off his bun.

"I don't mind," she answered, "but perhaps it's a story best suited for another time, not during dinner." Josh nodded, not wanting to press the issue. "How was it, by the way?"

"Very good, thanks," he answered, standing as she collected his plate and put it in the basin.

"Here," said Arya, grabbing a small bottle from the counter and pouring some of its contents into a stein before handing it to him. "Dessert." Josh took it and looked at the liquid: a bright, red, syrupy mixture. "It's nothing like the tea, I promise," she added, smiling.

He took a sip and immediately decided it was his new favorite dessert. It tasted like a mixture between raspberries and chocolate and had the texture of a very fine cream.

"This is brilliant," his voice echoed into the mug, taking another sip without hesitation.

"Thank you," said Arya with a smile, pouring a cup for herself. "If you're feeling up for it, we can go to the roof so I can properly show you the land and answer any questions you might have."

"Sure," agreed Josh with a shrug, feeling that he should at least get to know the place, no matter when he was going to end up leaving. They finished their desserts and Arya placed the empty mugs in the basin with the other dishes before motioning for him to follow her.

They ascended the iron spiral staircase and passed the second floor—which was simply a landing with one door on each side—before reaching a window at the top.

"Watch your head," said Arya, opening the window and leading them out onto the roof. Josh noted that it wasn't made of straw or wood but instead a smooth, tan leather he didn't recognize. "Mastrichon hide," she said when she saw him staring at it. "Very durable."

"Cool," said Josh, climbing out onto the roof with her. The sun was setting and cast a beautiful pink hue all across the horizon.

"I'm sorry?" she asked.

"Huh?"

"You said 'cool,'" she replied. "Is it cold to you?"

"Oh, no. Um…where I come from, 'cool' means that I think it's interesting," he explained.

"How very strange." She chuckled, standing up on the slanted roof. "All right, are you ready?"

"Yeah," said Josh, holding on to her shoulder to steady himself.

"Okay," she began. "Everything you see right in front of you is Ageria."

"Ageria," he repeated.

"It's mostly meadows, farmland, scattered groves, and small forests," she explained. "But there are plenty of villages. Almost everyone in Lumenaria lives somewhere here. It stretches for a while in all directions around us, all the way to the sea in the west and the mountains in the north. See them?" she asked, pointing at the mountain range Josh had seen earlier. He nodded. "That's the Endless Rise—a mountain range that goes on forever."

"Forever?" asked Josh.

"For a long while, anyway," she amended. "The rivers start somewhere up there and flow all the way down here and out to the sea. There are a lot of caves in the mountains with valuable crystals, so it's a pretty popular area among miners and archons and such."

"Archons?"

"The archons are an elite group of people who research new and more effective ways to use Essence. They're also extremely talented and well trained in combat and serve on the front lines whenever battle comes."

"Battle?" Although it didn't surprise him, Josh had inwardly been hoping that the evils of humanity had stayed away from this place.

Arya sighed. "Fortunately for you, you've arrived while we're at peace, but it wasn't always like this. There was a rampant war all across this province since before I can remember until I was about eleven."

"How old are you?"

"Eighteen," she replied stoically. "These past seven years have been wonderful, but anyone who's been around long enough will tell you it's just a matter of time."

"I see."

"You can ask my father, if you're curious," said Arya, stretching. "He's fought countless times for our land."

"Wow," said Josh softly. It made sense—Wester might have been getting along in years, but his air of confidence definitely gave him a refinement that made him seem much stronger than his physical appearance would actually suggest.

"You can't see them from here, but to the northeast are the Veran Hills," continued Arya. "All of our sport happens over there—the hills make good terrain for the grandstands and playing arenas."

"You have sports here?"

"Just one," said Arya. "Kingball. The rules are fairly complicated, but it's played around a large floating cube made of reinforced glass and inside a giant crystal sphere. There's a ball inside the sphere, and the object is to goal the ball in a hole at the top of the cube."

"It's played with teams?"

"Teams of seven each."

"How do the players get to the top?"

Arya smiled. "Essence. The matches are the only time that recreational use of Essence is sanctioned. It's quite something to watch."

"I'll bet," replied Josh.

"If you stick around long enough, you might even get to see a game," she continued. "Isaac—my father's friend—is the coach for one of the teams."

"Definitely."

"Anyway, beyond the hills is our prison, Synax," she said, her tone slightly subdued.

"Prison?"

"Some people here aren't as friendly as my family, I'm afraid," she said, frowning slightly. She continued on, obviously eager to change the subject. "In any case, to the south are the Sarcosian Salt Flats. The archons do a lot of their research and combat training in the flats where there's lots of space and not much they can damage."

"They damage things?"

"By accident, of course," replied Arya with a chuckle. "Most of them are very ambitious, so every once in a while one of them will devise a brand new way to use Essence and blow something up by mistake."

"How many ways *can* you use Essence?"

"Oh, there are so many—farming, medicine, craftsmanship...war..." She shrugged. "What the archons research is new methods to use and amplify it for combat purposes, although sometimes they come up with something that benefits all of us."

"Cool," said Josh, and Arya chuckled again.

"If you *do* watch a match of kingball, you'll see just how many different ways it can be used."

"So, what's that castle?" asked Josh, pointing at the towering, white structure to the northwest.

"That's the tower in the fortress at Danthian, our Grand Capital. It's actually a whole city; you just can't see the smaller buildings from here. The coast is beyond it and runs all the way from the Endless Rise to the flats." She paused for a moment. "Danthian is where we'll have to go to find someone who can help you get home—and where you'll learn to use Essence if you want."

"Okay," he said, absorbing as much of the information as he could. "You said this was a province. Are there other provinces out there?"

"There are, but we don't have much contact with them," she replied. "And you have to cross some nasty places to get to them."

"Oh?"

"The only two ways out of this province by land are over a mountain pass to the south or crossing a ravine in the east," she said. "Neither are particularly easy to get to, and in the east, past Synax, there's a forest that had to be walled off from Ageria because of the Nether in there."

"Nether?"

"Nether is the opposite of Essence," she explained. "You could say that if Essence is related to life, then Nether is related to death."

"Oh," said Josh, with some trepidation.

"You're right to be nervous," said Arya perceptively. "Essence and Nether have twisted and merged in there and created some nasty things."

"So, the next province is beyond that?"

"In a word, yes," said Arya, nodding. "The only gap in the mountains is guarded by a very large and dangerous chasm. To even make it there, you have to journey through the Deadlands, a wasteland that, as the name might lead you to believe, is devoid entirely of both Essence and Nether."

"How'd that happen?"

"In the last war there was a tremendous battle fought there," she replied, looking off into the distance. "There was an extremely powerful and zealous archon named Necanshin Desmarthe who disobeyed his Essence Restraint Order—orders given to limit how much Essence can be used at once—and in his frenzy overloaded the area by accident."

"Like filling a balloon with too much air?" asked Josh.

"Exactly. Anyway, he was the only one who survived. The explosion ripped the Essence in that whole area apart and turned it into the barrens that it is today."

"What happened to him?"

"Well, he was sentenced to death, but he had a lot of friends in high places and weaseled it down to exile for life. To prevent him from using Essence again, an underground prison was built in the heart of the Deadlands and he's been locked up there ever since."

Arya shrugged at the look of awe on Josh's face.

"I think he gets his food and water from old apprentices who are still faithful to him," she said. "I heard that the higher-ups in the government planned on him rotting in that cell, but he'd trained his followers very well and they figured out a way to keep him comfortable, not just alive."

Josh shook his head. "Wow."

"Look, there's Father and Isaac," she said, pointing at the curvy dirt road. A pair of figures on horseback were riding toward them from the cluster of buildings.

"Is that part of…Kendrall, was it?"

"Yes, that's the village center. We should go downstairs…Father doesn't like it when I come up here."

"Why not?" asked Josh.

"I imagine for the same reason that most loving fathers would give their daughters—he doesn't want me to fall and get hurt."

She climbed back through the window and down the stairs, Josh following carefully behind her.

They arrived in the kitchen just as Wester and Isaac came riding up the road on a pair of toffee-colored stallions. Arya went out to meet them and Josh tentatively followed, unsure of how to behave around the other man.

"Ah!" exclaimed Isaac, dismounting flawlessly from his horse. "You're up and about. Wester said you were faring better."

"Yes, thank you," replied Josh gratefully, shaking Isaac's outstretched hand.

He was an older gentleman, although his wrinkles hadn't deepened as much as Wester's. A mane of shaggy hair, a sandy-blond hue, covered his broad shoulders and his upper back. It was easy to see why this man was the head of a sports team, and Josh guessed he'd probably played the sport in years past. Given the way his shirt bulged, he could also probably lift the stallion he'd just ridden in on.

"Ari, take care of the horses fer me?" asked Wester, also hopping off his steed.

"Of course, Father." He gave her a quick hug before nodding warmly at Josh and heading inside. "Would you like to see the farm?" she asked, turning to Josh.

"See ya in a bit," said Isaac, touching the tip of his fingers to his brow in an impromptu salute.

"The stable's around back," she continued, taking the bridles and leading the horses gently around the cottage.

"Isaac seems nice enough," commented Josh once they were away from the door.

"He's an uncle to me," said Arya. "After my mother died, he helped my father get up and out of the house again—and helped me tend the fields when my father was grieving."

"Looks pretty strong."

Arya laughed at that. "He's one of the strongest men in the province." She smiled. "He played kingball in the years before the last war and then served directly under an archon during battle."

"You said that the other provinces are really hard to get to, right?" asked Josh as they reached the back of the house. There were great fields with rows of crops in the ground, and about two hundred feet away, a small, wooden stable with a hay roof. "If they're so hard to get to, how do they attack you?"

"We don't war against other provinces," answered Arya slowly. "Every once in a while someone will end up stumbling into some place where there's exposed Nether. It does great and horrible things to humans if it doesn't kill you."

"Like what?"

"Well, the last war was started by an ex-archon named Seras who had been convicted of conspiring to commit murder and treason, and was thrown in Synax," she explained. "He escaped the prison and fled into the forest, and instead of mutating him or destroying him, the Nether fused with the Essence in his body and made him powerful. Very powerful."

"So what happened?" asked Josh as they reached the stable. There were several more horses residing quietly inside, their attention all shifting to Arya when she and Josh entered.

"He used his new powers to breed an army of monsters in the forest…beasts spawned from Nether…mutated, strong, bloodthirsty."

"One man made war with the whole province?"

"He had help, of course," Arya responded with a shrug. She took the saddles and bridles off of the horses and tethered them into the stable. Reaching toward a nearby shelf, she took two brushes and handed one to Josh. "Want to give me a hand?"

"Sure," he replied. "What should I do?"

"Just be gentle," she answered with a smile, starting to brush the horse Wester had been riding.

Josh tentatively began to brush his horse, and was pleased when it didn't complain at his touch.

"There were plenty of students at the academy learning under him who were loyal apprentices, and they joined him in the forest when they learned of his escape," she continued.

"What's the academy?"

"The Royal Academy of Danthian," said Arya with a dramatic flourish. "It's where one goes to become an archon."

"Ah. So what happened to Seras's followers?" asked Josh.

"They were all either killed or captured," said Arya, putting some grain and water down for each of the animals. "When Seras was killed, the strength of all his creations and followers diminished greatly and they were overtaken."

"Oh."

"My mother was killed by him," she added softly, looking at the sky, which was growing pink.

"I'm sorry, I wouldn't have asked so many questions—"

"Again, you didn't know," she said, waving him off. "She was a wonderful woman. We used to play hide-and-seek in these fields when I was young. She'd always let me win, even though she could see me over the rows."

Josh put his hands in his pockets as they began walking back to the cottage. He couldn't bring himself to say anything as a lone tear fell down Arya's cheek. A gentle breeze picked up around them, warm and comforting. He watched thoughtfully as she closed her eyes and let the soft wind wash over her.

"She's always with me," said Arya softly, opening her eyes a moment later and turning to Josh. "Come on, we should get back. Father and Isaac probably want me to cook something for them."

"Dinner wasn't too long ago," commented Josh, still feeling content from the meal earlier.

"No, but they eat like men possessed." She managed a laugh, though her eyes were still slightly red. Josh discreetly watched her as they continued walking. She kept a very strong front, but he had the feeling there was more to it than that.

The sounds of manly laughter came wafting from the open window as they drew closer.

"D'you remember when tha' poor bastard tried to cure himself wit' only eight fingers?" roared Wester.

"War stories," whispered Arya to Josh as Isaac's laughter reached their ears.

"Do I? I was right next to the lad!" He laughed as Josh and Arya entered. "Kid had red spots on his face for a month!"

"Great big ones like hornberries, right?" interjected Arya, announcing their presence.

"Too right, too right," said Isaac, shaking his head and grinning.

"Could ya fix us up somethin' to eat?" Wester asked his daughter.

"Of course—sit," she commanded to Isaac, who had risen to help. He bashfully held up his hands in defense.

"Oh, Arya, when are you going to stop being so hard on me?" he said with feigned exasperation, sitting back down.

"When your team stops losing," she replied, sticking her tongue out at him.

"Now that hurt," he complained, frowning playfully as Josh laughed and sat down. "So, my lad—Josh, right?" Josh nodded with a smile. "What has Arya told you about the place?"

"A lot," he answered as Arya busied herself at the stove. "She told me about your sport. Kingball, was it?"

"Yeah," said Isaac chuckling, although there was a trace of trepidation in his voice. "Great game."

"What's funny?" asked Josh. Isaac gave Wester a look as if to say, "*spare me*," but Wester would have none of it.

"As Ari said quit' eloquently, his team's been in a losing stretch lately," he replied with a snort.

"S'not my fault," grumbled Isaac. "I'm coaching a bunch of slackers."

"How exactly is it played?" asked Josh. "Arya told me that there's a cube inside a sphere—"

Isaac held up a toughened hand to stop him.

"I could explain it to you, but you need a better knowledge of how Essence works before you'd really understand it," he said. "And actually watching a game would do wonders."

"I'd love to see one," commented Josh.

"Rainer's team has a match in a few days," said Isaac, glancing at Wester. "I can probably wrangle some seats out of him if you want."

"Should be good," said Wester.

"It should work out perfectly, actually," said Arya, walking over to the table with three plates of something meaty, brown, and steaming hot. "We need to go to Danthian, anyway."

"Why's that?" asked Isaac.

"Joshua would like to find out if he can go home, and if he can use Essence."

"Tha' righ', lad?" asked Wester, turning to him.

"Yeah," replied Josh, rubbing the back of his neck. "I don't know how long I'll be here, so I want to learn everything I can about this world."

"You're going to see Luther, then," stated Isaac.

"Who's Luther?" asked Josh as Arya nodded.

"The only man still here who isn't from here," replied Arya.

"Oh? Where's he from?"

"Um, someplace wit' an *L*," mused Wester. "Lumbon...Lundow..."

"London?" asked Isaac, and Josh's eyes went wide.

"Yeh," said Wester with a nod, pointing at Isaac. "Tha' was it."

Chapter Three:
The Grand Capital Danthian

A twelve-year-old Joshua stood in front of the hospital bed that his father was lying in. Various tubes and wires were connected to the thirty-four-year-old man's body and face in several places, hooked up to computers and monitors that beeped and whirred at random times.

"I've always told you to pay more attention in the car," said Annie, who was standing next to Josh. She sighed.

"The wanker T-boned me while I was stopped at a light," said Jacob weakly. "What was I supposed to do?"

"I'm going to the cafeteria to get some coffee," she replied, not answering him. "Stay with your father, Joshua."

Josh nodded as his mother left the room.

"Are you okay, Dad?" he asked, sitting in a chair next to the bed.

"The doctors say I'll be fine," he replied with a pained smile. "Just a few broken ribs and a concussion."

"What's a concussion?"

"It's when your brain gets bumped hard," replied Jacob. "Makes you feel rotten, and can do bad things to you if not watched properly."

"Okay…so why was Mum mad at you again?"

"She wasn't mad," said Jacob heavily, putting his hand on Josh's shoulder. "She's just upset and isn't handling it very well. She doesn't, in most cases."

"I don't get it, if you're going to be fine, why is she upset?"

"Well, she loves me," he replied with a shrug. "And I love her. It's a hard thing to watch someone you love get hurt."

"It doesn't seem like you guys love each other sometimes."

"Do you mean that, Joshua?" asked Jacob, his tone laden with sadness. Josh nodded. "Don't ever think that. We love each other...we just show it in strange ways."

"Why do you always fight, then?" he asked. "I hate it when you guys fight."

"I'm sorry," apologized Jacob. "I didn't know you felt so strongly about it."

"Both of you take me for granted a lot," said Josh. "I don't want it to be like that."

"You have my word, Joshua," said his father, taking his hand. "I'll be better to you."

"Thanks," he said, smiling.

Josh's sleep was interrupted by the sound of his door opening followed by Wester's rough voice.

"Wakey, wakey, lad."

"Five more minutes..." mumbled Josh, burying his head in his pillow.

He was relieved when he heard Wester's footsteps leave the room but was in for an unpleasant surprise when they returned a moment later, and shortly thereafter Josh found himself drenched in water.

"Bloody hell!" he yelled, jumping up and out of the bed. Wester stood there holding an empty pail, which was still dripping from the contents it had just been relieved of.

"I told ye to wake up," he said with a mischievous grin on his face. "Git dressed, we're leaving righ' after breakfast."

And he left the room without another word.

Josh groaned as he removed the now drenched clothes Wester had lent him to sleep in and found his own. Messily throwing them on, he stumbled out into the kitchen where Wester was at his usual spot at the table, Isaac to his left, and Arya at the oven.

"Sleep well, Joshua?" asked Isaac.

"Yeah," he replied, mussing his hair. "What time is it?"

"Just after six in the morning," answered Arya, nodding at the clock.

"Man," whined Josh, yawning quite tremendously. "Too early."

"We need to get an early start," said Isaac. "Danthian is a full day's trip, and we need to stop in the village quickly as well."

"How come?"

"Gotta git ye sum clothes," said Wester, as Arya placed hot plates of food in front of the three of them.

"Eggs?" asked Josh, looking up at her. Smiling, she nodded and brought her own plate over to the table. "I don't have any money for clothes."

"Dun worry about it," replied Wester dismissively. "I'll take care of ye."

"You don't have to—"

"I know I dun, but I want to. Besides, it's not like I'm gunna git ye anything 'spensive."

"All right," said Josh with a gracious smile. "So how are we going to get there?"

"Horses," replied Isaac, as if it were the most obvious thing in the world.

"I, um, I've never ridden a horse," he admitted.

"Never?"

Josh shook his head.

"Well, ye can ride with Arya, then," said Wester. "Dun want ye to get tossed if we have to go fast."

"Why would we have to go fast?"

Wester and Isaac shared a discreet look but said nothing further.

"Sometimes people get attacked by bandits who live in underground cities," explained Arya. "They come in small groups and rob people."

"Underground cities?" asked josh.

"Supposedly there's a huge network of tunnels and small cities under the countryside where thieves and other lowlifes dwell along with whatever family they may have," said Isaac. "I don't know how much truth there is in those rumors, though."

"Do people get held up often?"

"No, and it usually only happens to caravans," he answered. "I wouldn't worry about it if I were you."

"All right."

"Jus' be on yer guard," advised Wester.

The sun wasn't completely up yet as they steered the horses from the stable; drops of dew were still lingering on the grass, and the cool morning air made for a chilly ride.

"Um, how is this supposed to work?" asked Josh after Arya had pulled him up behind her onto the saddle.

"Just put your hands on my hips," she said, putting on riding gloves. "And you can use me for a pillow if you want."

Josh took her up on the offer and rested his temple against her back, falling asleep rather quickly.

It didn't take long to arrive in the center of Kendrall, where the local shops were beginning to open for the day. Arya gently woke Josh as they reached the outer buildings, and he looked on from behind her at the villagers who were milling about, either setting up carts to sell their wares or getting ready to make their purchases.

"Why is that man sleeping against the wall?" he asked, as they passed a man with unkempt hair and tattered clothes snoring loudly in one of the alleys.

"That's the town drunk," replied Isaac with a snort. "Don't mind him."

"Here we are, then," said Wester, slowing his horse to a halt in front of a shop with a great wooden sign nailed above the door which read ARLEN'S TAILORING in cracked gold letters.

"I'll grab the horses a drink while you're inside," said Isaac, tying his steed to a nearby post.

"Thanks," said Wester, tethering his horse to the post as well.

Arya helped Josh dismount and he followed Wester into the store. It was small, but there was enough space to move around comfortably. What light wasn't provided by the rising sun came from a single lamp hanging next to a door in the back, casting a golden glow over the shop. Clothes of all materials, colors, and varieties were folded neatly on the shelves—the nicer and more expensive stock hanging gently behind the counter. Wester immediately walked over to the counter and greeted the shopkeeper warmly.

"Wester Tremayne, good to see ya again," said the man—a tall, lanky fellow with long black hair. A gray smock covered the white shirt and tan pants he wore.

"Ye as well, Arlen," replied Wester with a warm smile, shaking the man's hand. "I'd like ye to meet Joshua Cooper."

"Nice to meet ya," said Arlen, extending his hand as Wester nudged Josh forward.

"Thanks," he replied, shaking the tailor's hand.

"He's new in town," said Wester. "I thought we migh' be able to git him somethin' to wear."

"New, eh? You wash up on shore?"

"Yeah," said Josh sheepishly.

"No need to be shy, lad. I've seen plenty of your type in my day…and here's the lovely Ms. Tremayne," he added, as Arya walked in the store.

"Hello, Arlen," she said, smiling.

"Beautiful as always, I see," he said reverently, with a slight bow of his head.

"It must be the clothes," she quipped.

"Aye, that it must," he said, laughing. "So what can I do for ya today?"

"Kid showed up with jus' what he's wearing," explained Wester. "Somethin' that'll make him look presentable in front o' Luther."

"Going to Danthian, eh? Well, a lad can't look anything but respectable in the Grand Capital," said Arlen, turning around and fishing for some clothes.

"Nothing too 'spensive now," warned Wester.

"Go soil yourself," said Arlen lightheartedly, his back still turned from them. "You saved my life in the war—everything is on the house like it always is."

"Whatever ye say, man."

"Here we are," said Arlen, turning around with a several pairs of pants and some shirts, all clean and pressed. "Go try these on so I can size them up for you."

"Thank you," said Josh gratefully. He took the clothes from Arlen and walked to the lone door in the back, closing it behind him when he was inside.

Everything was a little large for him, but that was the only complaint he had. The material was unlike anything he'd experienced back home; it breathed like cotton and kept him warm like wool but was as smooth and comfortable as silk. At closer inspection, he could see tiny grains of Essence woven right into the fabric, giving it the same slight shine as the silver horse Arya had made for him.

"How's it goin' back there?" Wester's voice came floating in from the other side of the closed door.

"About finished," called out Josh, returning to the storefront with the new clothes on. "They're a bit baggy."

"Oh, that's not a problem," said Arlen, taking all the extra clothes from Josh and spreading them out on the counter. "Hold still for a moment."

He lifted his hand at Josh, squinting his eyes and pursing his lips as he did so. A slight breeze picked up around them, and small trails of Essence began to swirl around Josh. It wasn't long before he noticed that the shirt and pants he was wearing—along with the other clothes on the counter—were shrinking gradually until they had reached the point where the fit was quite comfortable.

"Brilliant," said Josh in amazement, once Arlen was done.

"There we are," said the tailor, giving him a small leather bag to keep the spare clothes and his old ones in.

"Ye two go an' get the horses ready. I want a minute with Arlen here," said Wester, nodding Arya and Josh along.

"Of course, Father," agreed Arya, leading Josh out of the shop. The cool morning air hit them as they exited and found Isaac leaning against the post with the horses.

"Well, don't you look sharp" he commented, untying his steed.

"Thanks," replied Josh with a chuckle.

"Wester coming?"

"He's just chatting up Arlen for another minute or two," said Arya, patting the nape of her horse's neck.

"How come you didn't join us inside?" asked Josh.

"Arlen and I don't get along so well," said Isaac slowly.

"Why not?"

"We all make mistakes, son. His brother was under my command in the last war...and didn't make it."

"He blames you for it?"

"No...no, he doesn't," said Isaac, glancing in the window of the shop where Arlen and Wester were shaking hands, "but he hasn't completely gotten over it either, and I can't hold it against him."

"I understand."

Wester emerged from the shop with a smile and mounted his horse fairly quickly.

"Why y'all look so mopey?" he asked, looking at them. "We've gotta long way to go, so let's git a move on."

It didn't take long to reach the outskirts of Kendrall, and soon enough they had left the village behind for the lush, green landscape of the Agerian Fields.

"What exactly do people farm here?" asked Josh from behind Arya.

"Mostly crops," she replied. "Corn, wheat, oats, that sort of thing."

"So where does that...mastodon leather come from?"

"Mastrichon?" she asked. "Mastrichons are foul creatures that are incompatible with Essence and immune to Nether. I haven't been there myself, but I hear that the mountain range to the south of is full of them. I know that they also burrow in the Sarcosian Salt Flats every once in a while."

"So people hunt them?"

"Quite a few, actually, since much of their bodies has great value. Their hides are used for our roofs, as you saw, their horns are ground up and used by the archons to help amplify their power, their hairs are used for musical instruments, the list goes on."

"I see. Are parts of them used in what I'm wearing?"

"Arlen is the finest tailor in the entire province," replied Arya. "So it's reasonable to expect that no one knows what his fabrics are made out of but him."

"Fair enough," said Josh, smiling.

"You do look rather handsome, by the way," added Arya, a slight blush creeping up in her cheeks.

"Thanks." Josh was glad her back was to him, as his cheeks had gone a bit pink as well. "So…who is this Luther?"

"Luther was found on the beach about thirty years ago, from what I've heard. I've only met him once, but father fought alongside him in the war, and the two are good friends."

"What does he do?"

"I believe he's a…a *scientist*," said Arya thoughtfully. "I don't know much about science, but he works for the Grand Arbiter to help research new ways to use Essence outside of combat—for everyday use, that is."

"The who?"

"The Grand Arbiter? Lord Gainsburgh is the current holder of the position," she replied.

"What does the Grand Arbiter do?"

"Well, the way our government works is that any civil or criminal charge is brought before an archon, who makes a judgment on the matter. There is a publicly-elected council that reviews all decisions made, and if they feel a decision has been handed down erroneously in accordance with our laws, they give the case to the Grand Arbiter who makes a final ruling."

"So he's a powerful judge, then?"

"Basically."

"And this man Luther works for him?"

"It's the Grand Arbiter's duty to oversee the progression of civilization and keep order in the land when he's not deciding upon cases," explained Arya. "When it became apparent that Luther had knowledge that no one else here had—physics, I think he called it—the Arbiter asked him to assist."

"So he's from London." There was no question in Josh's voice.

"Yes, that's correct," said Arya, nodding. "Why?"

"I came not too far from there myself."

"Really?" she asked curiously. "I remember hearing things from my father about Luther's homeland…it sounded like a remarkable place."

"No more remarkable than here," muttered Josh.

"Well, in any case, you two should get along fabulously."

"Let's hope."

"I wouldn't worry, Luther is a very kind and wise man," said Arya. "As long as you're respectful, you have nothing to worry about."

"And he can teach me how to use Essence?"

"Well, I'd say it like this," said Arya. "He's one of the only people not from this world who figured out how to use it. He's the person who can probably get you home as well."

"If he can go home, why hasn't he?"

"Ask him yourself," she replied with a shrug. "Like I told you, I've only met him once, and it was years ago."

They rode in silence for a few minutes, only the rush of wind and beating of hooves on the ground permeating the morning air.

"How many people have washed up here?" asked Josh finally.

"More than I know about," replied Arya. "You're the second I've actually met, aside from Luther, of course."

"Who was the other?"

"She was about ten years older than me. Showed up when I was eight—right at the height of the war. She was killed in battle."

"What was her name?"

"Tanya. She was here for about four months."

"I guess I'm pretty lucky," said Josh quietly. Arya glanced over her shoulder at him.

"What makes you say that?"

"It's just all this talk about war and how many people you know who've died. I just feel lucky to be here while that stuff's not happening."

"I hope you stay around to see more of it," she said, returning her attention to the road in front of her. "It's not all bad, you know."

"I know," replied Josh, fumbling about in the bag for his old pants and taking the silver model horse out of the pocket. "I never thanked you for this, by the way."

"If you learn to use Essence, you can make me one as a thank-you," she said with a wink.

"It's a deal."

As the hours passed, the great city grew larger. More and more details became clear, and smaller buildings at the base of the fortress started taking recognizable shape. In time, the city's wall became visible, and—as they drew closer—guardsmen in shining mail atop the ramparts could be seen patrolling underneath red and white flags waving in the breeze.

The sun was setting by the time they approached the city gates, the sky glowing pink much like it had on the first night Josh had been there.

"Wow," he breathed, looking up in awe at the fortress towering above them—easily a thousand feet tall at its highest point.

"There's a reason you can see it from halfway across the province," said Arya with a chuckle. Their horses trotted up to the two open large wooden doors at the entrance. A massive portcullis was raised behind them, hanging peacefully from the chains that held it.

A guard clad in a suit of chain mail approached them as they came to a halt. Josh noticed that the armor was glimmering with Essence, much like the shirt from Arlen's.

"What business do you have in the capital this late in the day?" he asked.

"Bringin' a newcomer to see Luther," said Wester, nodding in Josh's direction.

"He wash up on shore?" asked the guard, shifting his gaze to Josh.

"Four days ago," said Isaac. "Found him myself."

"Coach Mathson is that you?" the guard suddenly asked, turning to Isaac. "I'm a huge fan of the Arrows."

"Glad to hear it," replied Isaac, though a bit tersely.

"Go on in then," said the guard eagerly. "Tell the guard at the fortress that Hodge cleared you already. I'm Hodge, by the way."

"Nice to meet ye," said Wester, nodding at the man as they rode past. The soft patter of hooves on dirt became clip-clops as the ground turned to cobblestone in the city.

"Who are the Arrows?" asked Josh curiously.

"Isaac's kingball team," said Arya. She seemed to be suppressing a laugh. "He, um...doesn't like to talk about it much in public."

"Why?"

"Cuz they can't win, tha's why," interrupted Wester, bursting out in laughter while Isaac glared mutinously ahead.

They emerged on the other side of the wall to find a vibrant market with people still milling about the various stands and shops before they closed for the day.

"It's like a big version of Kendrall," commented Josh.

"A very big version," said Arya. "Over one hundred thousand people live here."

"I'm not surprised," he said, looking around. "We won't have any trouble getting into the fortress, right?"

"It usually takes some time to get into the inner sanctum, but Father's pretty well-known by a lot of the chamber guards because he fought alongside most of them, so we shouldn't have a problem."

They continued on, Josh marveling at how alive the city was. As they moved farther into the city, the elegance seemed to increase. Outdoor markets became upscale shops, corner eateries became classy restaurants. The way the people dressed changed too—going from the clothes Josh had seen many of the farmers and peasants in Kendrall wear to beautiful robes, dresses, and other fashionable outfits each adorned with Essence, inlaid gold, or in one case, shining emeralds stitched right into the fabric.

By the time they reached the entrance to the fortress, the pink had faded from the sky, leaving it a deep blue. Another portcullis guarded the entrance, except unlike the one at the city gate, this was lowered.

"Hold," said one of the guards, walking toward them. "It's after curfew, do you have a residence permit?"

"We're here to bring the lad to Luther," said Isaac. "Hodge cleared us at the gate below."

The guard regarded them all carefully a minute before nodding.

"All right, then," he said. "Raise the gate!"

From above them on the lowest rampart, they distinctly heard another guard yell, "Raising the gate!" and a second later the chains clanked to life, lifting the steel grid that protected those inside.

The steady beat of horseshoe against stone echoed in the corridors as they climbed the sloping paths to the highest reaches of the castle. After what had to have been at least twenty minutes, they finally reached another arch, this one too short to pass through on horseback, and again guarded by a lowered portcullis. Two guards in full-plated armor stood on either side of the passageway flanking a third, although the third one was unlike any Josh had yet seen.

Clad in a strange, murky silver metal that he couldn't recognize, this person was slightly taller than the other two guards. A dark blue glow seemed to be coming from the skeletal armor itself, which wasn't ordinary plate either.

Several runic characters and symbols had been hammered into it, and what looked to be a high concentration of Essence had been infused into all the markings. The helmet completely blocked the guard's face from view; only two dark blue eyes could be seen from behind the metal helm that was just as decorated as the rest of the armor.

"That's an archon," whispered Arya to Josh as they approached. "You don't trifle with them."

"Wester Tremayne, Arya Tremayne, Isaac Mathson, and Joshua Cooper here to see the High Scientist," announced Wester.

"It's long past curfew," said one of the lesser guards, "and the High Scientist is working on a special project for Lord Gainsburgh. Come back tomorrow."

"We've traveled all day from Kendrall—" began Isaac.

"Do I look like I care?" asked the guard.

"Now see 'ere lad," said Wester dismounting. "I've fought in more wars than ye can care to think about, and if ye don't move yer arse, I'll make sure that the Grand Arbiter hears about it."

"He's away on business, I'm afraid," said a feminine voice to Wester's right. It took Josh a moment to figure out that it came from inside the helmet of the archon. "Rest assured, though, there won't be a need for it."

"Milady?" asked the guard.

The archon reached up and removed the helmet. Long golden hair flowed from where it had been kept up, and a woman no older than thirty stared back at them.

"Marilyn Fairbanks, is tha' ye?" said Wester with a grin, turning to face her.

"The same," she replied with a smile, reaching out and hugging him. "It's good to see you again."

"Ye as well, o' course."

"You—go and tell Luther that Wester Tremayne will be along shortly with a visitor," she said without looking at the guard.

"But, milady, the High Scientist is working on—"

A sudden burst of energy came from the inscriptions on Marilyn's armor, causing the hairs on the back of Josh's neck to stand at attention. The guard immediately snapped to and banged on the gate three times, which was apparently the signal to open up.

"You go as well," Marilyn said to the other guard, who nodded and followed the first through the arch once the portcullis was raised.

"Still gorgeous and menacing, as always," said Isaac slyly, stepping down onto the cobblestone as well.

"Still a flatterer, as always," she retorted, giving Isaac a hug as well.

"We have to leave the horses," Arya told Josh as they dismounted.

"Arya?" asked Marilyn. "My goodness, I haven't seen you since you were this high." She raised her hand to about her waist.

"It has been a while," replied Arya with a smile. "This is Joshua Cooper—he washed up four days ago next to the Tiras River."

"Hmm." Marilyn scanned Josh carefully, as if sizing him up. "He's not too bad to look at."

"Tha' really proper language fer an archon?" asked Wester lightheartedly, raising an eyebrow.

"Is that proper language for a lady?" added Isaac.

"No, but you both know I don't give a damn." She laughed. "Joshua Cooper, good to meet you... I'm Mary Fairbanks, and I pulled guard duty tonight."

"It's a pleasure," replied Josh, shaking her extended hand.

"D'ya think ye'll be able to put us up fer the night?" asked Wester. "Bit of a hike from Kendrall."

"I'm sure I'll be able to work something out," she replied. "I should warn you, though, Whitemane's been in a mood lately, so watch out for him."

"Why?" asked Isaac, as the two guards returned.

"Luther will be happy to see them," said the second guard. The first remained silent, though he looked rather annoyed.

"Let's go, then," said Marilyn, leading them through the arch and into a dark, narrow hall lit only by a few torches. "Six top-level students at the academy have disappeared in the past week," she said, lowering her voice to answer Isaac's question when they were out of earshot of the two guards. "Just vanished."

"Really?" asked Wester.

"Gainsburgh is worried about a revolt of some kind, apparently," continued Marilyn. "Here we are."

They emerged from the hallway to find themselves inside the great tower. Every inch of the walls was covered in either elaborate, beautiful frescoes or gold of some sort, and the ceiling was too high up to make out. There were balconies every thirty feet or so, with two huge ascending, marble staircases coiled around the walls of the cylinder, providing the smattering of people access to the different floors. Beautiful, ornate brackets were scattered about the walls, extending all the way up past the reaches of their vision, each holding a golden torch bearing a bright, white flame.

"Whoa," exhaled Josh, taking it all in.

"Indeed," said Marilyn with nod. "And you're going all the way to the top."

"The top," repeated Josh, still staring upward, and wondering how many stairs that was.

"Lucky for you I have access to the lift."

Marilyn led them off to the side where there was a small doorway sealed off by a pair of gold-plated doors. A small black panel was affixed in the wall next to them. Josh watched as Marilyn removed one of her gauntlets to reveal a jet black glove, with two more symbols on both the palm and back shimmering with Essence. She pressed her palm to the panel, and the two doors shook and slid open.

"After you," she said to Josh, ushering him in.

The inside was much like a normal lift—only where there should've been buttons for each floor, there were more symbols that were foreign to Josh. Once they had all gathered, Marilyn pressed her palm to the topmost one, and the doors shuddered closed.

"I hope you don't get motion sickness," she said to Josh.

"Why, does this thing go fa—"

It felt as if someone pulled Josh's legs up through his head as the lift roared to life and he crashed to the floor. Blinking the spots out of his eyes, he looked up at his four companions, who were standing quite normally, staring down at him with expressions of mirth on their faces.

"You've could've warned me," he said, returning to a wobbly standing base.

"Where'd be the fun in tha'?" asked Wester with a grin.

The ride ended a few seconds later, and the doors opened to reveal the top floor of the tower. Walking over to the railing, he stared down and could just make out the bottom far below. Looking up at the ceiling, he saw a very large painting depicting great black demons with burning red eyes bearing down on a beautiful lone woman who held a golden winged dagger up against them. Despite the dark shroud and stormy winds nearly encasing her, the dagger seemed to be protecting her.

"It's nice, isn't it?" asked Arya, coming over to him as the others gathered near one of the two doors on the floor.

"What is it?"

"From what Father tells me, it depicts the first war that ever took place here. The woman, Celestina, used that dagger to protect people from the Nether Wraiths that infested this land many centuries ago."

"Wow."

"The dagger is on display in the library three floors down," said Marilyn coming over to them. "I'm sure Luther would show it to you if you asked him nicely."

They heard sounds of laughter and turned to see the door open, and an older man with a kind face, curly silver hair and a warm smile embraced Isaac and Wester.

"Let's get you introduced then, shall we?" suggested Marilyn, steering Josh over toward the men. "Luther?"

"Yes, dearie?" asked the man with a faint British accent, chuckling.

"This here is Joshua Cooper. He washed up on shore a few days ago."

"Ah. Let's see him, then." Josh stepped forward to greet the man. He was wearing a flowing, dark blue robe that appeared to be made out of the same material as the clothes Josh had gotten at Arlen's. Luther reached into the chest pocket for a pair of oval glasses and put them on, appraising Josh carefully.

"Where are you from, lad?"

"Salisbury, England," he replied.

"You don't say?" replied Luther, taking off his glasses and replacing them in his pocket. "Well then, it should be rather easy to answer any questions you might have."

Josh nodded. "I have a few."

"Well, come on in," said Luther ushering him inside the room.

"You don't mind doing this tonight?" asked Isaac. "It is a bit late."

"Nonsense," replied Luther with a smile. "Anything for a friend, and I'm quite keen on hearing how things are back in my homeland."

"Right, we'll just leave you two at it then," said Marilyn. "I'll have everyone put up in the northern apartment, you can bring him along when you're done."

"Too right," said Luther with a nod, putting an arm around Josh's shoulders and ushering him inside.

The room looked rather like a medieval science lab. Long wooden tables were spread about, each with strange apparatuses on them—from a disorderly collection of chemistry tubes, beakers, and flasks with bubbling liquids to self-propelling models of planets and various star systems. One table was covered with several silver plates over which white flames of different luminosities were hovering.

"Why are some flames brighter than others?" remarked Josh, pointing at the nearest table.

"You don't waste much time, do you?" asked Luther warmly.

"I'm sorry," said Josh sheepishly.

"Oh, not at all…I was just as curious when I first arrived here."

"Thirty years ago, right?"

"One question at a time, lad," said Luther with a hearty laugh. "First, the flames."

He walked over to the table with the flames and beckoned Josh to him. Much to his surprise, Luther took his hand and placed it directly in the darkest. He removed it a few seconds later, holding the fire in his palm.

"You see this isn't natural fire like you are accustomed to back in merry old England," he explained, letting it flicker silently in his hand. "There's normal fire here too, before you ask. But this is something different. This is what Lumenarians call an 'Essence Spark.'"

"Combusting Essence?"

"Very astute of you," he replied with a nod, replacing the fire and wiping his hands on his robe. "You see like oxygen, Essence is also combustible but doesn't produce heat."

"What does it produce, then?"

"Nothing that modern science in our world can explain, but it's a bit like radiation."

"Isn't that dangerous?" asked Josh, leaning away from the table slightly.

"If it were, I think after thirty years I'd be feeling the effects, wouldn't you say?"

"True…so why are they different?"

"Different concentrations of Essence burn in different luminosities," said Luther. "The more concentrated the Essence, the brighter the flame."

"Rather like the difference between gasoline for an automobile and gasoline for a fighter plane?"

"Quite so." Luther nodded and walked down the length of the table. "You see the flames not only function as a light source but also as a battery of sorts for people who use Essence." He waved his hands gently and silver strands of

Essence siphoned themselves away from the one of the darker flames and began to take shape.

"So what's that black flame?" asked Josh, pointing at a simpering black flame, encased completely in a glass sphere.

"That's a Nether Spark," replied Luther after a minute. "Very dangerous. Don't go touching that."

"Why do you have it?"

"Experiments," he replied hesitantly. "I don't like using it, but it does yield impressive results if used properly."

"Does this have to do with that assignment from the Grand Arbiter?" asked Josh tentatively.

"Nothing gets by you, my boy," said Luther, appreciatively. "But no, that is another matter. As for this, the Grand Arbiter wants me to research ways we might able to use it in combat."

"Isn't that the archons' job?"

"You've learned a lot in the few days you've been here," commented Luther. "Normally yes, but with something this new and dangerous, I'm the man for the job in order to keep casualties to a minimum."

"Speaking of casualties, what's the painting outside?" asked Josh. "Arya told me it was from the first war here."

"It is," replied Luther with a nod. "The woman in the painting was named Celestina. She helped destroy the prominent presence of Nether in this world when humans first settled here."

"Wraiths, right?"

"Among other things. That painting was commissioned by the first Grand Arbiter after she passed away."

"And the dagger?" asked Josh.

Luther sighed and stared off into space. "The winged dagger. I don't know much about it. Supposedly, she brought it with her from…wherever she was from before she migrated."

"Migrated?"

"Well, based on historical writings, I feel that it's a safe assumption that the human presence here is not natural to this planet."

"Planet? You mean we're not in another universe or something?"

Luther regarded him carefully for a minute before smiling and walking over to a steel spiral staircase in the far corner that Josh hadn't seen. "Follow me."

Josh followed him up the winding metal stairs, and as he passed through the ceiling, he was greeted with a room so dark he could barely see his hands in front of his face. Luther was fumbling about for something next to him.

"Here we are," he said, flipping a lever. A large clanking sound came from above, and the ceiling rotated to expose the sky. Pale light from the stars combined with the glow of the city below them and flooded the room to reveal a massive telescope. "A unique quality of Essence—it makes astronomical observation so much easier."

He seated himself in the chair in front of the eyepiece and looked into it, fiddling with various instruments near him until finally he appeared satisfied.

"Have a look, lad."

Josh sat down and pressed his eye to the small glass piece and nearly fell out of the chair when he realized what he was looking at.

"That's…that's Earth? Pangaea?" he asked, stunned to see the single large continent he'd only read about in his science texts.

"Very good," commended Luther. "Earth, some two-hundred million-plus years ago."

"But…I didn't go back in time, did I?"

"No, this is simply the result of the fact that the effects of light aren't instantaneous; they must travel like everything else in this universe."

"I don't understand," said Josh, shaking his head.

"Well, have you ever watched a match of tennis in real life?"

Josh nodded.

"And have you ever noticed that when a contestant hits the ball, the racket makes contact with the ball slightly before you actually hear the noise it makes?"

"Yeah," agreed Josh, nodding again.

"Well, that shows you that sound travels—and it does—at a bit more than eleven hundred feet per second. Light is the same way. So to simplify things, the planet you and I call home is so far away from where we are now that it takes light two hundred million years to reach us."

"Wow." Josh paused, thinking. "So how did I get here?"

"Unfortunately, I'm unable to answer that question," admitted Luther. "You see, Essence doesn't obey the laws of physics. If someone on Earth had left this planet with Essence, they might be able to return if the conditions were correct."

He patted Josh on the shoulder and flipped the lever to close the roof. They walked back downstairs to the laboratory, the bright glow of the flames making Josh squint after his eyes had adjusted to the darkness of the observatory.

"I heard you might be able to send me home." It was more of a statement than a question.

"Normally, it would only be a maybe, but this time I actually know I can," replied Luther. "I happen to know a chap who lives in England that's been here before."

"You sent him home?"

"Aye, and he was right annoyed that I didn't go with him."

"Why?"

"He's my brother, you see," said Luther, the corners of his mouth turning upward slightly. "But I felt more at home here than I ever did in London, and he understood eventually."

"How do you know he got home safe?"

"See that painting over there?" Luther pointed to a small painting in the corner hanging above a bathtub. It was a picture of a dimly lit water closet. "Well, that place exists—there's another painting in that water closet of this room—and if you know what to do, you can travel between the two places or send messages."

"Wow," marveled Josh. "What do you need to do, then?"

"Well, you need water, Essence, and a drain. From what I understand, Essence helps facilitate the transition, and the draining water acts as a sort of jump point that will get you home."

"Okay."

"Are you that eager to return to your own land?" The old man laughed.

"Not yet, I have to see a match of kingball and repay Wester and Isaac for saving my life. But I do want to go home eventually."

"Whenever you're ready," said Luther with a nod. "I'll be happy to help."

"Thanks," replied Josh appreciatively. "So how does Essence work?"

"You know," said Luther, sitting down in a chair and reclining in it. "Even though I'm almost sixty years old, I still marvel at how simple questions can have such complex answers." He waved his hand and a chair flew over from the corner and came to a rest in front of Josh. "Have a seat."

Josh sat down as Luther waved his hand again, and a bottle and two glasses came flying from one of the corners of the room. He watched as Luther poured the dark red liquid into the glasses and handed him one.

"Hornberry juice," said Luther as Josh took a sip. He recognized it as the liquid Arya had given him on the first night he'd been there.

"I've had it before," replied Josh, drinking from the glass again. "I really like it."

"I have many bottles that I'm sure we can go through in your time here," said Luther warmly. "Now then, how Essence works." He gazed up at the plain, tan ceiling in contemplation for a few moments. "I take it you don't know much about physics, my boy?"

"No, they don't teach that until the last year of secondary school."

"Well, there are natural forces in this universe, things like gravity and magnetism. As I said earlier, Essence does not obey the laws of physics—for example, it has a mass greater than the atmosphere here, yet it floats. It should sink, normally," he added, seeing the puzzled look on Josh's face. "Living beings on this planet can manipulate it rather like how a potter shapes clay."

"So it can do anything?"

"There are limitations, of course," replied Luther. "That's why the archons spend so much time in the flats—to figure out just how far they can stretch the limits."

"And you can teach me how to use it?"

Luther regarded him for a moment before speaking.

"Since you've been here, have you felt anything different about yourself?"

"Not really. There was a time when Arya was telling me about her mother and everything seemed more…alive? I don't know," he said with a shrug, shaking his head. "You must think I'm a bit mad."

"On the contrary, that is a very good sign," replied Luther, drinking deeply from his glass. "Essence isn't something that people here simply know how to use when they're born. Children usually end up causing a reaction by accident before they're three, but I've heard of it taking years, sometimes twenty or more, before some people are able to use it efficiently."

"What do you mean, 'causing a reaction by accident'?"

"The manner in which Essence interacts with humans is via reaction, just like any you might find in chemistry or physics. I have no idea how it works exactly, but when the correct conditions exist in the body, and the brain sends the correct electrical impulses, we're able to manipulate the environment. As for what kind of reaction happens, it can be anything," said Luther, waving his hand dismissively. "Usually it's just some sparks, or they'll make something float or shrink. Most of the time there's some underlying emotion like fear or love that's at the root of a desire to cause the occurrence."

They sat in silence for a little while, Josh contemplating Luther's words while Luther remained quiet and pensive.

"It doesn't happen overnight, you know," he continued, breaking the silence.

"I didn't expect it would," replied Josh with a resigned nod.

"I can try to teach you, if you'd like," he offered, putting his glass down. "I understand you're seeing the match in three days and will be here until then."

"You think I might be able to do it that quickly?" asked Josh, raising his eyebrows.

"No, but if you do what I tell you to after you leave the city, you might have a shot before you go home," he replied with a wink.

"All right."

"We'll start tomorrow," said Luther. "It's a bit late to start anything now. Was there anything else you were curious about?"

"Um, if you can't tell me, I'll understand, but I heard Marilyn saying something about people disappearing?"

"Ah yes, that's been quite a problem," said Luther solemnly. "Students vanishing from the academy."

"What does it mean?"

"Well, anyone who's been here long enough would tell you that it means some archon has decided to try to organize a revolution, but I don't think that's the case this time."

"Why not?"

"I knew two of the students personally," stated Luther. "Kristopher and Mareth Rothwyn."

"Brothers?"

Luther nodded. "Twins, in fact, and a more sinister pair of young men you'll never meet."

"So you think it's them?"

"I always questioned their motives," said Luther thoughtfully. "They were ambitious, powerful, maybe even a bit power hungry, but they never voiced any problems with Gainsburgh. Even so, when I first met them ten years ago, they were fifteen and had been secretly researching ways to amalgamate metals for two years."

"That doesn't seem too malicious," commented Josh.

"Except for the fact that amalgamating metals here isn't the same as creating an alloy on Earth," said Luther. "You saw the armor Marilyn was wearing, right?" Josh nodded. "Well, that's a special man-made plate with Essence infused into it along with various metals."

"I thought it seemed a bit strange."

"It's powerful," said Luther sagely. "If we hadn't brought them into the academy when we did, they might've turned into..."

"Into what?"

"Something unpleasant," said Luther evasively. "Now then, you've asked me a fair share of questions. Tell me about good old England."

"It's been raining a lot lately," replied Josh with a wry smile.

Luther laughed. "When hasn't it been?"

"You'll have to forgive me," said Josh, "I've been really wrapped up in my studies. I haven't been paying much attention to the outside world."

"I think, perhaps, you picked the better choice," said Luther with a smile. "Now then, it's getting late, and if you want me to try and get you accustomed to the finer points of using Essence, you should get a good night's sleep."

"Of course," replied Josh with a curt nod. "Thanks for answering my questions."

"I'm sure you'll have many more in the days to follow," said Luther, standing up. "Now come, let me show you to your quarters."

"You don't have to—"

"You think you could find them by yourself, then?"

"Er...no."

"Let's get a move on." Luther smiled and steered Josh toward the door.

"You said that people migrated here," said Josh inquisitively, looking up at the painting again once they were on the landing. "From where?"

"Who knows?" said Luther with a shrug, leading him toward a staircase. "Just being here tells one that the humans on Earth aren't alone in the universe like most of them suppose. I'm guessing that elsewhere in the cosmos, there are other planets that support life, just like the one you and I come from."

"It's weird," said Josh as they walked down two sets of stairs and emerged on a landing with at least a dozen doors all leading off in different directions. "I always assumed that if there was other life out there it'd be, you know, not human."

"Well, to me, anyway, it seems that the odds tend to favor human-type life forms for intelligent life," replied Luther. "After all, I'm sure that somewhere out there, there are amphibious, vegetarian squids with three heads whose diet consists of grass and seaweed, but I doubt they could engineer an airplane."

"I never thought of it like that."

"Opposable thumbs, standing on two legs, oversized brains...*Homo sapiens* is ideal for invention, and as you can see, the species exists on multiple planets, which only strengthens my theory, would you agree?"

"Definitely."

"Here we are," said Luther as the two of them arrived at a small, wooden door. He knocked loudly twice, and the door opened a moment later to reveal Wester clutching a rather large stein filled with some sort of mead. Josh could see Isaac in the background sitting at a table, with an identical flask in front of him.

"Oy lads!" cheered Wester, embracing them both sloppily. "Come in fer a drink!"

"I can't stay, I'm afraid," said Luther. "Much work to do still. And young Joshua here needs his sleep, he has a busy day tomorrow."

Wester laughed drunkenly. "Ah yer both a bunch o' old hens." And he stumbled back off toward the table.

"Nine o' clock tomorrow," said Luther, turning to Josh. "Try not to be late."

"Of course not, sir."

"Luther, Josh," he replied with another smile. "I'm not old enough yet to be called 'sir.'"

Josh grinned and nodded as the old man left, closing the door behind him. Their quarters were small—a sitting room with a table and several other doors leading to what Josh assumed were their personal rooms. There seemed to be a small cooking space behind the sitting area.

"Arya's out on the balcony if you want to talk to her," said Isaac as Wester took a tremendous pull from his drink. "Through the kitchen."

"Thanks," replied Josh with an appreciative nod, keeping himself from laughing when Wester nearly fell out of his chair.

He walked through the kitchen and saw a small archway leading out to a balcony where Arya was standing, head propped up on her hands with her elbows resting on the railing. The stars—combined with the Essence in the sky and their altitude—gave her an almost angelic aura.

"I like the dress," said Josh, shyly. The nightgown she was wore was a soft yellow and fell just to her ankles.

"Yes, well, normally I'd just sleep in my old work clothes." She laughed. "But for some reason, being here makes me want to be more proper."

"It might be the city," suggested Josh. "Whenever I go to London I feel like I have to be more dignified than I am at home."

Arya smiled. "You're probably right."

"Gorgeous night," he commented, looking out over the railing. "And we're really high up."

They were, in fact, so far up that the lights from the buildings looked rather like Christmas lights wound around a tree that they were perched on the very top of.

"It's absolutely beautiful up here," said Arya. Her brown hair fluttered in the breeze as she gazed out into the sky. "Every time I visit the citadel, I can't help but stand out on the balconies for hours on end."

"There's no moon," remarked Josh offhandedly.

"Not here," said Arya. "Though I hear there are some planets nearby that have them."

"There are other planets near here?"

"I don't know for certain," she replied. "I remember hearing Marilyn talk about it to my mother when I was much younger."

"As in Marilyn, the archon I just met?"

"She and my mother were great friends," explained Arya. "My mother mentored her when she was a young girl, taught her the history of this world, and helped her get into the Academy. Until tonight, I hadn't seen her since I was nine."

"So the archons study more than just Essence, I take it?" asked Josh.

Arya smiled. "One of their fundamental teachings is to be well versed in all aspects of our world and whatever may lie outside it, not just Essence. I remember Marilyn came by one time when I was about eight complaining to my mother about learning maths."

"A woman after my own heart," quipped Josh.

"I don't know much about them myself. We all tended to the farm as a family, so I was taught how to make the land grow."

"Where I come from, all the kids have to go to school," he said softly. "I wonder what they're all doing right now."

"Out looking for you, I'm sure," replied Arya.

"I'll have to get back," said Josh, looking up at the stars. "I'm sure my parents are worried…if they've stopped fighting long enough to notice I'm gone," he added bitterly.

"They don't get along?"

"To put it mildly."

"So what is your moon like?" asked Arya, not wanting to press him.

"It's round like the sun," he replied, thankful for the change in subject. "Only it's white most times, not yellow, and it doesn't hurt your eyes to look at. It comes out at night and if you're somewhere where there isn't a lot of light from buildings and such, it gives everything around you a pale glow."

"It sounds wonderful." She smiled. "I'd love to see it someday."

"I bet Luther could show it to you, actually," said Josh thoughtfully. "He actually showed me my home through the telescope."

"Are you serious?" asked Arya incredulously, turning to face him. "That's amazing!"

"I was a bit shocked," admitted Josh. "It was pretty weird."

Arya nodded. "I believe it." She let out a yawn and stretched. "It's getting late, and I'm sure you need rest for tomorrow."

"You know about that already?"

"I have ears, Joshua Cooper," she said with a playful smile. "I did manage to hear Luther over my father's drunken ramblings."

"Sorry," he said sheepishly. "And yeah, I should get to sleep."

"Your room is next to mine," said Arya, pointing to a door that was visible through the kitchen. "You can always come get me if you need anything."

"How about a wake-up call?" he asked with a chuckle.

"Six o'clock, sharp," she replied, smiling.

"Think I could sleep in?" groaned Josh a bit lamely.

"Seven, then."

"See you in the morning," replied Josh with a nod and headed off for his room.

Chapter Four: The Stadium

"You have to relax. Don't focus on your mind, it's only a piece of the whole. Essence is part of everything around us, so you must be in tune with your surroundings to use it."

Joshua and Luther were sitting in an antechamber of the laboratory on two piles of plush cushions. It was the day Josh and the others were to leave for the kingball match.

"I still don't know what I'm trying to do," said Josh, opening his eyes and touching one of the quiet, flickering specks of light near his fingertips.

"It can be very frustrating trying to learn," said Luther with a solemn nod. "I remember it took me several years before I was able to use Essence for even the most basic and rudimentary tasks."

"How'd you finally do it?" asked Josh.

"Patience, practice...a good emotional outburst seems to help facilitate things," he added with a wry smile.

"Like what?"

"Oh, well, the first time I used Essence, I was rather upset at a certain archon that was being a bit of a self-righteous arse, if you will."

"What'd he do?" asked Josh bemusedly.

"Nothing worthy of note," replied Luther with a dismissive wave. "Criticisms, arrogance, and a lack of respect for those he saw as inferior."

"Doesn't sound too friendly."

Luther laughed. "Quite accurate. He's the High Archon now. Might not be the friendliest bloke, but he does get the job done."

An extremely loud banging from the laboratory door startled them both.

"Luther!" came a rough, annoyed voice.

"Speak of the devil," said Luther with a sigh, rolling his eyes. He clapped his hands on his thighs and stood up as another series of loud bangs resounded throughout the lab. "I'm coming, hold your horses!"

He opened the door to reveal a tall, burly-looking man. He had a jaw like steel and ragged brown hair, some of which was growing on his chin in a scruffy stubble. He was wearing the same kind of armor Marilyn had, though his seemed slightly more ornate. His helmet was grasped firmly in his left hand, which looked big enough to crush a cantaloupe.

"High Archon Whitemane, to what do I owe the pleasure?" asked Luther with a tinge of sarcasm.

"What's this I've heard about you training some runt?" he said in a brusque voice, disregarding Luther's facetious tone.

"That 'runt' is right over there," Luther said, pointing to Josh. "He washed up on shore five days ago, and he wants to learn how to use Essence."

"Gainsburgh isn't keeping you up here so you can give newcomers charity. You know what you're supposed to be working on, now get to it."

"Listen here, Derecks," said Luther dangerously, stepping close to the man. "There was once a time when you held authority over me, but that time is over. I answer to the Grand Arbiter alone now."

"And while he is away, I am in command in his stead," replied Derecks. "Get to work." He turned and left, slamming the door behind him.

"See?" said Luther, turning to face Josh with a look of annoyance.

"Yeah, wow," he replied, shaking his head.

"I'm sorry you had to see that. He tends to bring out a less cheerful side of me. Oh, bollocks, it's half past noon," said Luther, glancing at his wall clock. "I have to get you back downstairs, you'll be leaving soon for the match."

"Yeah," said Josh with a slightly regretful nod, following Luther out of the lab. "Why is the Grand Arbiter away?"

"I'm afraid his lordship has taken slightly ill," he replied. "He's gone to the neighboring province of Mafaelia to see a well-renowned physician—keep that to yourself, though, we don't want the people worrying."

"Of course. So what's the project you're working on, anyway?"

Luther stopped walking and turned to face Josh.

"There are some things I cannot tell you about—things that are between myself, the Grand Arbiter, and High Archon Derecks Whitemane, understand?"

Josh nodded.

"You cannot speak of such projects to another soul. It is government business and must remain as such."

"Why did Derecks talk about it in front of me, then?" asked Josh, curiously.

"Because he is a wanker, and didn't give it a second thought." Josh laughed at that. "In all seriousness, though, promise me you will not mention it to anyone."

"I promise," said Josh seriously.

Luther smiled warmly. "Thank you, lad. Now then, let's get you ready for your first kingball match, shall we?"

"Definitely," said Josh with a nod as they reached his quarters. Wester was snoozing, slumped over on the table in the sitting room, while Isaac and Arya were bringing their belongings out of their rooms.

"He had a bit of a late night last night," remarked Arya, spotting Josh and Luther chuckling softly.

"He had a bit too much to drink, is what he had," countered Isaac with a laugh, dropping a large sack by the door. "Wake up, you drunkard."

"Five minutes," mumbled Wester.

"Let me get this one," said Josh quickly, the opportunity too good to pass up. He jogged over to the kitchen and found a pot. Pouring some water into it, he carefully walked back over to Wester and dumped the liquid all over him. Wester jumped to his feet spluttering and looking around wildly for the source of the disturbance when his eyes fell on Josh holding the pot.

"Yer a sly bastard," he grunted, wiping the water out of his eyes. Laughing, he stood and clapped Josh on the shoulder. "We're all square now, got it?"

Josh chuckled. "Too right."

"Well, then, I'll take my leave," said Luther, shaking hands with Isaac and walking over to Wester. "Ease up on the drink, man."

"Ah, ye know me," replied Wester with a yawn, rubbing the back of his head. "Good to see ye, old friend."

"You as well." Luther nodded, embracing him. "Enjoy the match."

"I will."

"Take care of our young friend here, Lady Tremayne," he said with a smile, nodding at Josh.

"As if I haven't been doing that already," replied Arya with a lighthearted wink.

"Remember what I've told you," Luther said to Josh. "Practice and patience."

"Thank you very much," said Josh, nodding and shaking Luther's hand.

"Until next time," said Luther with a wave, leaving the quarters and closing the door behind him.

All too soon, the four of them were mounted and departing through the same gates they had arrived at three days earlier.

"Are you excited?" asked Arya as the city began to slowly shrink behind them.

"I'm still trying to figure out how to use Essence," said Josh, trying to calm his mind.

"I'm sure Luther told you this, but you need to have a very singular goal in mind when using Essence—you have to truly want the result."

"What do you mean?"

"Put it like this—when my mother died, all I wanted for the longest time was to have her back."

"You can't bring people back from the dead though, right?"

"Of course not," affirmed Arya. "It's quite impossible. But since that was all I really wanted, I couldn't use Essence effectively until I finally started getting over her death."

"So, then, someone who had a sick child might not be able to use Essence to harvest crops because that wasn't where their heart truly was?"

"In a word, yes," she said with a nod. "You have to be able to focus so distinctly on your goal that you block out all other potential wants."

"Okay. That helps a bit…I think."

"Glad I could be of some service to you," she said, turning and smiling at him.

"Just add it to the list of favors I owe you," replied Josh dryly.

"I hope that's not why you're staying around," said Arya, quietly glancing sideways at him. "You don't have to repay us."

"It's part of the reason," he admitted. "But I also like it here. It's so much different from the life I have back home."

"You're an interesting man, Joshua Cooper," she said, returning her focus to the road in front of her. "And I'll admit, it's been nice having someone close to my age around."

"I imagine that it must get a bit monotonous for you also from time to time."

Arya nodded. "It does. There hasn't been much spark in my life since my mother passed."

"Maybe that'll change."

"I can't complain. There's peace right now, and that's all I can ask for."

"You know, after I go home, if I find a way back here, you should come to my world for a little while so you can have a break," he suggested. Arya turned to look at him properly, strands of sun-touched hair blown across her face.

"I'd like that," she replied with a smile, and Josh thought it was the most genuine smile he'd seen her make.

The trip to the Veran Hills was much shorter than the one from Kendrall. The sun was still shining brightly overhead through a cloudless sky by the time the landscape began to change.

The once flat farmlands and fields transformed into a great range of verdant, moderately sized hills with crops growing on stepped lands near cottages sprinkled here and there. Curved roads took them around the slopes of most of the green protrusions, but when they finally rode to the summit of one, Josh gaped at the sight that lay before him.

A great valley lay below. In the center of the depression resided a massive amphitheater which would easily rival any football pitch in Europe in terms of size. In the middle of the stadium sat a great sphere, inside of which was a cube positioned rather like a spinning top; one of the corners was nearest to the bottom of the sphere with the opposite corner nearest to the apex—except those corners had been cut off, and a great shaft had been drilled through the cube from the top to the bottom. Several solid, transparent beams reached out from the inner walls of the sphere to hold the cube in its place, perfectly centered inside the great crystal ball.

Thousands of people were already in the stands, though they were only specks and blurs of color from a distance. Far beyond the hills, Josh could distinctly see a gray ominous-looking fortress sitting between them and a dark shroud that enveloped the land past it.

"Is that the prison?" he asked Arya as they began to descend into the valley.

"Synax, yes, and the Forest of Andromar beyond it."

"You said there's exposed Nether in there, right?" Arya nodded. "Why is the prison next to it? Aren't most of the people in there the type who would use Nether for evil?"

"Make no mistake, lad," said Isaac, riding up to them. "Nether is very powerful and can do horrible things, but it takes a real genius and master of Essence to not die from it—let alone use it—and almost no one is that strong."

Josh nodded and looked on as they continued to draw closer to the stadium. A short time later, they found themselves next to a massive queue of people lined up around the outside, each person eagerly waiting to be a spectator during the match. Josh was mildly surprised—and relieved—when they passed the line and rode over to a smaller entrance on the other side.

They dismounted and tied their horses to nearby posts before approaching the entrance.

"Isaac Mathson, now since when do you scout other teams like a good coach?" the man guarding the gate asked with a laugh as they got close. He was a bit lanky and wearing purple and red pants and a matching shirt, which Josh assumed was his work uniform.

"I'm the best coach in the league, and you know it, Giff," retorted Isaac, puffing out his chest.

"Sure, sure." The man named Giff laughed. "These all with you?"

"Of course, you've met Wester Tremayne before, yeah?"

"Oh, too right, too right," said Giff extending his hand to Wester. "How be ya, man?"

"Good 'nuff," replied Wester with a nod.

"Well, go on in. Match is supposed to be a good one today," he said, handing each of them a program.

"Thanks," said Isaac with a grateful nod as they walked through the gate.

They were immediately greeted by a set of steep stairs that appeared to go right to the top of the grandstand.

"Who was he?" asked Josh as they began to climb.

"Just a guard who works here," said Isaac tersely. "We get to use the back entrance because I'm a coach, see?"

"Right," said Josh, holding his hands up in defense.

"No more comments about the losing streak then, got it?" He directed this more at Wester than Josh.

Wester laughed. "Oh, quit yer whinin'. Let's go."

Up close the transparent playing arena looked even more impressive. The great crystal stanchions supporting the hollow ball and cube inside it were larger than any tree trunks Josh had ever seen in his life. The sphere itself was at least a hundred feet in diameter, and two large, metal poles were anchored into the ground on opposite sides outside of the globe, just as tall.

"They play inside that?" asked Josh skeptically, following the three of them through the stands.

"They certainly do," replied Isaac, gently excusing himself as he maneuvered around an older gentleman. "The ball starts at the bottom and both teams try to goal it at the top, then it falls back down and they do it all over again."

"What are the poles for?"

"It's how they keep score," replied Isaac.

"How long are the games?"

"Games these days are up to seventy-five minutes," said Isaac, "five periods of fifteen minutes each."

"Why's it 'up to'?" he asked as they found their seats. The seats were very good—Josh's eye level came up to just above the center of the sphere.

"Well, they score each period individually," explained Isaac. "They have to recharge the Essence in the sphere often—"

"Which is why tha periods are only fifteen minutes," interrupted Wester.

"Right," said Isaac with a nod. "So at the end of each period whoever's scored more goals wins the period. First to three wins."

"Why do they do it like that?"

"In the old days, they used to play for ninety minutes just on straight score," said Arya. "But there would be cases where one team would be up by, say, ten at the first break. Made the rest of the match a bit boring, you know."

"Top marks," said Isaac with an appreciative nod.

"Ninety minutes also drained too much o' Essence," added Wester. "Especially when the score was even. Games could go on fer ages."

"How long?"

"Long," deadpanned Isaac. "If, after the last fifteen minutes the score is tied, they play for a golden goal winner, but the problem is that it can be very hard to score in this game."

"I'm sure I'll see why?" asked Josh.

Wester grinned. "Quite righ' ye will, laddie. Ah, it's good to be back," he added, stretching. "I haven' been to a match in ages."

"How come?"

"Gotta tend to me farm after all," he said with a smile.

"So how long was the longest game?"

"Never finished," said Isaac, looking on as more and more people began to fill the stands around them. "It was an irrelevant game near the end of the season and neither team was in the running for the championship, so after they postponed the game on eight separate occasions owing to darkness, the officials finally called it a draw—the only one in the history of the game."

"Now they start removing players from each team after every five minutes if it's all tied up," said Arya. "Makes it finish faster."

"Does that happen often?" asked Josh.

"Every once in a while," replied Isaac. "Maybe once a month or so."

"How long is the season?"

"Nine months. We can play year round, so there's just a short break to allow the competitors some time off after the championship."

"Right," said Josh, trying to take it all in. "So how do they get inside the sphere?"

"You'll have to wait an' see lad," said Wester with a laugh. "Match should be starting soon. Want anythin' to eat?" he added, motioning at the vendors carrying trays of assorted food and drink who were walking up and down the stairs of the grandstand.

"What's on the menu?"

"Oy lad!" yelled Wester to the nearest vendor. "Whatchoo got?"

"Sheep's leg!" the vendor yelled back. Wester looked at Josh, who nodded.

"Three!" he replied, holding up three fingers. "You want one?" he asked, turning to Isaac who had pulled out a pair of strange looking binoculars and was focused on what appeared to be one of the team benches.

"Nah," he replied.

"Jus' the three," said Wester to the vendor, who had come up beside them.

"Sure thing, that'll be thirteen fifty."

Josh watched intently as Wester opened a sack of coins that was tied to his belt and handed the man one gold coin, three silver ones, and five that looked to be bronze. Josh recalled a conversation he'd had with Luther the previous day.

"So what's used for currency here?" he asked.

"It's a fairly simple decimal system," said Luther while preparing them some lunch in the laboratory. "Everything is in coins, you see. The smallest unit is copper and is referred to as a cera. There are ten-cera coins, which are made of bronze, and henne coins, which are silver. There are a hundred ceras in a henne—which you might say is the equivalent of our pound."

"So how high up do the denominations go?"

"Oh, I've seen thousand-henne coins cut from emerald before," he said. "Supposedly, there are diamond ones worth ten thousand, but I've never actually heard of someone who was in possession of one."

"And they're minted here?"

"About a hundred feet below your shoes, actually," replied Luther with a nod. "The fourth floor is where the mint is, but don't try to go exploring in there. It's very heavily guarded and they don't take too kindly to unauthorized people snooping around."

Do you mind if I see one of those coins?" asked Josh as Wester handed him and Arya their food. "I'm curious to see what they look like."

"Sure, jus' make sure I git 'em back." He opened the sack and handed Josh a few coins—one copper, one bronze, and one gold.

Sure enough, inscribed around the edge of the copper coin were the words ONE LUMENARIAN CERA. The bronze and gold coins had similar carvings; TEN LUMENARIAN CERAS and TEN LUMENARIAN HENNES, respectively. Josh noted as he handed the food to Arya so as not to drop it, that as the value of each coin increased, the diameter got slightly bigger, and the markings more elaborate. Each had a hint of Essence infused into the metal and had the crest of Danthian—a sword and rose crossed together—inscribed on one side, and to Josh's surprise, the winged dagger on the other.

"I thought you said that the story about Celestina and the dagger wasn't well-known," said Josh, turning to Arya.

"It isn't," she replied, taking a bite of the sheep's leg. "You would think more people would know about it, given that most of us see it every day, but it isn't the case."

"I shouldn't be surprised, actually," said Josh, giving Wester the coins back. "I couldn't name most of what's on the notes of my country's currency."

"Notes?" asked Arya.

"We use paper notes as well as coins," he elaborated. "Never really thought about why, though."

Arya smiled. "How odd. This is really good today."

"The lamb? It is," he marveled, looking down at it. "I've never had anything with so much flavor before."

"Tha's because it's all farm-grown fresh right here," said Wester, chewing happily on his. "None of tha' mix-and-match meat ye have back home."

"How do you know about that?" asked Josh.

"When we were in tha war, Luther would talk about home from time to time," said Wester. "He used to say tha' even though we were fightin' tooth an' nail, tha food was better here than it ever was back where he came from."

Josh nodded. "It is. The only really good food back home is expensive, and not everyone can afford it."

"Don't people get sick, then?" asked Arya.

"Yeah," said Josh with a sigh. "And then, of course, that's if you're lucky enough to be able to afford food."

"That doesn't sound too pleasant," she said.

"There are some very unfortunate people where I come from," said Josh, his mind drifting to the homeless men he frequently saw on his walks home from school. "That's why I like being here. There's a lot less misery."

"Enough depressing talk," said Isaac, still looking through his binoculars with one hand. "Here, Joshie, take a look down there at the benches, you can see them warming up."

Josh took the binoculars from Isaac and could tell the moment he looked through them that Essence had been used in their creation, much like Luther's telescope. There was no need for a focus—the view was automatic based on how far one was looking, and the picture was so flawless that he could distinguish individual blades of grass on the ground if he tried.

Josh scanned the stadium until he saw one of the benches with about three dozen people standing around it, wearing dark blue shirts with golden stars on the front and various numbers on the backs.

A few were stretching independently or with others, and a couple were talking to a man in fancy white shirt who looked like the coach, but it wasn't until Josh saw six players standing in a circle that he really started to pay attention.

There was a simple brown leather ball in the middle of the circle. He watched in amazement as one of the players pointed his hand at it and a bolt of white energy erupted forth, bouncing the ball about twenty feet into the air. Each player took turns volleying the ball to others in the circle, never letting it hit the ground. When it finally did, they started it all over again. Josh observed that much like Luther had said, when brighter Essence was emitted from the players' hands, the ball would move faster and bounce higher.

"Are the extra players backups?"

"Yep," said Isaac. "It's an incredibly tiring sport to play, so new players are substituted in when the current ones get worn out."

"Neat, innit?" asked Wester, leaning over to Josh.

"It's wicked," he said in astonishment. "Is this a contact sport?"

"Physical contact isn't allowed," said Isaac.

"Oh," said Josh, somewhat dejectedly.

"But nothing says you can't use Essence to beat the other team around," said Isaac thoughtfully.

"That's legal?" asked Josh, intrigued.

"Oh, wait until ye see it," Wester said with a wink.

Josh heard a snort from beside him and turned to see Arya chuckling while shaking her head and mouthing something that distinctly looked like the word *men*.

"You can hold on to those for the match, by the way," said Isaac, pointing at the binoculars.

"Thanks," said Josh appreciatively.

The officials appeared on the field a short time later and the players headed out to the center of the pitch, right underneath the center of the sphere. After a short pregame conversation, the reserves headed off to their respective benches while the three officials and fourteen players walked out from underneath the sphere.

"Here we go," said Isaac.

Josh watched intently as the man appearing to be the lead official was handed a ball from one of the guards stationed at the bottom of the grandstands. With a curt nod to his co-officials, he raised a hand into the air.

"What's he doing?" asked Josh a moment later.

"Wait and see," said Arya.

He looked through the binoculars, and it was only then that he saw the raised hand of the official was glowing pale white. He barely had time to register the thought when the man brought his hand down in front of him as if he was slapping the air around his waist. An enormous burst of energy emanated from underneath him, and he rocketed skyward, landing softly on top of the sphere a moment later.

"Oh, you've got to be joking," said Josh in awe.

It wasn't a joke, in fact, as the other sixteen men followed suit a moment later, all meeting at the very top of the sphere. The head official had opened a small trapdoor in the ceiling and one by one they all clamored through, using jets of Essence to slow their descent to the cube, and subsequently the bottom of the sphere.

"That is so cool," said Josh, not taking his eyes off it.

"And to think, the match hasn't even started yet," commented Isaac with a lazy smile.

"Who are we rooting for?"

"The lads in the red shirts," replied Arya. "They're the Devils."

"The boys in blue are the Comets," said Isaac. "And they're a point ahead of us in the standings, which is why we don't want them to win."

"A point ahead of the Arrows, you mean."

"Right," said Isaac with a nod. Just then, a booming voice emanated from all around the stadium.

"Lads and ladies, welcome to today's match between the Devils and the Comets!"

A loud cheer went up from the stands, which had filled to maximum capacity since Josh had last paid attention.

"The starting lineups and officials can be found on page four of your program, so without any further delay, would you please rise and remove any hats you may be wearing for the Provincial Anthem."

Josh stood and was slightly surprised to hear a single trumpet start playing throughout the arena. He looked on in amazement as the crowd began to hum along to the tune, but no words were sung. After a minute or so, the piece ended and everyone applauded fervently, some people even shooting sparks of Essence into the sky.

"How come there aren't any words?" asked Josh, clapping with everyone else.

"I couldn't tell you the exact reason," answered Arya, "but to me it seems that words are for poetry—which is perfectly fine. But an anthem is music, and music is supposed to mean more than words, it's supposed to evoke deep-seated feelings inside you, and give you a sense of pride when you hear it, not tell you a story that you might not even understand."

"I never thought of it that way," he said thoughtfully.

"Oy, they're about to start," said Wester, nudging Josh.

"All right, what am I watching?"

"See that official standing on top of the cube with the ball?" asked Isaac.

"Yeah."

"He's going to drop the ball down that chute in the middle of the cube. When it clears the bottom, anything goes."

"Anything?"

"Well, not anything," revised Isaac. "But you'll see."

A loud, long beep sounded around them, which Josh assumed was the signal for the countdown to start, as numerous short beeps followed thereafter.

"Five, four, three," Isaac counted down—Josh guessed for his benefit—"two, one…"

A loud whistle blew and the official released the ball, which went whizzing down the tube and emerged at the bottom.

Instantly great flashes of white light began shooting from all directions inside the sphere. In the surprise of it all, Josh had temporarily looked away, only to have Arya physically turn his head back toward the action.

Four of the players on the red team were locked in what looked to be individual duels with players on the blue team toward the bottom of the crystal globe. Of the other three on the red team, two were protecting the third—who was carrying the ball—all of whom were being pursued by the remaining members of the Comets up the side of the sphere.

"Watch, he's going to jump," said Isaac loudly over the roar of the crowd. Josh quickly spotted the ball carrier through the binoculars and noticed his right hand was glowing like the official's before the match.

An instant later, the player slung his hand toward the ground and the built-up

Essence erupted underneath him, sending him rocketing into the air. In a move of dexterity Josh found difficult to comprehend, the man extended his free hand at one of the horizontal beams holding the cube. He wrapped his arm around it and flipped to the top of the beam, and to half the crowd's pleasure and the other half's dismay, he landed cleanly on his feet and sprinted toward the cube, the leather ball tucked safely under his left arm.

"What?" yelled Josh. "How?"

"Jus' keep watchin'!" yelled Wester over the crowd.

The man had reached the cube and was laboring toward the top when one of the blue players who had been in pursuit fired a bolt of Essence from underneath the glass structure. The energy passed right through the glass and struck the man carrying the ball square on the feet, sending him flying away from the prism and loosening the ball from his grip in the process.

"Perfectly legal," called out Isaac, seeing the look on Josh's face.

"I guess," said Josh, laughing, the hairs on the back of his neck standing up at attention from all the energy crackling in the stadium. He could feel himself getting pulled into the frenzy of the match and soon was cheering wildly as the Devils fought tooth and nail for the ball.

Soon enough, one of the Comets from the bottom of the sphere had picked it up and was busy rocketing from stanchion to stanchion, trying to avoid the attacks of the red players. Suddenly, another player in blue came shooting up from below, all the way above and beyond the cube.

"Oh hell," said Isaac worriedly.

Isaac's worries were justified, as the player holding the ball saw his teammate fifty feet above him. Quickly charging Essence, he hammered the ball upward in a fashion much like a volleyball serve. It got to the player right as he reached the apex of his flight, and in a very graceful maneuver, he slammed the ball toward the goal with his fist, delivering it soundly into the aperture.

"Damn it," grunted Isaac, waving a hand in disapproval as a Comets banner was raised up to the top of the pole near their bench, while the players sitting on it cheered.

The next hour was much like the first few minutes—fast-paced and a lot of acrobatics that Josh had trouble comprehending. At one point late in the third period, a member of the Devils had actually defended a pass successfully by ricocheting a bolt of Essence off the inside of the sphere and striking the ball with it before it could reach the intended recipient.

As the fourth period drew to a close, the match was tied 2-2 (the Comets, after winning the first period three to zero, gave up seven goals over the next two periods before winning the fourth by a slim two to one victory).

"I can see why this is a popular sport," commented Josh, as the fifth period started.

"Bes' game in tha world, lad!" yelled Wester as the Devils gained possession of the ball.

"Only game in the world," quipped Arya with a sly grin.

Josh was watching carefully as they moved the ball up toward the goal when he saw a pale red glow from behind the far grandstands. Adjusting the binoculars, he saw a dark red ball of light hovering in the air, getting brighter.

"Hey, Isaac?"

"Yeah, lad?"

"What's that over there?"

"What's what?" he asked, turning.

"That," said Josh pointing at it and handing him the binoculars. "Is that part of the game?"

"I…I have no clue," he said, looking. "I don't recognize it."

"Oh, what are ye on about?" asked Wester, annoyed at having to turn away from the match.

"That light, what is it?" asked Isaac. Josh could see that it was starting to grow slightly into the shape of an orb, though it wasn't opaque—he could see through gaps in the light as if it were a thick spiderweb, and parts of the light were ripping away from the surface like solar flares.

"What?" asked Wester, looking around. "I don't see any—"

He froze.

"What is it, Father?" asked Arya, her brow furrowed in concern.

"Tha's not good," said Wester quietly. The whole stadium had gotten quieter too as others had also begun to notice the expanding orb.

"Wester?" asked Isaac.

"Git out o' here."

"What?"

"Run!" he screamed at them. "It's gonna blow—"

His sentence was never finished. An unearthly pulse emanated from the light and washed over the entire area, affecting everyone in the stadium.

It was like a strange dream—instead of devastation, everything had stopped in suspended animation, as if it was all frozen in time. Players midair inside the sphere were floating peacefully as if weightless. Wester's mouth was still open in a silent scream.

Josh could only watch in shock as nearby specks of Essence began to be drawn toward the now-pulsating orb at an alarming rate, which was continuing to grow larger by the second. After a few moments, when at last the final few grains of Essence had been absorbed, the orb turned a pale gray and collapsed on itself.

The resulting explosion was tremendous. Josh barely registered throwing his arms up to protect his head before the shockwave hit, sending him flying into the air along with pieces of the obliterated grandstands. He opened his eyes a crack, saw the ground quickly speeding toward him, and braced for impact.

He landed hard, bouncing into a destroyed gate while pieces of fiery wood and metal rained down around him. Still covering his head, he turned to see Arya slide to a stop a few meters nearby. He made to crawl over to her, but a screaming pain in his left side prevented him from getting onto his knees. Clawing his way through the grass, he reached Arya and rolled her onto her back. She squinted painfully up at him, her mouth contorted in discomfort.

"Are you all right?" he asked, although he couldn't hear himself speak over the ringing in his ears. He barely registered Arya weakly mouth *What?* as more debris came crashing to the ground nearby. Instinctively, he covered her body with his to keep her from getting hit.

As his hearing slowly returned, he could make out screams of pain and horror coming from all around him. Slowly, he backed off Arya and looked at her properly.

She was covered in blood; a deep wound had been opened across the right side of her face, and her left arm was bent at a strange angle. She was breathing slowly, her eyes half closed as she lay on the wreckage-strewn grass.

"Can you hear me?" he asked, moving to her side so she could see him. She nodded almost imperceptibly. "Are you all right?"

"My father?" she asked weakly.

"I don't know, I didn't see him." He finally managed to rise to his knees and look around, scanning for any sign of Wester. He saw Isaac about ten meters away, kneeling over the limp body of his longtime friend, hammering his fist into the latter's chest.

"Come on, man!" he yelled, pounding harder with each stroke.

"Arya, Wester's—"

But she had lost consciousness, her body lying just as unresponsive as her father's.

Josh felt his eyes start to burn and made to wipe them but was met with excruciating pain in his left shoulder as he tried to move his arm. Falling weakly to the ground, his eyelids fluttered as he barely caught sight of a wave of archons descending on the area. Then darkness overtook him.

Chapter Five: Aftermath and Escape

Time was endless—an eternity.

Josh found himself floating in a sea of darkness, unable to move. Only a dull echo of indistinguishable sounds penetrated the everlasting black surrounding him. Murmurs, dull whispers, sharp yells, and suddenly, very distinctly, muffled sobs.

His eyes opened and his senses were immediately offended by a bright white light. His pupils adjusting, he saw that the glare was coming from spots of sunlight shining through the edges of a linen sheet covering a skylight in the roof above him.

How did I end up here? he thought to himself. The last thing he remembered was sitting in the stands, watching the match of kingball, when he had seen a dark red light.

The light...

The explosion...

He pinched the bridge of his nose as the memories came rushing back to him. Suddenly, a soft sniffle to his right made him turn his head. Though he was still groggy, there was no mistaking Arya, who was lying with her back to him on the bed to the right, crying softly.

"Arya?"

The crying instantly stopped and she sat up and turned to face him.

"Joshua?" she exclaimed. "Thank goodness you're all right!" She summoned an older-looking nurse with curly gray hair and a white apron to his side.

"What's going on?" he asked. "I thought you were injured. You're okay?"

"I'm fine. The nurse here is very proficient at healing injuries."

"With Essence?"

She nodded. "Yes, but you were worse. We didn't know if you were going to make it. You've been out for two days."

"Was I? Where's everyone else?"

"I'm right here," said Isaac, walking through a pair of closed doors on the left.

"Glad to see you're all right," said Josh as the nurse looked him over. "Where's Wester?"

Isaac looked at Arya who in turn looked away discreetly. Finally, after an uncomfortable silence, she looked up at Josh.

"Father didn't make it," she said, barely above a whisper.

"What?" asked Josh, shocked. "But I thought…I saw you with him, Isaac—"

"He was dead before I got to him," said Isaac, sitting down heavily on the bed next to Josh. "I don't know how the bastard did it, but in the split second between the shock breaking and the explosion, he discharged some sort of shield to protect us. It's why we're alive."

"So we're the only survivors?" he asked, horrified.

"No, no…" said Isaac slowly. "There were thirty thousand people at the match. About four thousand lived."

Josh was too stunned to respond. He simply stared up at the ceiling, trying to comprehend the gravity of what had actually occurred. After a few minutes, he looked over at the girl to his right.

"Arya?"

"I'm not ready to talk about it yet," she said quietly. Josh understood and said no more.

"What caused it?"

"You mean who caused it," corrected Isaac. "And I don't know. I think the archons have a few leads, but they're not releasing information to anyone."

"So where am I?"

"You're in the infirmary inside the tower of the citadel," said Luther, striding into the room briskly, "and I've come here to warn you that the High Archon has learned you're awake. He's coming down here to question you right now."

"Question me?"

"He's been questioning everyone," said Isaac. "Arya and I went through it yesterday."

"Anyone who survived the match," added Luther, nodding in agreement. "I should tell you, he's not in a good mood."

"I wonder why," muttered Josh, as the doors to the ward banged open and Derecks Whitemane strode in, accompanied by two other archons fully clad in their armor.

"You three," he said, pointing at Arya, Isaac, and the nurse. "Out."

"Hey now, this lad here is in our charge and—"

Derecks's entire suit of armor flashed white, briefly blinding Josh.

"I won't. Say it. Again."

"We'll be outside," said Arya, standing up and walking out the door with the nurse.

"Good luck, Joshua," said Isaac, putting a reassuring hand on his shoulder before following the women.

"Are you sure you don't want me to leave too, milord?" droned Luther.

"Enough," said Derecks impatiently, sitting down next to Josh. "Tell me what you remember."

"I remember watching the match," said Josh. "The fifth period had just started, when I saw a dark red glow coming from behind the grandstand on my right."

"You were in the coach's box, yes?"

"I think so," said Josh. "I know we went in the private entrance because of Isaac's connections."

"I told you," said Luther. "This was a one-man job—"

"Just because all the witnesses said it came from near the prison doesn't mean it was a one-man job," spat Derecks.

"One-man job?" asked Josh confusedly.

"Did you see anyone suspicious while you were watching the match?" the High Archon continued, ignoring Josh's inquiry.

"No."

"It didn't occur to you to look around and see maybe what was causing the light?"

"I was watching the game," defended Josh. "Things move so fast, I had no clue what was going on until Wester started yelling."

"Ah yes, the late Lord Tremayne," said Derecks, snapping his fingers at one of the archons, who produced a sheaf of paper and handed it to him. "Pity he had to die, I would very much have liked to know how he managed to save the three of you."

"Lord?" asked Josh, surprised.

"What, you didn't know?" countered Derecks, raising an eyebrow.

"He's been here for just over a week, you nit," said Luther. "He doesn't know anything."

"The mere fact that this occurred right after he appeared makes him all the more suspicious," said Derecks, resuming looking over the paper.

"I'm a suspect?" asked Josh incredulously. "You can't be serious! I don't even know how to use Essence!"

"You could've helped facilitate the offender's escape."

"I was busy trying to make sure Arya didn't die!" yelled Josh, now getting irritated.

"I suggest you watch your tongue," said Derecks, looking him in the eye.

"Oh, stuff it, Whitemane," said Luther. "This boy is no more guilty of treason than you or I."

"We'll see," said the High Archon after a moment. "Newcomers are the easiest to manipulate, after all. I'll be around."

And without another word he stood and strode off, the other two archons hurrying to keep up with him.

"Is he always like that?" asked Josh as Isaac, Arya, and the nurse returned.

"Of course," replied Luther with a dry laugh, sitting down on the bed opposite Josh. "Now that he's gone, I can actually bring you up to speed on what's happened in the last two days."

"There's been more?" asked Isaac, and Josh was actually somewhat thankful he wasn't the only person out of the loop.

Luther sighed. "Oh yes. We'll start at the beginning, and of course, this conversation doesn't leave this room." Everyone nodded, at which point Luther looked at the nurse who was tending to an unconscious patient in another bed. "That goes for you too, Janice."

"I would never abuse patient-doctor privilege, you know that," she said kindly.

"Thank you, luv," he said gratefully. "So…the explosion went off, many were killed, the rest were injured, and the entire archon task force from the prison arrived on the scene to do damage control—this much I assume you all know."

"That's when I passed out," said Josh, nodding.

"Right. Well, unfortunately that wasn't the last of it," elaborated Luther. "While all the archons were busy at the amphitheater, there was a prison break at Synax."

"What?" breathed Arya. "Who escaped?"

"Tyran Nazerf and six others from Seras Falrider's inner circle."

"You're going to hunt them down, right?" said Isaac quite suddenly. "I mean you can't just let them go—"

"It's easier said than done," interrupted Luther, holding up a hand. "They escaped into Andromar."

"Well, problem solved, then," said Isaac with a shrug. "They won't survive in there."

"Maybe," he replied pensively. "There's um…a bit of a catch." No one said anything; they just looked at Luther expectantly. "Seras isn't dead."

"What?" whispered Arya venomously, her eyes narrowing.

"Seven years ago, when the war ended, word was spread that Seras had been killed so that the public wouldn't worry," he explained. "But the truth was that Derecks himself had secretly led a team of archons into the forest and ambushed Seras. By all rights, he should've died, but the Nether had warped him so much that he couldn't—not while he was surrounded by what was fueling him. So, to prevent any further bloodshed, Derecks locked Seras in stasis, buried him underground in the forest, and sealed the burial site."

"What's stasis?" asked Josh.

"You remember that time-lapse shock right before the explosion?" asked Isaac. "Stasis keeps you in that state, unconscious."

"It's why Derecks was promoted to High Archon," commented Luther.

"If any of the stories about Nazerf are true, we don't have anything to worry about," said Arya, although her tone and expression were unreadable. "He was a genius, yes, but his gifts at the uses of Essence weren't anything special."

Luther nodded. "That much is true, but—and the High Archon does not share my point of view on this manner—I believe the people who broke him out can destroy the seal holding Seras."

"Who?" asked Isaac.

"The Rothwyn twins," he muttered, resting his elbows on his knees. "Most of the guards at the prison were killed, but one who survived correctly identified Mareth Rothwyn entering the area where the prisoners who escaped were kept."

"So, Kristopher, was it? Set off the bomb?" asked Josh.

"That is what I believe, although as I said, Derecks doesn't agree with me."

"How do you know it was them?" asked Arya, somewhat half heartedly.

"The other four missing students from the academy were found by some miners in the Endless Rise north of the forest, and they'd had the Essence depleted from their bodies."

"Depleted?" Josh glanced at Isaac whose expression was one of slight repulsion.

"Everyone, whether they're born here or not, has a bit of Essence in them," explained Arya. "For people born here, they're surrounded by it during conception, the gestation period, and birth, so they have a much higher concentration of Essence in their bodies. It's why it's much easier for natives of this land to learn how to use it, opposed to people like Luther and yourself."

"Correct," said Luther agreeing. "Because there's so much Essence in the body, you can forcefully take it from the victim and transfer it to yourself if you know how."

"It's not a pleasant way to go," grimaced Isaac.

"So if it was the twins, there may be something to worry about," finished Luther.

"What are you going to do about it?" asked Arya.

"I can't do anything until Lord Gainsburgh returns. Derecks has never—and probably will never—listen to my opinions. And…"

"And what?" asked Josh.

"He's going to detain you," finished Luther heavily. "Both of you, actually," he added, looking at Arya.

"Why?" asked Isaac incredulously.

"You heard it yourself, Joshua," said Luther with a sigh. "You're a suspect because you're new here. As for young Miss Tremayne, well, by all rights you three should be dead, but you're not. She's the only living relative of Wester, and Derecks wants to know how he saved you."

"What about me?" asked Isaac.

"As far as I know, you're free to go," he said with a shrug.

"No," said Isaac, shaking his head. "No, this is unacceptable. I'm not leaving without these two."

"You probably won't have much of a choice," said Luther. "I'm sorry."

"Sorry doesn't cut it!" exclaimed Isaac, slamming his fist down on the bedside table. "What are you going to do about this? You can't just let Derecks Whitemane of all people keep these—for all intents and purposes—*children* here because of some stupid hunch he has!"

"And what would you have me do?" yelled Luther, standing up. "Do you not think that I'm just as saddened by the passing of Wester Tremayne as you are? I fought alongside him against Seras himself! I am limited by my position here, and I cannot do anything without being scrutinized by that self-righteous, arrogant excuse of a man who just happens to be in the highest position of power right now!"

Josh watched carefully as Luther took a few deeps breaths to calm himself.

"Okay, then," said Isaac, subdued.

"It's all right," replied Luther. "We're all a little tense right now."

"So what am I to do, then?" asked Isaac.

"Marilyn will see you home to Kendrall," said Luther. "I personally requested she be the one to escort you back since you both are well acquainted."

"Thank you," replied Isaac with a nod.

"You should probably get going," said Luther. "I'll come back in a bit to check on you two."

"Thank you," said Josh gratefully as Isaac stood.

"Take care of her for me, will you?" he said quietly in Josh's ear. Josh nodded as Isaac walked over to Arya and hugged her tightly.

"Be strong," he said.

"Always," she replied.

Luther gave them both a strange look as he left with Isaac, almost as if he wouldn't be seeing either of them again for a long time.

Once the doors had closed, Arya immediately walked over to Josh's bed and sat down next to him.

"You know I can't stay here," she said softly.

"I had a feeling you'd be saying something like that," he replied.

"Derecks is a man of politics," said Arya. "He'll drag his feet—and anyone he wants along with him—until he has concrete evidence. I can't be held here while Kristopher and Mareth try to start another war, the people of this land couldn't take it…and I have to avenge my parents, especially now that I know Seras is alive."

"I understand," said Josh, sitting up and pushing the comforter off his legs.

"Where do you think you're going?" asked Arya.

"With you, of course."

"Don't be foolish, I'm liable to be executed if I get caught on the run," she said, shaking her head. "You still have a home to go to. Luther is coming back soon, and I'm sure he'll get you out of here before any real trouble happens—"

"I gave Isaac my word," interrupted Josh. "And I owe you for saving my life."

"You don't owe me anything—"

"Then I owe it to your father to try to help you," replied Josh. "He gave his life to save ours. I'd be insulting him if I didn't go with you. Besides, *my* father taught me to never take the good people in life for granted. I'm not going to leave you to do this by yourself."

"They'll hang you too," she warned, in a last effort to dissuade him.

"So be it," said Josh, getting out of the bed. "My entire life I've always wondered why people risk their lives to protect their country, why people go thousands of miles overseas to kill others only because they were told to—by old men who sit comfortably in armchairs, no less." Arya watched him gently. "This place may not be my home, but it's more beautiful than any place I ever saw or read about where I come from. Here, the people are honest, kind, and seem to care about the well-being of everyone, not just themselves. If that's not worth trying to protect, then nothing is."

Arya stood silently in thought for a moment before sighing resignedly. "Wrap your arms around my waist, then," she said softly, extending her arm to him.

"All right?" said Josh confusedly, doing as he was told. It was a bit awkward, as he was slightly taller than Arya, but he managed without much trouble. She had placed her left arm over Josh's shoulder and was holding onto his back, when the nurse suddenly reappeared.

"This looks friendly," she commented without much emotion.

"Janice," said Arya. "Please don't try to stop us."

"Stop what?" asked Janice. "One minute I turned my back, the next you were both gone. But I will have to call for the guards," she warned.

"Could you give us a small head start?" asked Arya.

"I think I could manage that," said the nurse, nodding. "Please be careful, milady."

"I won't forget your kindness," replied Arya thankfully, her right hand beginning to glow a pale gray.

"Good luck," she said, before turning her back to them.

"How exactly are we getting out of here?" asked Josh, watching the glow around her hand get brighter.

"We're going to jump, of course."

"Aren't we rather high up?" he asked with a nervous laugh.

Arya nodded. "Oh yes. Trust me," she added softly, seeing the sudden panic on Josh's face.

"Isaac's going to be right sore with me if we die in the next minute." Her hand glowed brighter still.

Suddenly, Arya leaned up and quickly kissed Josh's forehead.

"We'll be fine," she reassured, her hand having turned white. "Three…"

Josh tightened his grip.

"Two…"

He closed his eyes.

"One…"

Much like at the kingball match, she threw her hand down and the energy exploded from underneath them, sending them rocketing up through the sheet and out the open space in the ceiling. Josh opened his eyes a crack and nearly let go from the shock.

They were falling through the air away from the tower, picking up speed much faster than he would've liked.

"Hang on!" yelled Arya, taking her arm away from Josh's back and raising it in the air. "And don't look down!"

In an instant, a brilliant flash of light emanated from her outstretched hand, and Josh looked up to see the many flickers of Essence above them being dragged down to their falling bodies. Suddenly, a thick cord of a strange material appeared in her hand, and a moment later, a massive, glimmering parachute had appeared above them.

The effects were instantaneous. The decrease in speed was so great, Josh almost lost his grip. Looking down briefly, he saw that they were poised to land just outside the fortress.

"When we land, we're going to have to find a spot to hide, and fast," called out Arya. "They'll be looking for us already."

And suddenly, their feet found cobblestone. They crashed together in a tangle of limbs, the parachute floating down gently on top of them.

"Come on," said Arya, rising quickly to her feet and pulling Josh along. Once they were a few steps away, she waved her hand and the parachute was instantly incinerated.

Their outlandish escape had attracted attention; several people out doing their routine errands and such were pointing and staring.

"You'd think we'd just fallen out of a building, the way people are staring," quipped Josh breathlessly as they ran by another crowd of onlookers.

"Hide now, joke later," replied Arya. They came to a gap in the buildings where there was a darkened alley along with some piles of trash. "In here."

They quickly ducked into the alcove and hid behind a heap of old fruit peels.

"Won't people have seen us go in here?" asked Josh, making a face. The stench of rotting garbage was causing his eyes to water.

"I'm counting on it," said Arya. "Grab my waist again."

Josh did so, and after a moment, she rocketed the both of them up to the roof of the nearest building.

"Lie down," she commanded, and they both pressed their bodies flat to the roof. The distant sound of clanking mail and plate had reached their ears, and it was drawing closer.

"Which way did they go?" they heard an angry voice ask a bystander.

The person must have pointed down the alley, for the clanking got closer and moved nearly directly underneath them. Josh glanced over at Arya who put her index finger to her lips. Finally, after a few minutes, they distinctly heard the archon tell the guards to move on, and rolled over onto their backs with a relieved sigh.

"That wasn't too bad," said Josh, still breathing hard.

"You handled yourself well," praised Arya. "If you ever learn to use Essence, you might even make a good kingballer."

"One step at a time," he replied dryly. "What now?"

"Now we have to get out of the city," said Arya, peeking over the ledge of the roof. Josh crawled up next to her. Two guards had been posted at the entrance to the alley, and there were at least half a dozen more in view running through the streets with an occasional archon. "We'll have to jump from roof to roof."

"And here I was thinking we'd gotten through the hard part."

"We can take a minute to breathe, though," she said.

"Are you...okay?" asked Josh, trying to carefully broach the subject of Wester.

"I'm fine. Essence heals injuries extremely well if they're tended to quickly enough."

"I meant about your father. Although I had been wondering about that," he added, moving his shoulder around easily without any pain.

Arya sighed. "My father...I miss him dearly, but I know him, and I know he wouldn't want me to wallow in despair over his passing." Josh nodded. "There will be time for grieving after this is all settled, but for now, we have to get out of here."

"Right," said Josh, getting onto all fours.

"The alleys aren't too wide," said Arya. "I'll jump first, so if it's too far I can use Essence to help get me over. If you aren't going to make it, I'll use it to pull you to me. Sound good?"

"No, but it'll have to do," he replied nervously. "I have a feeling I'm never going to want to be in a tall building again after this."

"Stop whining," she said, although it was with a lopsided smile. "Let's go."

He watched as she got up and took a run at the building on the other side of the alley. The gap wasn't too far, only seven or eight feet. She cleared it easily, waving him over once she was on the other side. Josh took a few steps back and chuckled a bit to try to calm his nerves. Taking a quick breath, he took three long strides and catapulted himself into the air, tucking his legs into his body and rolling across the roof on the other side.

"You made it," said Arya with an amused smile. Indeed, Josh had made the jump with about five feet to spare. "Come on."

Over the next twenty minutes, they jumped from roof to roof, slowly descending out of the center of the city. Eventually they reached a gap at least twenty feet wide that Josh was sure he couldn't cross. Arya, having already made the jump with the assistance of Essence, was standing on the other side willing him on.

"I promise, I'll get you over," she said. "We've come so far, you can't want to stop now."

"I don't, it's just…I know you say you can do it, but it doesn't make this any easier."

"Joshua, please," she said, looking him in the eyes. "You have to."

"All right," he conceded. "I hope this works."

He stepped back far enough to get a full running start. Sprinting at the edge, he jumped as hard as he could, sailing into the air. Just as he was about to start falling, a burst of light emanated from Arya's outstretched hand, pulling him over the gap and right into her body, and sending both of them sprawling on the roof.

"Nice landing."

"Sorry," he muttered, rolling himself off her. "Let's not do that again."

"I'll try to avoid the big ones from now on," she said, getting up and brushing herself off.

Suddenly, a loud yell came from somewhere behind them, followed shortly thereafter by one of the guards on the street shouting, "They're on the roofs!"

"Oh no, someone must have seen us from above," said Arya hastily. "We've got to move, come on."

She was right. A moment later, three great bursts of energy went off and a trio of archons landed on top of the building two behind them.

"You two! Hold!" yelled one, holding out his arm.

"Damn it," she muttered, turning to face them.

"What do we do?"

"When I say so, grab on real tight, and don't let go."

The archons had begun to advance on them—they were already on top of the adjacent building. Arya was hiding her hands behind her back and Josh could feel the hairs on his arms stand on end as if he had touched a doorknob after shuffling around on a carpet with socks on.

"Put your hands in the air!" the archon closest to them commanded. "Do it now!"

"Now," said Arya, barely moving her lips.

Immediately, Josh threw his arms around her waist. A split second later, they were rocketing through the air, bolts of what looked to be fire chasing after them.

"They're gonna hit us!" yelled Josh.

"Not if I have anything to say about it!" Before Josh even knew what happened, they had been encased in a great blue-white bubble that halted their momentum.

"We're...we're floating?"

"Yes, but don't let go," replied Arya as one of the bolts of fire came speeding right at them. However, instead of popping the bubble, it struck the outer shell and propelled them clear past the city walls, three farms, and into a small grove of trees where they finally came to a rest on the ground.

"So, does everyone know how to use Essence as well as you?" asked Josh, once they had regained their bearings.

"No," replied Arya with a dry laugh. "My family has always been very gifted. My mother was a genius with academics, my father with Essence, and I got the best of both worlds."

"Apparently," marveled Josh, sitting down against the trunk of a tree. "Why aren't you in the academy?"

"They asked me to join," she replied, sitting next to him. "But I turned them down. I wanted to stay with my parents on the farm. My father was thrilled, of course. He didn't want me going off to fight wars."

"I guess you can't avoid some things."

"Perhaps not."

"What do we do now?" asked Josh. "I mean, how do we go about stopping these people from bringing Seras back?"

"We have to get into Andromar," replied Arya. "But we'll die unless we're prepared."

"How do we prepare?"

"There are only two men alive that I know of who have been into the forest and survived," she said. "One is chasing us right now."

"Who's the other?"

"Do you remember me telling you about the archon who disobeyed his Essence Restraint Order and blew part of the province away?"

"Yeah, the guy in the Deadlands, right?

Arya nodded. "Necanshin Desmarthe. He doesn't have any ties to Derecks, so he won't give us up, and he might be able to tell us how to survive the forest."

"Didn't you say he was imprisoned in the middle of that wasteland?"

"Yes. We'll have to travel through the Deadlands to get to him, which means we need to stock up on food, water, and probably some Essence Sparks."

"Where can we get that stuff?"

"Isaac will be able to supply us," said Arya. "We'll go back to Kendrall first. Fortunately it's one of the last major villages before the flats, so if we make it that far, we should be fine."

Josh was silent for a moment, trying to assemble his thoughts. "Suppose we make it into the forest, stop the Rothwyn twins, and bring peace to Lumenaria. What then?"

"What do you mean?"

"I mean, if we do all that, will we still be fugitives, or will Derecks forgive us?"

"I doubt he'll forgive us," said Arya. "But maybe, if we get lucky, he'll let us go quietly."

"We've gotten ourselves into a lot of trouble, haven't we?"

Arya looked at Josh sadly. "Yes. We'll have to make do, though."

"I know," said Josh, standing and offering her his hand. "And we will." She took it and stood up.

"That's the Auroman River over there," she said, pointing to a winding body of water not far away. "We should find a crossing and hide under it until nightfall. That way we can travel with less chance of being seen."

"Let's go, then," he said with a smile.

"Joshua?"

"Hmm?" he asked, turning to face her.

"Thank you," she said, embracing him gently.

"We have a long way to go before you can thank me," he said, smiling again and returning the hug. "But you're welcome."

Chapter Six: Enemy of the Enemy

Three days passed uneventfully after their escape from Danthian. Traveling at night had worked out exceedingly well—Arya's speculation that the cover of darkness would make them difficult to spot had proven accurate.

Stiffness in Josh's back woke him from an uneasy sleep. Opening his eyes, he remembered that he had been sleeping on a mixture of rocks and dirt underneath a small bridge.

It had been Arya's turn to keep watch, and she turned to look at him when he moved.

"What time is it?" he asked, yawning.

"The sun's just gone down," she replied. "I was going to wake you in a few minutes."

"Did it rain earlier?" he asked, glancing out from under the bridge at the still wet grass around them.

"Yes. The clouds will give us good cover tonight."

"Good," he said, sitting up and stretching. "Do we still have any of those berries that we found?"

"Here," she replied, tossing him a small sack. "That's the last of them."

"Do you want any?" he asked, opening it and peering inside.

"I'll be all right," she replied, turning her back to him.

"You've barely eaten since we escaped," commented Josh, popping a couple berries into his mouth.

"I haven't been hungry."

Josh looked at Arya for a moment before scooting over next to her.

"You know, there's a difference between not grieving and not eating," he said carefully.

"I'll be fine," she said, still not looking at him.

"You need your energy if we're going to save the world," he pointed out. "And I'm sure your mother would say the same thing."

Arya finally looked at him, and he was pleased to see the corners of her mouth turned up slightly.

"She would," she replied, taking the bag from his outstretched hand. "You're absolutely right about that."

Josh smiled. He waited for her to finish the last of the fruit before urging, "We should get moving."

"Yes," she agreed, quickly washing the bag in the river. "We still have a ways to go."

"Do you know where we are?" asked Josh.

"I have a vague idea," said Arya as she poked her head out from under the bridge to check that no one was around. "Let's go."

They kept near the water so that if anyone passed by they could hide in the riverbank.

"I'd guess we're about six days from Kendrall on foot," she said, as they walked quietly through some tall grass. "This would be so much easier if we had horses."

"It'd be a lot harder to stay hidden, though."

"True."

They continued on, moving at a comfortable pace.

"It's a bit strange, the Grand Arbiter growing ill at the same time everyone goes missing, don't you think?" asked Josh.

"I agree, but I'm not ready to start believing conspiracies," said Arya. "Lord Gainsburgh is quite the resilient man. I'm sure if he had to go to Mafaelia for treatment, he had no alternative."

"Speaking of lords," said Josh, "how come no one ever told me that your father was a lord?"

"It never came up," she replied with a shrug, though Josh missed it in the darkness. "My entire family is descended from royal lineage."

"You're joking."

"No. Actually, I once heard my mother telling a friend that we were descendants of Celestina—you remember the woman in the painting?"

"Seriously?" asked Josh.

"I don't know if it's true or not," she replied. "I do know that I'm related to the third king of Lumenaria. I don't remember his name, though."

"So you're a princess?"

She pursed her lips. "Technically."

"I thought there was just the Grand Arbiter?"

"That's how it is now, but hundreds of years ago royalty ruled in this land."

"Wow. So if you're royalty, how come your family lived out on a farm?"

"Do you think less of me because we chose to help the land grow rather than have people do it for us and be spoiled rotten?"

"I think more of you because of it," said Josh. "It's the kind of thing I was talking about back in the infirmary."

"You mean with people being better here than where you're from?"

Josh nodded. "Yeah. I don't know anyone who would pass up an easy life to take care of the land."

"Is there a lot of war where you come from?"

"Quite a bit."

"You can't really blame them, then, can you?"

"Why not?" he asked.

"After you see so much fighting, you stop believing that the world is worth helping," said Arya softly.

"Yeah, but these people haven't been to battle. They don't even have relatives fighting—"

"War affects everyone," said Arya, stopping. "Even if it doesn't seem like it immediately."

"I…I'm sorry. I didn't mean to offend you."

"You didn't," she replied, resuming her pace. "But don't be so quick to judge people. Everyone is just trying to get by as best they know how."

Josh thought carefully but didn't say anything. There was undeniable truth to her words, but he was unsure how to respond. His choice was made for him, however, when Arya suddenly stopped and pulled him down to a crouch.

"What is it?" he asked.

"I'm not sure," she whispered. "I thought I saw movement up ahead."

They waited silently in the river bank, trying to determine if they were alone.

"Wait," whispered Josh, squinting. "There."

The outlines were barely distinguishable in the night, but three horses were standing at the edge of the river about fifty feet in front of them, lapping at the cool, clean water. Each looked to be mounted by a rider.

"Archons?" he whispered.

"Can't tell," replied Arya. "It's a bit strange for them to be out at night, and they almost never travel together. They have their own units to command."

"Should we wait or go around?"

"We should wait," she replied. "We'll have to go too far away from the river to avoid them."

"It sounds like they're talking," said Josh, who could barely make out dull sounds of conversation over the quiet flow of the water.

"We might hear something useful," suggested Arya. "But they could be farmers for all we know."

"I think we can move up a little without being heard," said Josh, peering around Arya at the dirt and mud in front of them.

"Stay low," she whispered, starting to crawl forward on her elbows.

"This is good," breathed Josh almost inaudibly as they got closer, the indistinguishable mutterings turning into words.

"...rotten bastard was holding out on us," said one of the riders in a deep, bass voice.

"Whaddaya expect o' Jones," said another. "He's as dir'y as they come."

"Yeah, but how can you, in good conscience steal from your brothers?" said the third, and it sounded like he was speaking through his nose.

"Oh hell," whispered Arya. "Bandits."

"We don't have anything of value," said Josh, crawling up next to her to get a better view. "What would they want with us?"

"Well...usually when there are people wanted for crimes, the government offers rewards for their capture."

"Say what?"

"I'm sorry for not saying anything," she apologized. "I thought it would upset you."

"Nah, I just wish I'd known," whispered Josh. "It's rather cool, actually."

"You're taking it fairly well," commented Arya.

"As long as Isaac won't turn us in when we get to him, then life's no different, is it?"

"Well, other people might try to—"

"Shh," hushed Josh as the riders had glanced over in their direction.

"Did you hear something?" the third man asked.

"Yea," said the second.

"It's probably just the fish jumping," the first man said.

"Might want to check it out. You know they said the young Miss Tremayne and some whelp escaped not too far from here."

"Miss Tremayne," said the second with a haughty laugh. "I reckon it migh' be worth tryin' ta pillage Kendrall jus' ta get a crack at her."

Josh put a hand on Arya's shoulder at hearing this, though he wasn't really sure why.

"Come on," the same man said. "We gotta git back ta camp before sunup."

Josh and Arya watched as they rode away before letting out a mutual sigh of relief.

"That was close," she said, leaning against the silt wall of the riverbed.

"A bit, yeah," he replied with a nervous chuckle.

"I'm sorry for not telling you about the reward," reiterated Arya. "I didn't even remember until two days ago, and I wasn't sure how to bring it up."

"Don't worry about it," replied Josh. "It is a bit strange being on the lam, but every experience makes us stronger, right?"

"And we must always strive to improve," she said with an approving smile, offering him her hand. "Let's get moving."

"You know," said Josh as they started up again, "I keep thinking about what Luther said about the twins and how he seemed to know it was coming."

"Luther is extraordinarily perceptive," said Arya. "In all fairness, I bet the situation could've been prevented if Lord Gainsburgh hadn't fallen ill—he and Luther have always gotten along famously from what I've heard."

"Yeah, Derecks is really a pain in the arse."

"Speaking of Luther, have you come any closer to figuring out Essence?"

"You saw me practicing?"

"Yesterday," she admitted. "I woke early and watched you for a bit while you were keeping lookout."

"I'm rubbish at it," he said ruefully. "I can't feel a bloody thing."

"It takes time and determination. If you keep at it, you'll get there eventually."

"We'll have to wait and see then."

"You know, I didn't manage to do anything until I was six—"

"GOTCHA!"

A huge net made of thick black ropes descended and dragged them to the ground. Josh doubled over, the wind knocked out of him. Arya too looked as if she'd been punched in the stomach.

"It's an anti-Essence net," she grunted. "I can't do anything."

"Yer right it is," said a familiar voice. "Knew I heard sumthin'."

"And spot on about who they were," said the man with the deep voice, lighting a candle. He was very dark-skinned, bald, and had multiple piercings in each ear. "Tremayne and the runt."

"Let's git 'em bundled up and head for camp."

The three men pushed Josh and Arya around so they could grab the corners of the net, which they tied off. The large man with the deep voice made a strong beam out of Essence, which he placed across two of the horses, against the saddle horns.

"Why do we have to ride with them?" asked the third man.

"Because I said so."

Using Essence, the man lifted Josh and Arya off the ground and tied the net to the beam so they were hanging in it between the horses.

"Let's get moving. Garcia will pleased," he said, extinguishing the light.

"One hundred thousand hennes!" whooped the man with the nasally voice as the three men mounted their horses.

"Is that a lot?" Josh whispered to Arya.

"Yes. A bit more than I thought it was going to be, actually. Derecks must really want us badly."

"Keep yer voice down, you twit," the second man said as they starting riding.

"Twenty-five equal shares, that's…that's…"

"Four thousand each," called out the man who appeared to be the leader.

"Well, I was always awful at math!"

"Is this bad?" asked Josh over the noise of the horses' galloping.

"Probably," said Arya ruefully. "By the sound of it, they're taking us back to their camp, where their leader will decide our fate. They'll probably send us off to the archons to collect their money, and we'll be hung."

"I think I would've preferred you lie to me there."

"You did ask for the truth," she said with a sigh, then, "Ouch!" as they went over a particularly large bump.

"Are you all right?" asked Josh, concerned.

"I will be," said Arya, rubbing her back. "This net is a pain in the ass."

"Literally," replied Josh flatly.

"You never cease to amaze me, Joshua Cooper. We could be staring death in the face in two days or less, and you still have a sense of humor."

"I learned a long time ago that fear isn't a very sensible emotion to have," he replied. "I can't be emotionless. I don't really know anyone who doesn't feel anything, so I just use humor to deal with things."

"That's very mature."

"When I was in primary school, I was often bullied out of my lunch money," he explained as they went over another nasty bump. "Well, one day I just got sick of it, and I told the wanker to beat me up and take it if he wanted it so badly. He scoffed and walked away, and I never heard from him again. Ever since, I haven't let fear affect my life."

"Oy! No talking ye two!" yelled one of the riders.

"You know," whispered Josh, "I think I can reach through this net and maybe grab a rock to saw through this rope."

"It'll hurt pretty bad to fall going at this speed, and don't you think they'll notice?"

"You'll be able to use Essence, though," said Josh, sticking his arm out through one of the holes in the net. He slowly lowered his hand until he could feel blades of grass brushing against his fingertips.

"Watch out for sticks," warned Arya. Her words came a moment too late as a twig snapped against Josh's hand forcing him to withdraw it and shake it out violently.

"Damn it," he muttered sucking on the bruised spot.

"I'll help," said Arya, reaching out through the net.

"You don't have to—"

"Why? Because I'm a girl?"

"No...I just don't want you to get hurt..." he replied lamely. Arya looked at

Josh and gave him a wry smile.

"Very chivalrous of you, but I'll be all right."

She reached down, and after a moment came back up with a round, smooth, baseball-sized rock.

"I don't think this'll cut through much," she said, frowning and discarding it.

"Let's keep at it."

It took them many tries and several minutes before they found a rock that was suitable. Josh promptly started hacking away at the ropes, passing the rock to Arya when his hands got tired.

He was rubbing the cramps out of his hands when he saw flickers of light through the nearby trees as they went flying past.

"Hurry," he whispered urgently. "I think we're almost there."

Arya glanced up and—upon noticing the gradually brightening glow of campfires—began chopping frantically at the net.

"I've almost got it," she grunted, blood trickling down her fingers. A moment later, the rope broke free and they crashed to the ground hard, rolling to a stop a few seconds later.

"Ugh," groaned Josh. Picking himself up, he glanced around only to discover that they were in a clearing surrounded by tents, small campfires, and about two dozen very brutish and amused-looking men. He helped Arya to her feet as a tall, lanky man with a thin black beard and long black hair stepped forward into the clearing. He wore an elegant ruffled black shirt, with matching pants, shoes, belt, and bandanna. Josh thought he looked like a pirate.

"Arya Tremayne and Joshua Cooper?" he wondered aloud. "It appears Lady Luck truly has eyes only for me."

There was a commotion from behind him, accompanied with a very loud yell.

"HOW DID YOU LET THEM SLIP AWAY FROM RIGHT UNDER YOU?"

"Morris!" called the tall man inside the clearing, his eyes never moving from his prize.

"Boss!" said the dark man, stumbling forward. "You're not going to believe what Smithey and Rowan just did. We had Tremayne and the boy, and they let them get"—his eyes glanced over to where Josh and Arya were standing warily—"away?"

"A pity," said the boss, as the other two men joined their companion. "But thankfully, I seem to have found them for you." The assembled crowd laughed at the men, who looked properly embarrassed. "Bring them to my quarters."

As he turned his back, Arya thrust her hand toward him, a jet of bright white light erupting from her fingertips. The man's reaction was almost as if he expected it—with a simple wave of his hand, a great white screen appeared between the incoming bolt and himself. Arya's blast slammed into it with an earsplitting crash but left the man completely unharmed.

"Now then," he said, without turning around. "Refrain from attacking me or my men from here on out, please, or I will be forced to hurt you. You three," he added, looking at Josh and Arya's captors. "You come too."

Arya looked at Josh apologetically as the five of them followed the leader into his tent—the largest in the camp. The interior was about what Josh expected for a bandit captain: a comfortable-looking bed, a large table in the middle with what looked to be a map of Lumenaria laid out on it, several bottles of assorted liquids, a wardrobe, and many other trinkets and oddities Josh couldn't identify.

"Morris," said the leader, turning around to face him.

"My lord."

Josh nearly jumped when the bandit leader pulled out a dagger and thrust the point of it at Morris's throat.

"You had a hundred thousand hennes in your back pocket, and you almost let them get away?" he asked in a dangerously quiet voice.

"I was riding up front. Smithey and Rowan were supposed to—"

"They're a pair of bumbling idiots," said the man as if the two others weren't present in the room.

"Ay, now, tha's not nice—"

"Shut up, Rowan," hissed the boss. "I don't expect much from those two, but if these"—he glanced sideways at Josh and Arya—"children had escaped under your watch, we'd be using you for mastrichon bait in the morning."

"I understand, sir. My deepest apologies."

"And as for you two," he added, lowering the dagger. "Go read a book, or do something that will make it so you aren't as stupid as rocks."

"Yes sir," the man called Smithey answered sullenly. "Let's go lads."

The three men left the tent, and as the flaps opened, Josh noticed that there were four or five men standing outside the entrance—whether they were guarding the tent or eavesdropping, he didn't know.

"Before we begin, let me tell you that this tent is made out of the same material as the net my men used to capture you. So don't bother trying anything."

"You're bluffing," said Arya. "I didn't feel anything when we entered."

The man paused and looked at her, the corners of his mouth turning up. "You're the daughter of Wester and Rae Tremayne, no question there. Regardless, there are two dozen men outside who will do everything to stop you if you try to escape, and trust me, they'll not all as stupid as the ones who captured you."

"They were smart enough to do that," countered Josh.

"Indeed. My name is Garcia Theron," he said extending his hand toward Josh, who did not shake it. Smiling, Garcia withdrew his hand and sat down at the table. "I am the leader of the Kalrazal Bandits."

"Kalrazal, hmm?" asked Arya appraisingly.

"I should think you've heard of us before?"

"Does it matter?" she asked. "What are your plans for us?"

"Well, that depends, of course."

"On what?" asked Josh.

"The manner of how you came to be here."

"Your men captured us and brought us here," deadpanned Arya.

"You are as witty as you are beautiful," he said with a wink.

"Don't even think about laying a hand on her," said Josh, taking a step in front of Arya.

"And if I did, what would you do?" asked Garcia, standing up. "Would you hit me?" He walked up to Josh and held the dagger out to him. "Would you kill me?"

Josh took the dagger from him and looked at it—it would be easy to just thrust his hand forward and kill this man who was likely going to sell them to Derecks Whitemane for his riches.

"No," he said, tossing the sharp piece of metal to the ground. "I'm not a killer. Not yet, anyway."

Garcia regarded him carefully for a moment before smiling and returning to his chair, not bothering to pick up the dagger.

"I'm glad to hear that," he said. "And you needn't worry. I may be a thief, but I have rules, rules that both my men and I follow, and one of them is that we do not harm women or children."

"You think women are incapable of fighting?" said Arya skeptically, crossing her arms.

"You are so incredibly tetchy," replied Garcia with an irritated sigh, leaning back. "Relax."

"You could be sending us to our deaths in a matter of hours," Josh pointed out. "She has a right to be upset."

"Fair enough," said Garcia. "But there's no guarantee I'm going to do that, is there?" He sighed audibly when neither of them answered. "I do not harm children because they aren't capable of defending themselves. I do not harm women—not because they can't defend themselves—but because I consider it a sin to damage a thing of beauty."

"Surely you don't mean to tell me that you find all women beautiful," challenged Josh.

"What I find to be truth is irrelevant," answered Garcia. "Beauty lies in the eye of the beholder, one man's trash is another man's treasure."

"We've heard the proverbs," said Arya, annoyed.

"My point is that unlike men, every woman is beautiful to someone in this world, and I will not do damage to such a type of being."

The image of Josh's incredibly rude lab partner, Tricia, crossed his mind and he had to stifle a laugh at the thought of anyone finding her self-centeredness beautiful.

"I see young Joshua disagrees with me," commented Garcia amusedly.

"I was just remembering someone," he replied, not offering any more information. Arya glanced sideways at him, but Josh shook his head slightly and she made no effort to press him.

"So, then, back to the matter at hand. I've heard stories about your escape, and they all sound like a load of bureaucratic dribble. I want to hear what actually happened from the source."

"We were at the kingball match when the explosion happened. The High Archon was planning to detain us afterward, because he believed me to hold some unnaturally strong power and Joshua to be suspect," said Arya.

"And why would the High Archon believe either of those things?"

"My father sacrificed his life to save us, and Joshua is new to these lands," replied Arya tersely, not offering any further explanation.

"That's nice, but you've not really answered my question," said Garcia. "I digress. Why did you run?"

"We can't tell you," replied Josh quickly.

"You had better, lad, else I'm liable to turn you over to the authorities for a great deal of money."

"We have no choice," said Arya to Josh quietly. "No one would believe a bandit, anyway."

"I'm insulted to hear you speak so lowly of my noble profession."

"Killing and looting qualifies your profession as noble?" questioned Arya.

"No, no, no, you have me confused for one of those evil bandits," he replied, waving his hand dismissively. "I'm a less-evil bandit. I only steal from the wealthy and corrupt, and I don't kill if I can help it."

"And do you give your plunder to the weak and defenseless?" countered Josh.

"Er, no," said Garcia flatly after a moment. "That's not the point! Tell me why you ran, or I'll have a new net thrown over you two."

"You know about the explosion at the match, but you don't know that while everyone was panicking and all the archons were busy, there was a prison break at Synax."

"Who escaped?"

"Tyran Nazerf, among others. And there have been disappearances at the academy," she continued. "Six top students went missing, and four turned up dead, bodies depleted of Essence." Garcia made a grimace at this. "We know who the other two are, and we think they're plotting something big."

"How do you know this?"

"One of the guards identified one of them during the break-out."

"I see," hummed Garcia. "And how many men did he have with him?"

"It was just him, I believe," replied Arya. One of Garcia's eyebrows went up considerably at this, but he said nothing. "There's one other important thing."

"Yes?" he prompted, after a moment.

"Seras Falrider isn't dead."

The bandit leaned forward in the chair and rested his elbows on the table.

"So I assume what you're getting at is that these students who've escaped and freed Nazerf plan to travel to parts unknown and meet up with Seras, thus bringing about another war to this kingdom?"

"That's the short version, yes," said Josh with a nod.

"Fascinating," said Garcia appreciatively. "But you *still* haven't told me why you ran."

"Okay, look," said Arya, slamming her palm on the table in frustration. "You know who I am, you know my lineage. There isn't a damn person in the province who doesn't. What kind of person would I be if I soiled my family's name and let a war come to Lumenaria, having been fully capable of preventing it?"

Garcia appraised her carefully for a moment.

"All right," he said, satisfied. "And what about you?" he asked, nodding at Josh.

"She and her father saved my life," he replied. "I want to help her."

"I wonder, Joshua Cooper, if that is all you want."

"It is," he replied confusedly. "What else would I want?"

"I guess you're still at the age when innocence outweighs hormones," said Garcia with a smirk, standing up. "Never you mind, then. So, what is your plan to accomplish all of this?"

"Boss!" yelled a man, running into the tent. "You've gotta come quick, there's somethin' wrong wit tha' horses!"

"Don't try anything funny now," he warned, beckoning for them to follow him.

The scene was chaotic. Several of the bandits were trying to calm down fifteen or so horses that were bucking wildly, while the others were attempting to pull the animals to the ground with ropes. The horses' eyes were burning red, with flickering black flames for pupils.

"We should break for it," whispered Arya to Josh.

"Something's wrong here," he replied. The flames in the animals' eyes looked oddly familiar. "I've seen something like that before."

"Something like what?"

"The black flames. Nether?" he wondered aloud, remembering the flame in Luther's laboratory.

"Did you just say Nether?" asked Garcia, spinning around to face him.

Josh didn't have time to answer when huge shards of ice materialized in the air around them and fell to the ground, encasing the entire camp in a frozen cage. Over the angry shouts and screams of disapproval, a loud dark voice spoke through the air.

"Quiet."

Instantly, the entire area went silent, a lone figure descending slowly from above them. He—at least Josh assumed it was a he based on the voice—was garbed in a full black robe and hood with maroon trim. Rivers of a glimmering substance coursed all over the garment, but it wasn't Essence. Instead, it looked rather like liquid obsidian.

"Pure Nether," whispered Arya. "This isn't good."

"Ah, here we are," said the figure, touching down on the ground lightly. He lifted his head slightly, and piercing blue eyes were visible beneath the hood. "I'm not one for monologues, so I'll make this brief. *You*"—he said pointing to all of them—"are the scum of this land. And *I*"—he continued, pointing to himself—"am the man who will cleanse it of you."

From beneath his robes, he procured a great bowling-ball-sized orb. Beautiful incandescent colors of blue and orange swirled about inside it while small translucent flames licked its surface. As he did so, three bandits to the left charged at him, using Essence to shield their attack.

Without so much as blinking, the rivulets of Nether flew off his robe in great, long strands like ropes, punched through the shields of Essence, and wrapped around the necks of the attackers.

Instantly the air was filled with screams and the stench of burning flesh. Josh cringed and looked away as the tentacles of Nether burned through the skin of the bandits, and he pretended not to hear the three thuds a moment later.

"My brother and I have evolved beyond you people," the man said. "We have unlocked a power greater than the gods themselves, and now it is time to pay for your treachery."

A man whom Josh had seen trying to calm a horse stepped forward.

"My lord, may we pledge our services to you in return for mercy?"

There was no answer. Instead, the cloaked figure lifted the orb slightly and it floated from his hand. In an instant, the man was engulfed in blue and orange flames, writhing in agony, his mouth twisted open in a silent scream. A moment later his blackened body fell to the ground, lifeless.

"I didn't say," the attacker replied, replacing the orb in his robe. "Though you certainly will not see any mercy from me."

Josh's fists clenched slightly as the man laughed at his own remark.

"I will soon stand on the remains of your people, your men, your women, your children. That's right," he added, seeing the shocked looks on the faces of some of the bandits. "I know all about the underground network of cities you use to hide your families in. Rest assured they will not remain hidden for long. But for now, I will deal with each of you. Sit."

Everyone in the clearing lowered themselves to the ground, no one willing to test the man's patience. He began walking around the camp, assessing each person individually. When he reached Josh and Arya, he stopped.

"You two aren't bandits," he said, crouching down next to them. Up close, Josh could see a young face, no older than twenty-five staring back at him—yet there was no mistaking the absolute evil coursing through this man. "What are you doing here?"

"There's a reward out for them," said Garcia. "My men captured them and they were brought here."

"Ahhh, Garcia Theron," said the man with a cold, shrill laugh, standing up. "How I've been looking forward to this."

"And who would you be?" asked Garcia.

"Surely you haven't forgotten?" asked the man, in mock indignity. "After all we've been through!"

"Enough of your games, will you tell me what relation we have or not?"

"As part of the Razorback Guild, you raided my hometown of Laeton ten years ago, and killed almost everyone, including my parents."

"I didn't kill anyone, it was that idiot who called himself captain that was leading us," said Garcia, spitting on the ground. "And if you remember correctly, he was sent to the executioner publicly in the Grand Capital not three days later."

"The sins of the father," replied the man, a crazed look in his eyes. "My name? My name is Mareth Rothwyn, and tonight, I am *your* executioner…but I have an idea before that."

He turned to glance at Josh and Arya quickly, before forming a table out of Essence next to them. "Stand up." They did as they were told, and Mareth produced a dark bottle from his robe, uncorking it as he put it on the table. A moment later two glasses had appeared next to it. "Since neither of you are bandits, I feel it is appropriate to not kill both of you."

"How generous," muttered Josh.

"This here," he explained, pouring a black liquid into each glass, "is a Nether drink that will, if consumed in great enough quantity, kill you quite painfully. So we'll have a little game. You'll both drink until one of you dies. The other will be healed and let go."

"That's horrible!" exclaimed Garcia. "They're just children!"

"What's horrible is being forced to watch a bandit murder your parents when you're fifteen," spat Mareth, thrusting his hand at Garcia. A flash of white light blinded them all, and when they could see again, blood was dripping down and off the bandit leader's cheek from where a great wound had opened. "You obviously seem keen on these two, so I will extend you the same courtesy of having to watch someone you care about die."

Josh and Arya looked at each other nervously.

"I'll drink fast," said Arya quietly, her gaze shifting downward. "If I can't save Lumenaria, at least I can save you."

"We do this fair," insisted Josh. "I'm not any more thrilled about this than you, but you're not dying to save me."

Arya said nothing, she only looked at the glasses on the table.

"Well, go on, then," said Mareth. "Get on with it, or I'll kill you both."

Josh nodded and picked up a glass, Arya the other. Sighing, he smiled sadly at her.

"Bottoms up."

He touched the glass to his lips and took a great pull. It was as if he was drinking death itself. The liquid, while flavorless, drained energy from his body with each swallow. After four gulps—and just as Josh was sure he wouldn't last a fifth—a sudden warmth engulfed and rejuvenated him, and somehow he found the strength to keep drinking. Chancing a glance at Arya, he saw her looking straight forward, her right hand holding the glass to her lips and her left glowing a pale white at her side where Mareth couldn't see it. The thought that she was sacrificing herself to save him passed through Josh's mind, but he realized that Arya was drinking just as strongly as he was and not faltering.

After a few more seconds, Mareth walked over to the bottle and picked it up, peering inside to examine the contents.

"Should have worked by now," he muttered, not noticing that Arya had raised her glowing hand and pointed it straight at him.

A tremendous amount of energy exploded from her, sending Mareth skyward. She quickly threw the glass down and waved both her arms above her head, encasing the entire camp in a great, transparent shield, which Mareth landed on a moment later. Withdrawing the orb with the flames, he held it out at arm's length—yet the only thing that happened was several black burn marks appeared on the barrier all at once.

"Interesting," he said, in the same loud, echoing voice he had used to quiet the bandits. "I didn't know everyday peasants had talents to rival academy students. What is your name, girl?"

"My name is Tremayne!" shouted Arya. "And that is all you will learn of me!"

"I should have guessed," replied Mareth, his tone almost one of amusement. "I hear it was your father who managed to stop some of the effects of my brother's gift at the match, after all."

Arya's eyes darkened in anger, but her barrier remained intact.

"So this is it, out doing the dirty work for your brother?" she taunted. "Cleaning up the country while Krissy goes and romps through the forest with

Tyran?"

"You know a lot," said Mareth appraisingly. "How very interesting."

"You're insane if you think the archons don't know what you're up to," said Arya. "You will never bring back Seras Falrider."

"You think we're bringing him back so we can make war on Lumenaria with him?" he replied with a demented laugh. "You go on thinking that. As for now, I have other business to attend to." He replaced the orb in his robe and a black glow appeared around him. "Until we meet again, Miss Tremayne."

And he disappeared.

"Is he gone?" asked Josh, looking around. The horses had begun to calm down and the ice melted.

"It seems so," replied Arya. She didn't lower the barrier, however.

"You two go wait in my tent," said Garcia, using Essence to heal the wound on his face. "I'll be with you in a minute."

"What makes you think we'll take orders from you?" asked Josh.

"If the princess can materialize a shield that powerful, you two could've put up a hell of a fight, and she knows that," said Garcia accusingly, pointing at Arya. "Just wait for me, I'll only be a minute."

Josh glanced sideways at Arya before shrugging, walking into the tent ahead of her and sitting at the table.

"You can hold the shield up from in here?" Arya nodded and shrugged. "I guess Derecks was right to be suspicious of you," he said thoughtfully after a moment. Arya looked at him, her lips curving up slightly.

"Maybe," she replied in noncommittal fashion. "You're new to this world, Josh. I can't tell you everything immediately."

"I didn't ask," he replied, holding his hands up. "Merely just remarking at how much arse you kicked out there."

"I did a bit, didn't I?"

"More than a bit."

"My entire family—not just my father—has always had an exceptional gift with Essence," said Arya. "And certain other things help. When we have a private moment, I'll tell you more."

"Speaking of private moments, looks like this one is about to end," said Josh, as the silhouette of Garcia appeared at the entrance to the tent.

"All right, there's obviously something you're not telling me," he said entering, looking at Arya.

"Makes two of us," commented Josh.

"Funny. As you were saying?" she asked Garcia.

"At first, I thought you were mad," he said, regarding her carefully. "But after that display out there, maybe you have a chance to do what you want to."

"This isn't news to me," said Arya, folding her arms. "What of it?"

"Mareth killed good friends of mine tonight," said Garcia. "And if he truly knows about our underground dwellings—"

"Yes, I'm interested about that," said Arya. "This network of underground cities and towns."

"His information is incorrect, just as his desire for vengeance," replied Garcia, dismissively. "We have hideouts and small communities hidden about the land, but nothing more. If he knows where they are though…" He trailed off, staring vacantly into space. "I have no family, just my men. My men, however—who are my brothers by all rights—have wives, sons, and daughters. I cannot let them perish without a second thought."

"What are you going to do about it?" asked Josh.

"Join up with you two, of course," he replied as if it were the most obvious thing in the world. "If you'll have me."

"And what of your troupe?" asked Arya.

"Disbanded. I don't want them out gallivanting after riches while their loved ones are in peril."

"This was okay with them?"

"After what they just saw, everyone thought it might be better to take a breather."

"And what's to say you won't turn us over to the archons at first chance?" asked Josh. "You are a bandit, after all."

"You don't know much about banditry, do you?" Garcia sighed and shook his head. "I can't turn you in. I'd have to pay a farmer to do it and get the money from him afterward, assuming he didn't run off to parts unknown to begin with."

"Why can't you do it?" asked Josh.

"Because I'm a thief," said Garcia exasperatedly. "You think the archons don't have a price on my head as well?"

Josh raised an eyebrow at Arya, who shrugged.

"I can provide horses."

Still, both of them remained silent.

"You want a better reason? Why are you helping her?" countered Garcia.

"Because she saved my life. You know that."

"We share common ground, then," he pointed out. "Truth be told, I've been growing weary of this life. It's not very healthy, and I've been aching to get out and see a bit of the country."

"That's a surprise," deadpanned Josh. "What do you think?"

"An extra pair of eyes never hurt," remarked Arya. "And horses will make our trip much easier. Just as long as we're clear that if you try any funny business, I'll kill you," she added, staring down Garcia.

"You have my word, milady, that I will help you to the best of my ability."

Arya looked at Josh, nodding.

"All right," he said shrugging. "What the hell."

Chapter Seven: Return to Kendrall

Because they'd been relieved of traveling strictly along the river, the detour to the bandit's camp had shortened the remaining trip to Kendrall considerably. Along with the horses Garcia provided, they were set to arrive three days early.

"What's in Kendrall?" asked Garcia, stoking a small fire they had made one evening.

"Supplies," said Arya, not offering any further information.

"You know," began Garcia thoughtfully, "I know that you don't trust me, but I'd still like to know how we're going to accomplish saving the world."

"We'll tell you when we get to Kendrall," replied Arya. "That way we'll at least be able to ride there before you call us delusional and leave."

"I wish you'd have more respect for me than that," he replied sullenly.

"You are a thief," Josh pointed out.

"Right, right."

"We're almost out of food," remarked Arya.

"I'll find some," said Garcia, getting up. "I could use some time to myself, anyway."

Arya raised an eyebrow skeptically at him.

"I'll leave the horses," he added with an exasperated sigh, rolling his eyes.

"Be back in twenty minutes," said Arya, returning her gaze to the fire.

"No problem, Princess," said Garcia, wiggling his eyebrows suggestively at Josh.

"Don't call me that," she warned, her eyes narrowing. Garcia shrugged at Josh, who arched an eyebrow skeptically and watched as the bandit walked off toward a nearby field.

"You've been edgy lately," he commented after a few moments.

"Have I?" she asked shortly. Josh said nothing as he watched her carefully, hands in his pockets. Looking down, she sighed. "I'm sorry. I don't like bandits all that much."

"I can understand that," he replied with a dry laugh, looking at the dark blue sky. "You don't have to do this all yourself, you know. I might not be able to use Essence, but I'm a good listener."

Arya looked up and smiled at him.

"I know you are," she said, looking him in the eye. "And thank you…it means a lot to me that you've stuck with me through this."

"Why are you so obsessed about this, though?" asked Josh. "I understand you wanting justice for your father, but there's obviously something else." Arya lowered her eyes but said nothing. "What haven't you told me?"

She sighed and looked at him gently.

"I haven't been completely honest with you. My parents weren't always farmers. They were both archons, once upon a time."

"Really?"

"Yes," said Arya with a nod, her gaze returning to the fire. "Skilled fighters like you couldn't imagine, and well liked by the entire land."

"What happened?"

"Me," she replied with a reminiscent smile. "When my mother became pregnant, they decided to hang up the armor and move from Danthian to Kendrall and live a quiet, peaceful life." She sighed heavily and rested her chin on her knees, hugging them to her chest. "When the war with Seras came, my mother heard that Marilyn was being sent off to the front. She'd just graduated from academy and wasn't experienced. My mother had always looked at her as another daughter and went with her regiment as a healer."

Arya looked away as her eyes began to well up slightly.

"Seras found out somehow, and the opportunity to kill someone from one of the royal lineages was too great for him to pass up. One night he snuck into their camp and killed her himself and left everyone else unharmed."

"Why?" asked Josh incredulously.

"He wanted to make a statement," she replied. "No one, nowhere was safe from him. Shortly after Derecks Whitemane received word of her death, he led the charge into the forest and ended the war." She paused and wiped at her cheeks discreetly. "My mother, and father now, died protecting people they loved from those who would undo this land. I could never forgive myself if I didn't make the same effort."

"I understand," said Josh quietly. "So…how did you learn to use Essence so well?"

"When you're the daughter of two ex-archons, you pick up a thing or two," she replied with a small chuckle, finally looking at Josh properly.

"Pity I can't use it," he lamented. "It'd be right useful to have you as a teacher."

"Keep practicing, then," encouraged Arya. "I wonder if our thief is going to be back with something to eat anytime soon."

"I think he will," said Josh. The words were barely out of his mouth when Garcia wandered into to the camp holding a small brown pouch full of something. "You find anything?"

"Hornberries," said Garcia, tossing him the sack. "Don't eat them all."

"Just a couple," he replied in thanks, popping two into his mouth and handing them to Arya.

"You know, I was thinking…"

"About what?" asked Josh after Garcia trailed off.

"I remember you mentioning something about the forest when we were all back at the camp," he mentioned thoughtfully, pointing at Arya. "Do you mean to go in there?"

She turned her gaze toward Josh, who shrugged.

"We're going to do whatever it takes," replied Arya. "If that means going into the forest, so be it."

"You're mad. Both of you," he added, grinning at Josh. "But no matter. It'll make for a fine story one day, in any case."

"Indeed," muttered Arya. "We should get moving soon, it's getting dark enough."

"I'll ready the horses," said Garcia, getting up.

"He seems really eager," she commented, rising to her feet.

Josh nodded. "He does."

"I wonder what he's not telling us."

"Everybody keeps a bit of the truth for themselves from time to time," quipped Josh.

"Right," replied Arya with a slight laugh, waving him off as Garcia came riding up to them with their horses.

"We should be able to reach Kendrall by tomorrow night," he said from atop his mount.

"I'm still not a great rider, you know" grunted Josh, struggling to pull himself up onto the saddle.

"Just keep your heels down on the stirrups and lean forward," coached Garcia.

"I know, I know," said Josh, finally getting himself situated atop his chestnut stallion.

"Ready?" asked Arya.

"As ready as I'll ever be."

"Hyah!" yelled Garcia, tearing off down the bank of the river. Josh quickly rode after him as Arya brought up the rear, just in case they were attacked or if Josh fell off his horse.

Despite his earlier reservations, Josh couldn't help but absolutely love riding with speed; the warm, night breeze flying through his hair as he galloped forward. He'd had driving lessons in preparation to get his license, but driving a car was incomparable to riding. The raw power underneath him was exhilarating, and it gave him a chuckle to think of three hundred miniature versions of the animal he was on top of packed underneath the hood of a sports car.

The night passed without incident, and with the dawn came time for Josh to keep watch while Arya and Garcia slept.

He was leaning against the bank of the river. He glanced over at Arya and Garcia, each of them curled up next to their mounts, and rubbed the back of his neck. Sighing, he looked down at his hands and flexed them, trying to will the beautiful glimmers of light in the air to bend to his will.

He sat patiently for hours, trying to calm his mind and feel his surroundings, when Arya shifted and opened her eyes, squinting at him.

"What time is it?" she asked groggily.

"After midday," replied Josh, wiping the sweat from his palms on the grass.

"Ugh," she grumbled, rolling over and sitting up. "I suppose it's my turn, then."

"You can sleep a bit more if you want," said Josh. "I'm still trying to get the hang of this."

"Great cities aren't built in a day, Joshua Cooper," she said tiredly but with a smile, sliding over to him and covering his hands with hers. He could feel a warm energy coming from them. "And you haven't slept in nearly twenty-four hours. You certainly won't be able to use Essence unless you're rested."

Josh's nodded—his eyelids were already closing of their own volition.

"I'll wake you when it's time to go."

Josh laid his head down on the grass, his eyes closing a moment later, and he failed to see Arya smile softly at him before focusing her attention to the landscape.

When nightfall came, she shook Josh awake gently. The three of them wasted no time in mounting their horses and galloping at full speed toward Kendrall.

Not too long into their ride, Josh looked up and saw Garcia slowing down slightly, pointing at a dark mass in the distance.

"That's the Ferris Crossing!" he yelled over the wind, as he drew even with Josh. A large, wooden bridge extending out over the rushing water of a nearby river became visible as they approached. "We're going to cross there! Not too long to go now!"

Josh nodded as Garcia picked his speed up again, resuming his position in the front.

"What did he want?" asked Arya, riding up alongside Josh.

"He said that this is the Ferris Crossing," he called out, as they rode over the bridge.

"We'll be there within the hour, then," she replied.

They rode on, although Josh's legs were growing tired and sore; they'd passed a particularly bumpy patch of ground and the results had been somewhat painful for him.

Finally, after what seemed to be much longer than an hour, Garcia slowed to a stop in front of a small grove of trees, Josh and Arya trotting up behind him.

"Are you all right?" Arya asked Josh, who winced as he dismounted.

"I think I need an athletic protector for this," he groaned, walking around and stretching.

"You'll get used to it," said Garcia with a sympathetic smile, clapping him on the shoulder. "We'll leave the horses here so you can walk it off. The village is just beyond the trees."

"Hang on," said Josh, as they tied the bridles to a log. "Do you smell something?"

"Now that you mention it," replied Garcia, sniffing the air. "I do smell something."

"Smells like…."

"Fire," whispered Arya, running off into the grove.

"Arya!"

"Princess!"

Josh and Garcia ran after her, the trees and bushes whipping at their limbs and faces as they hurried through.

They emerged on the other side to a blinding red and orange blaze, the buildings of Kendrall burning in the night.

"What...what happened?" breathed Arya, falling to her knees.

"There's no Essence," noted Josh, looking around. Indeed, the minute points of light that normally glittered in the air were missing.

"It was Mareth. It had to be him," said Garcia, stepping toward the well in the center of the square. "Even the water's dried up."

"We have to find Isaac," said Arya, getting up. "Follow me."

They ran through the square and down one of the streets, covering their heads as chunks of burning wood and ash flew from the buildings and rained down on them.

"How much farther?" called out Garcia.

"Just at the end, here," replied Arya, jogging up to a smaller cottage that was completely immersed in flames.

"Well, if he's still in there, he's not going to be happy," said Garcia, gazing at the burning house. Arya turned and looked at him murderously. "What?"

"We've got to find him," said Josh, trying to change Arya's focus. "Where would he have gone?"

"If he escaped?" asked Arya. "Maybe Danthian, but I doubt he'd ride through the night, not with things like this happening."

"So where then?"

Arya thought for a moment before looking at Josh.

"Let's go see if the farm is still standing."

They returned to the horses and saddled up, riding around the trees towards the path that led to the Tremayne acreage.

"I don't see any fire," said Garcia, squinting.

"And the Essence is starting to come back," added Josh, looking around.

"So why didn't he burn this too?" wondered Arya aloud.

"Too far from the main village?" suggested Garcia.

"Or maybe he was trying to make a statement," said Arya, glancing meaningfully at Josh.

As they approached the cottage, a loud voice shouted at them from what sounded like the roof.

"OY! DON'T YOU COME ANY CLOSHER OR I'LL HIT YOU WITH SHOME POWERFULL TECHNIQUESH YOU HEAR ME?"

"McPhearson, get off my roof, you twit!" yelled Arya as they got close enough to make out the town drunk perched on top of the building, a bottle of something in his hand.

"Oh, Lady Tremayne," he said, scrambling to his feet. "I'm shorry, I didn't notish—whoa whoa!"

The three of them looked on as he tripped over his own feet, fell flat onto his face, rolled down the incline and tumbled off, landing at their feet with a dull thud.

"All right, then," said Garcia, dismounting and helping the man to his feet. "Up you get."

"Thanksh...s-shorry 'bout that," he slurred, bowing rather ungracefully.

"Why are you here?" asked Arya concernedly.

"The whole town'sh in there," he said. "Matheshon brought ush all."

"Well, at least everyone's safe," said Josh, dismounting and tying his horse next to Garcia and Arya's.

"He'sh hurt, though," said McPhearson. "Got hit wit' shomethin' reallllll powerful."

"Damn it," said Arya, pushing her way past him and inside, where the kitchen was filled with a few villagers, some wounded, others trying to help the wounded. "Where's Isaac?"

A woman tending to a man with blood-soaked bandages around his leg pointed to the bedroom Josh had stayed in. They quickly hurried inside to find

Isaac lying on the bed, a damp rag draped over his face.

"That you, Jocelyn?"

"No, it's me," whispered Arya, hurrying to his side and kneeling next to him. "Joshua is here too."

"You got away?" he asked, and his words were laced with relief.

"Yes, and unharmed."

"I'm very glad to hear that," replied Isaac, sitting up and removing the rag. A long mark on the left side of his face was all that was left of what had probably been a very deep gash. "Oh, don't worry about me," he added, seeing Arya's eyes widen in worry. "One of the local nurses healed me up nice. I was just a bit overheated from going into the houses."

"You went into a burning building?" asked Josh.

"Four, actually," he replied with a wry smile. "Gotta do what I can to help. You know how it is."

"I do."

"And who are you?" asked Isaac, noticing Garcia standing behind Josh and Arya.

"My name is Garcia Theron, and I am helping Princess Tremayne in return for saving my life," he said reverently, bowing his head slightly.

Arya whipped around to face him.

"If you call me that one more time," she warned, her eyes flashing.

"Knock it off," replied Isaac. "He's probably just being an ass." Garcia grinned widely at him. "Theron, you say?"

"Yes, what of it?"

"You're a bandit lord, aren't you?"

Josh and Arya turned to look at Garcia, who scuffed his boot along the dirt floor.

"That'd be my father," he said, rather hesitantly. "We don't get on too well."

"Right," nodded Isaac skeptically. "Do you trust him?" he asked to Arya.

"Not in the slightest."

"Well, that's good enough for me then," he said, lying back down. Garcia gave him an affronted look but said nothing of it. "So what brings you here? You obviously wouldn't risk capture by going to a populated area if you didn't have a reason for it."

"Father told me, um…" She turned to Garcia. "Could you give us a minute?"

"I suppose," he replied, disappointed. He turned and exited the room. Josh made to leave as well, but Arya held him up. "Stay, Joshua. You deserve to hear this." She turned back to Isaac. "Father told me that if anything ever happened to him, that you'd have something for me…something you kept safe for him after the war."

"I had a feeling that was it," said Isaac, sighing.

"And we'll also need supplies. Food, water, and a few Essence Sparks would be good."

"The food and water will be easy enough, but all of the Essence has been depleted from the town. That bastard drained it all with that orb of his."

"It was Mareth, then," said Josh, dismayed.

"Seems so," said Arya.

"We need Essence here to keep the townsfolk healthy," said Isaac. "You're better off going south to the flats and finding a spring or geyser. There are some scattered down there."

"It'll add a few days, but we'll manage," said Arya turning to Josh, who nodded.

"As for what your father left you, it's in a lockbox under my bed in my cottage."

"Your cottage was on fire. We went there before we came here."

"It'll survive, trust me, but you'll have a hard time getting to it. By the time the fire goes out, there'll be archons swarming all over the place."

"What do we do, then?" asked Josh.

"You might ask your friend the thief," said Isaac, nodding in the direction of the door.

"Someone say my name?" asked Garcia, poking his head in.

"Were you eavesdropping?" asked Arya in a very annoyed tone of voice.

"Not in the least," he said waving her off. "But when I hear the word 'thief,' my ears just prick up, you know?"

"Can you get something from a burning building for us?" asked Josh.

"Without Essence?" he asked. "It'll be a bit tricky, but I'll manage."

"Let's go," said Arya, dragging the both of them from the room. "We'll be back within the hour."

"Best of luck!" called Isaac, placing the damp cloth back on his face.

"Get a skin of water and some rags," instructed Garcia.

"Why?" asked Arya, glaring at him.

"Because I don't want to end up in the same state as the house I'll be going into," he deadpanned.

"Fine," she huffed, stalking off to grab some water from the sink.

"Why d'you think she hates me so much?" Garcia asked Josh.

"She doesn't hate you, you just make her edgy," he replied. "She'll come around."

"Certainly acts like a princess, though, doesn't she?"

"I'd probably stop calling her that if you want her to come around," said Josh in a neutral tone. "And she's not always like that."

"Always like what?" asked Arya, handing Garcia the water and torn scraps of cloth.

Garcia smiled. "Nothing," he replied charmingly. "Let's be off, shall we?"

"Yes," she replied, looking at him skeptically. "Let's."

They were back in the village within ten minutes. The buildings were still ablaze, but the amplitude of the fires had diminished in the time they'd been gone.

"Now what?" asked Josh, as they pulled up in front of Isaac's cottage, the wood and thatching still crackling away in the night.

"Now," said Garcia, jumping off his horse and fishing around in a satchel tied to his saddle, "I put this on."

"This" turned out to be a cloak imbued with Essence that he draped over the back of his horse as he dumped the water all over himself and the rags. Wrapping the rags around his hands and neck, he threw the cloak on and turned to face them.

"It's under the bed," said Arya, nodding at the cottage.

"Right. If I'm not back in five minutes, try to put the fire out, will you?" he asked, tying a bandana around his face to shield his nose and mouth.

"Will do," affirmed Josh. Garcia winked at them and charged through the broken door.

"Such an ass," muttered Arya, dismounting.

"He's just trying to lighten the mood," said Josh.

"You're defending him?"

"I'm just trying to get you not to hate him so much."

"I don't hate him," argued Arya. "I just…he puts me off, you know?"

"He doesn't mean anything by it."

"Doesn't stop him from being irritating."

"Don't let it get to you," suggested Josh. "He's trying to help us."

"I don't know why he bothers me so much…"

"Calling you 'princess' probably has something to do with that."

"Oh, goodness, I hate that," said Arya, shaking her head. "I want people to know me for who I am, not for some title."

"You could do both, you know."

"It's not that simple," she said, shaking her head.

"Why not?" asked Josh.

Arya sighed and looked at him.

"One time when I was about six, my mother took me to Danthian for a couple days. She had official business to attend to, and father needed to spend all his time harvesting the crops. My mother left me in the care of one of her friends while she took care of her business, an archon who taught at academy.

"I went to the class and sat in the back, just trying to take everything in—it all looks very impressive when you're six—but the students teased me mercilessly about my lineage and how my parents left the capital to live simpler lives."

"That's horrid."

"I know," said Arya. "I don't mean to be so ill humored, I just never took too well to being baited."

"You don't have to apologize to me," replied Josh. "I never cared for it much either."

"Were your peers unkind to you in school?"

Josh nodded. "Some, but I learned to take the bad with the good."

"That's very mature of you," said Arya admiringly. "It took me forever to get used to..."

She trailed off, looking down the road leading out of the village and toward the capital.

"What is it?" asked Josh.

"Nothing good," she replied, squinting.

A cloud of dust was gathering at the edge of their range of vision and appeared to be drawing nearer.

"Hurry it up in there!" Arya yelled into the cottage, her eyes not moving from the road.

Garcia took that exact moment to come crashing out through one of the windows—his cloak steaming from the evaporating water—and a large, metal chest clutched in his arms.

"Feel free to help at any time," he wheezed, stumbling over to them. They quickly lifted him to his feet, and he deposited the chest into the satchel on his horse. Mounting it a moment later, he pulled the bandana and cloak off and stuffed them in with the chest.

"We need to get out of here," said Arya, jumping into her saddle.

"Let's ride, then!" yelled Garcia, rallying his horse to a sprint.

They tore from the village and back down the path that led to the farm.

Arriving a few minutes later, they jumped from the horses and hurried inside, quickly returning to Isaac's side.

"Here," said Garcia, placing the chest on the floor next to the bed. "How do we open it?"

"I'll do it," said Isaac, swinging his legs over the side.

"Hurry," urged Arya. "I think the archons were getting to the village just as we left. They'll be here soon."

"Jocelyn!" yelled Isaac, concentrating on the chest. A young woman in a nurse's outfit came into the room.

"Yes, Isaac?"

"Get my friends here some food and water, enough for a week."

"Right away."

"Leave it by the horses?" asked Arya. The nurse nodded and left, leaving the four of them in silence waiting for something to happen.

"Here we go," said Isaac, the tips of his fingers glowing a pale white. They heard several clicks come from inside the box, and a moment later the top sprung open. Smiling, he handed it to Arya, who took it tentatively.

"We'll give you a moment," said Josh, heading out of the room with Garcia.

"No, stay," she said, and Garcia raised an eyebrow. "You too, thief."

"Of course, milady," he replied, giving her a gracious, yet toothy smile.

Arya opened the chest and her mouth opened in a silent *oh* when she saw its contents.

Two ornate silver pendants lay inside, with small runic inscriptions on each. Underneath them lay a sheaf of parchment. To Josh's surprise, Arya carefully moved the pendants aside and took the paper, her eyes welling up slightly as she did so.

"It's the deed to the farm," she said with a sniffle.

Isaac nodded. "Rightfully yours. Wester always used to brag about how you'd be the best farmer in the province once he'd gone."

"What are those?" asked Josh, referring to the necklaces.

"Archon medallions," said Arya, replacing the deed in the chest and picking one up. "All archons wear one. They help amplify Essence from the body, which causes a tremendous increase in power."

"Oh, that's right, your parents were archons before they moved here," said Garcia.

"You knew?" The question came not from Arya, but from Josh.

Arya sighed. "I'd guess most everyone over the age of twenty knows." She gazed at the medallion with an expression of longing. "They did great things in their day."

"They did," agreed Isaac.

"I see."

"Come on," said Garcia. "We should get going before the archons arrive."

"You prepare the horses. I need to finish up here," Arya directed him. Garcia raised an eyebrow at her. "Please?"

"All right," he said with a nod, and left the room.

"Isaac, can you take care of this for me?" asked Arya, handing him the chest with the deed and one of the pendants inside.

"Of course, but don't you want both of these?" he asked, pointing at the medallions.

"I can't harness that much power, I don't trust that one"—she nodded in the direction of where Garcia had departed—"and you could use it to help the people here."

"That I could," he said thankfully. "Do be careful out there."

"You know me," said Arya with a smile, kissing him on the cheek.

"Good luck, lad," said Isaac, shaking Josh's hand firmly. "Keep watching over her, will you?"

"I'll do my best, sir."

"Oh, don't call me that," he said, smiling. "Makes me feel older than I am."

"Ready?" asked Arya.

Josh glanced at her and nodded.

"Is something the matter?" she asked once they were out front.

"Why couldn't you tell me?" asked Josh, watching Garcia load their supplies onto the mounts.

"About my parents?"

Josh nodded.

"I didn't want you to think less of me or my family," she admitted.

"Why would I think that?"

"When you arrived, you seemed so entranced. There was such wonder and amazement in your every word...then when I brought up the war, and the violence that has come to this land in the past, your awe diminished somewhat. You didn't seem angry or incredulous, but disappointed, sad even. I figured it was because you expected something more, that maybe the beauty of the land was reflected in the hearts of the people," she said, looking sideways at him. "I didn't want you to think less of my parents, knowing they had played such a major role in the bloodshed of years past."

Josh thought about this for a moment before speaking.

"I was a bit disappointed," he conceded. "But it's irrelevant. I try to not judge people—it's hard, because it's in our nature to, but I try. I trust you enough so that if you told me your parents had risked their lives to kill a thousand enemies in battle, but had done so to protect the ones they love, I would only think more of them, never less."

"You really are quite remarkable," she said softly, as Garcia finished packing the bags. "I'm sorry for not telling you."

"We're human," he said, smiling. "We all make mistakes. The only thing that matters is whether we're mature enough to ask for forgiveness."

"How are you so wise at your age?" asked Arya as Garcia began walking over to them.

"I've learned a few things from my family—when we get a private moment, I'll tell you about it," he parroted with a grin.

"Tell you what?" asked Garcia.

"That you stepped in horse droppings," said Arya, breezing by him.

"What?" asked Garcia, looking over his shoulder to check the bottoms of his boots.

"She was joking," said Josh with a laugh, walking past him.

"That's not funny."

"I thought it was," said Arya with a wink, mounting her horse.

"Right," said Garcia following suit. "So you still haven't told me where we're going."

"Very astute of you."

"Care to clue me in?" he asked, after a moment of silence.

"The flats first," she replied. "To get enough Essence to last us the journey."

"You can make Sparks?" asked Garcia.

"With this, yes," said Arya, fastening the archon pendant around her neck. "After that, we make for the Deadlands…and the prison of Necanshin Desmarthe."

"You cannot be serious."

"Can't I?" she asked coyly. "The full trip will take ten days, and we have enough food for seven."

"Let's not waste time, then, shall we?" said Josh, pulling hard on the reins in an attempt to spur his horse into a gallop. Instead, the animal reared back, unseating its rider and causing him to land flat on his back.

"Graceful," said Arya, trying to stifle a laugh.

"My middle name," groaned Josh, getting back up.

"Last one to the flats is a rotten hornberry," cheered Garcia, taking off to the south.

"Well, I don't fancy being one of those," said Josh to Arya, climbing back on his mount.

"Nor I."

"Let's make sure it's him, then."

Neither of them saw Isaac standing in the doorway as they sped off, holding on to the frame for support.

"Godspeed," he said softly, before returning inside the cottage, closing the door behind him.

Chapter Eight: A Friend in Need

The group reached the edge of the Sarcosian Salt Flats on their second day out of Kendrall. After miles upon miles of farmland, fields, and green landscape, a great silver floor appeared on the ground in front of them. Shimmering with Essence and minerals, the flats extended for hundreds of miles, ending at the base of a long mountain range to the south.

"Sarcosia," said Garcia, patting his horse as the three of them came to a stop. "Like a frozen ocean shining with brand new ice, and unknown dangers and treasures lurking beneath its surface."

"Dangers?" asked Josh, raising an eyebrow.

"Mastrichons," said Garcia with a sadistic smile.

"Oh right. They burrow here, do they?"

"Do they ever," he scoffed. "I ran into one last year."

"What happened?" asked Arya.

"I was with six of my men at the time," he said distastefully. "It killed two and wounded a third, but we managed to down it. Gave all the money from the sale to the families of my men who passed on."

"Why didn't you just run away?" asked Josh. "Two men seems like a pretty steep price for one hunt."

"Son, you can't run from these bastards," said Garcia grimly. "If they see you, it's kill or be killed."

"That fast, huh?"

"They are," affirmed Arya. "I had no desire whatsoever to come down here, but we have to gather enough Essence for a few Sparks, or we'll never be able to make it through the Deadlands."

"How do we do that?" asked Josh.

"Well, we need to find a geyser or a spring," explained Arya, fishing around in one of the satchels tied to her horse. "And use this"—she pulled out a glass jar—"to catch what we need."

"Where will we find something like that?"

"No clue," she replied, shrugging. "Springs and such aren't marked down on maps because then people with ill intentions could just find them rather easily and gather up whatever Essence they wanted."

"Only archons know the exact locations of them," chimed in Garcia.

Arya nodded. "And they're sparse. Father once had to come down here as an archon to harvest some Essence for use in the academy—it took his regiment three days to find a spring."

"We might as well make camp here, then," suggested Josh. "The sun's starting to set, and I don't fancy galloping around at night with big beasts wanting to eat me on the prowl."

"Not a bad idea," agreed Arya. "And I'd rather sleep on grass than hard compacted salt."

"I'm all for that," said Garcia, dismounting and beginning to unpack.

"We should sleep early," said Arya. "We'll need our energy these next few days."

"You don't really think something bad will happen, do you?" asked Josh.

"Joshua, when you've lived in this land long enough, you learn to plan for everything."

"Yeah, I suppose you're right."

Josh lay back and looked up at the pink sky while Garcia and Arya began preparing a fire. He breathed deeply and tried to calm his mind, something he'd been doing every night in an attempt to figure Essence out.

"What'cha thinking about, lad?" asked Garcia, noticing him.

"Just practicing," he replied, closing his eyes.

"Essence?" he asked.

"Don't disturb him," chided Arya. "How is he supposed to concentrate and make conversation at the same time?"

"It's all right," said Josh, sitting up. "I haven't been having much luck anyway."

"It doesn't mean you shouldn't keep at it," she said. "I have faith that you'll figure it out."

Josh smiled and nodded his thanks.

"What'd they teach you to do?" asked Garcia.

"Just to be calm and to focus my desires on how I want to use it."

"You know what works for me?" he asked, tossing some tinder into the small, growing pile of wood, dried grass, and other assorted foliage. "I think about what would happen if I failed to use Essence in that exact moment."

"That's a trick that some archons use in the heat of battle, actually," commented Arya, raising an eyebrow at him. "Did you come up with that on your own?"

"Well, since I'm a thief, I should lie and say 'yes', right?" he replied with a smirk. Arya huffed and resumed building the fire. "No, I didn't."

"Who'd you learn it from?"

"An archon," replied Garcia passively. "An old friend of mine, someone I haven't seen in a very long time."

"Who?"

"Doesn't matter," he said, brushing off the question.

"Since when are archons friends with thieves?" asked Arya, not looking up.

"Since when are princesses friends with thieves?" he countered, though in a playful manner.

Arya glanced up at him in annoyance.

"Hey, you set up me up for that one," he defended. "*Miss* Tremayne."

"I suppose," she muttered.

"So when you're doing that, do you think of something bad that might happen?" asked Josh, returning to the topic at hand.

"Well, it's different in each situation, but for the most part, thinking of a worst-case scenario helps," said Garcia. "For example, I might use Essence to start this fire. But what should happen if I can't? Maybe we won't be able to eat tonight. Because of the lack of nourishment, we are unable to defend ourselves when attacked by a fierce mastrichon with an extra muscle in its hind quarters, giving it substantially greater speed and clawing force. As a result, we all are chewed slowly and thoroughly, resulting in a very painful and lasting death."

Josh and Arya looked over at him, both with looks of shock and revulsion on their faces.

"I never said it was pretty," he said innocently, holding up his hands in defense.

"Effective, though, I'm sure," said Arya, shaking her head.

"You get the idea," said Garcia.

Josh nodded. "I do. Thanks, I think."

Night came, and with it, restless sleep for Josh.

He was standing in a field behind the Tremayne cottage, but was alone. A light breeze picked up, causing him to look around.

"Yer in over yer head, lad."

"Wester?" asked Josh, looking for the source of the voice.

"Aye," replied the voice.

"I thought you were dead."

"Oh, I am," came the reply, with a hint of mirth. "Dyin' in this land ain't the end by any stretch o' the imagination, ye know."

"I didn't."

"Well, now ye do. I appreciate what yer doin' fer Arya, but ye could die, Joshie."

"So could she."

"She can use Essence," pointed out Wester.

"I'm trying to learn," argued Josh. "Just because I can't do it yet—"

"I know ye been tryin'. I dun want ye to think I'm not grateful fer ye helpin' her, but yer gonna wind up like me if yer not careful. My time is short," said Wester. "I bes' be goin'."

"Wait!" called out Josh.

"Yeh?"

"Do you have any tips to help me use Essence?"

There was a pause before Wester spoke.

"Follow yer heart."

"It's time to wake up, Joshua," a soft voice said.

Josh cracked his eyes open to see the sky just starting to get lighter. Arya was kneeling next to him and Garcia was putting out the last remnants of the fire.

"So early?" he muttered.

"It gets hot in the flats during the day," she explained. "We'll need to rest at some point to prevent heat exhaustion, so we should get an early start."

He slowly sat up with a yawn, blinking.

"Sleep well?"

Josh nodded, rubbing the back of his neck.

"I dreamt your father spoke to me," he said, wanting to tell her. She looked intrigued, but not shocked.

"What did he say?"

"That I was in over my head. And to follow my heart if I wanted to use Essence."

Arya smiled and sat down on the ground next to Josh. "Sounds just like him. After my mother died, I had a couple dreams where she spoke to me."

"Do you think they're real?"

"You mean, do I think they're really speaking to us from beyond the grave?"

Josh nodded.

"I don't know, to be honest," she replied. "But either way, it's comforting knowing that they're still with us, even if it is just in our minds."

"He said that dying in this land wasn't the end."

"Well, your mind could've made that up, you know," she replied wryly. "If I had to guess, I'd say that there's more to existing than life and death, but maybe that's just me wanting to believe I'll see my parents again."

"I feel kind of bad," said Josh. "Since I've been here, I really haven't missed my parents all that much."

"You should be glad you have them. Didn't your father tell you not to take good people for granted?"

"He did," said Josh, smiling because she had remembered. "And I love my parents, I just love them more when they're not in the same room together."

"I wouldn't know what that's like," said Arya. "My parents never fought in front of me."

"Well, I suppose some good came of it," he replied. Arya raised an eyebrow at him. "If I hadn't gotten out of the house after they'd been arguing, I'd never have found myself here, would I?"

"You never know," said Arya with a smile. "You might have come to Lumenaria regardless."

"I'd like to think that."

"If you two are done flirting," said Garcia, loading a satchel onto one of the horses, "can we get a move on?" They regarded him warily, but each failed to notice the slight pink tinge in the other's cheeks.

They finished packing up camp and soon enough were off, each of them hoping to spend the least amount of time in the salty desert as possible.

Arya's description of the heat in the flats was a bit of an understatement. By the time noon rolled around, sweat was pouring down Josh's forehead. He'd tied a spare shirt around his head to give his face some respite from the burning sun, but the cooling it afforded was minimal at best.

"Five hours and nothing," groaned Garcia. "We going to rest soon?"

"Now should be fine," said Arya, slowing her horse to a halt. "We'll hang a cloth for shade."

The three of them set to assembling a makeshift tent, and ten minutes later they were lying peacefully underneath it, the horses cooling off next to them.

"It's a desert out here," said Josh, drinking from a skin of water enthusiastically. He handed it to Arya and wiped his mouth with his sleeve. "I feel like I'm going to shrivel up."

"It's a bit worse than I thought it'd be," she admitted, also drinking deeply.

"At least we haven't run into anything," said Garcia, drinking from his own canteen.

"Would we be able to see a mastrichon coming?" asked Josh.

"It depends," he replied. "Mastrichons are incredibly intelligent and alert creatures. There might not be any burrow holes nearby, but if we walk over one of their tunnels, they won't hesitate to break through the ground and catch us in an ambush. That was how it happened the last time I was here."

"Great."

"Well, with any luck we'll find a spring today and be out of here by tomorrow," said Arya hopefully.

"Wouldn't count on it," said Garcia, holding a hand to his brow and peering out at the landscape. "Nothing for miles."

"That we can see," Arya pointed out. "We'll rest for another half an hour or so. The sun won't be directly overhead then."

"Sounds like a plan," replied Garcia, lying down and draping a damp cloth over his eyes.

"It's quite unpleasant here, isn't it?" asked Arya, turning to Josh.

Josh nodded, though he was grimacing. "Yeah. It amazes me that Essence gathers out here in vast quantity."

"It's because of the climate. Without people here to use it up for farming or medical purposes and whatnot, springs and geysers can pop up when too much gathers in one place."

"Makes sense."

"Do you feel any closer to being able to use it?"

"Not really," he replied with a sigh. "No matter how much I practice, nothing seems to happen."

"I've heard it can be very frustrating," she sympathized. "My mother once told me that some people here don't learn it as quickly as most of us."

"Really?"

Arya nodded. "I understand there was one case where a young man was in his twenties before he first used it."

"Wow."

"Don't get discouraged," she said with an encouraging smile. "I have faith in you."

"Thanks."

They lay in comfortable silence for a few moments—the shade finally starting to cool them—before Arya turned her head to Josh.

"You don't talk much about yourself, you know?"

"Don't I?" he asked.

"I've been telling you stories about Lumenaria, and my parents, and Essence, and you haven't told me anything about who you are, really."

"I'm sorry," he apologized, shrugging. "I don't mean anything by it."

"Don't say you're sorry, just tell me something about you," she replied with a light laugh.

"Well, um, I'm seventeen years old—"

"You're only seventeen?" she asked in astonishment.

"I hadn't mentioned that?" he asked. Arya shook her head. "Well, yeah, I am."

"Go on," she encouraged.

"I don't know," he said, laughing. "I haven't lived the most exciting life."

"That doesn't mean that there haven't been important events that you hold dear to your heart."

Joshua smiled and sighed. "All right. There was this one time last year...I was at my school during lunchtime. There's a sport we play back home called football—you basically run around a pitch with a small ball and try to kick it into the goal without using your hands or arms."

"Simple enough."

"It is. So our school's football club is all eating lunch at the same table. I'm sitting a few tables away, minding my own business and all that. One of the players gets up to put his tray next to the bin, and his mate trips him as a joke. He goes flying, headfirst, into the wall and crashes into one of the fire alarm pull boxes—"

"What's that?"

"If there's a fire, you're supposed to pull the lever on one of these boxes, and it makes an alarm go off so that people can evacuate the building."

"That's a good idea," commented Arya.

"It is. It also happens to turn on the sprinklers. They're these metal devices that shoot water from the ceiling to help prevent the fire from spreading." Arya nodded and Josh chuckled at the memory of what he was about to say. "This bloke goes sprawling into the fire alarm and sets it off, and the sprinklers with it. So now we're all running toward the exit to keep from getting drenched, and in the middle of it someone threw a pie at someone else and started a great food fight." Arya laughed. "In the end we were all soaked to the bone, covered in cafeteria food and whatnot, and given detention."

"Did you partake in the food throwing?" asked Arya, the corners of her mouth quirking upwards in a tiny smile.

"I may have thrown an egg at a girl who didn't do her half of our lab assignment and made me do all the work instead," he replied, smiling sheepishly.

"Perhaps she had it coming, then."

"I like to think that," he said, laughing.

"Were your parents upset that you got into trouble?"

"Yeah," he replied, his laughter subsiding. "And then they argued for two hours on how to punish me."

"You don't talk about your parents much," she noted.

"For good reason," he replied. "All they do is argue."

"You did say you picked up a few things from them," she persisted.

"I learned how not to act," answered Josh. "To me, all their arguments seemed really silly. It always looked like there was a clear-cut solution, if one of them would budge on how they felt just a little. They were always both too stubborn to do it."

"It must not have been easy."

"Well, like I said, I wouldn't be here if it weren't for them," he said. "But the most valuable thing I learned was not to take myself too seriously. Nobody's perfect, so that means there's always room for us to improve. Until the day I become perfect, I'll always listen to what anyone else has to say. I might not agree with it, but if I don't, then I'll explain why, and hopefully they'll listen and both of us will grow a little. Or something like that."

"That's a very smart way to live your life," she said appreciatively. "And don't be afraid to speak up if you have any ideas. You always seem so quiet when we're discussing our plans for saving the world."

"I tend to not pretend I know things that I don't," he said. "Not being from here is a fairly big disadvantage in that regard."

"Even a blind mouse can find some cheese from time to time. You'll never know unless you try. And if I don't agree, then I'll explain why," she parroted.

"Fair enough," he said with a chuckle.

"Tell me more about your home."

"It rains a lot," he deadpanned. "It's very different from Lumenaria."

"How so?"

"Well, for example, we have these devices called computers. They're complex machines that have a ton of uses, but what most people my age use them for is to access something called the Internet."

"Which is...?"

"It's hard to explain in a sentence," he replied. "If I had to, I'd say that the Internet connects people all over the world and lets them share information with each other."

"You mean you can send something to someone on the other side of your planet using this?" she asked, impressed. "That's a very useful thing to do. How long does it take?"

"Seconds."

Arya looked at him as though he'd grown another head.

"You're mad."

"I'm serious," he said, smiling. "It's really changed how we live our lives."

"I can imagine," she said, astonished. "If we had that kind of technology here, well, I'm not sure what we could do, but I bet it'd be quite a thing to witness."

"You do have Essence," Josh pointed out. "And to be honest, if I had the opportunity to trade you computers for Essence, I might take it."

"I guess both things are equally as impressive to people who know nothing about them."

"That's probably true."

"Do you think if I had a computer, you and I could send things to each other once you go home?" she asked thoughtfully.

"It would be nice," he said, closing his eyes. "But it doesn't work like that— and even if it did, according to Luther it would take over two hundred million years for something to get from here to there or visa versa."

"That's too bad."

"I'm sure we'll work something out," he said, glancing at her. "I rather like this place. It'd be a shame to not try and keep a part of it in my life."

"I'm glad," replied Arya, smiling at him. They lay there for a couple moments just staring at each other, before Arya seemed to realize what they were doing. Looking away, she coughed and sat up. "Looks like the sun's gone down a little bit. Has it been half an hour already?"

"Time flies when you're having fun," said Josh, and Arya blushed slightly. "Oy, wake up!"

He tossed the damp rag he'd been using to cool down at the bandit, and landed it squarely on his face. Garcia jerked up suddenly, looking around to see what had interrupted his nap.

"Time to get moving," said Arya sweetly.

"Ugh. Yes, Mum," he said lamely, clamoring to his feet.

"We'll head southeast," said Arya, taking down the sheet. "That way, if we get lucky, we're closer to the Deadlands."

"All right," said Josh, climbing onto his mount.

Five minutes later they were packed and moving again. There was no conversation; it was much too hot to talk aimlessly, and their attentions were needed to watch for any unwanted visitors.

A thin gust of wind blew by them, and with it, a strange cracking sound reached Josh's ears.

"Did you guys hear that?" he asked, glancing over his shoulder at Arya.

"Hear what?" she asked.

"I didn't hear anything," grunted Garcia.

"Sounded like rocks scattering on the ground," he said, scanning the horizons for any sign of trouble.

"Just keep an eye out," said Arya.

"There it is again!" he exclaimed urgently, the noise getting louder. "Can't you hear it?"

Garcia halted his horse and dismounted, dropping to a knee once he was on the ground.

"What is it?" asked Arya, catching up with them. Garcia said nothing, only held a finger over his lips indicating a need for silence. Slowly, he leaned down and placed his ear to the ground, listening intently.

A minute passed before he got back up, wiping the dust off his pants as he did so.

"Did you hear it?" asked Josh.

"I thought I did," said Garcia. "We should hurry away from here."

"Why?"

"Because the noise stopped when we did," he said. "If there's something underneath us, it's smart enough to know to be quiet when we're listening."

"We won't be able to ride at full speed in this heat," said Arya.

"We'll have to make do," said Garcia. "The farther away we get, the bet—"

A huge eruption came from below the salty surface and sent them flying off their mounts and crashing to the ground. The horses scrambled to their feet and dashed away as a deafening roar came from within the huge hole that had appeared not twenty feet away.

"Oh no," whispered Arya, shielding her eyes with her arm.

A giant black claw the size of a schoolteacher's desk emerged from beneath the surface and latched onto the ground with a resounding crunch. A gigantic beast, at least fifteen feet tall, pulled itself up and out of the hole, another equally large claw appearing a moment later next to the first.

Four large, silver tusks were sticking out of the monster's face, pointing straight at the three of them. As the behemoth's hindquarters emerged, a great, black, scorpion-like tail came into view, with three very long and very sharp-looking quills sticking out at the end. Muscles bulged from every inch of the creature's body, which was covered in the same thick, dark brown hide that Josh and Arya had stood on just after his arrival in Lumenaria—something that seemed like a lifetime ago.

The three of them watched as the beast bared its teeth menacingly while looking them over with glistening, black eyes. A low, guttural growl sounded with every breath it took, each of which smelled like rotting flesh mixed with last month's milk.

"What's the plan, then?" asked Josh, frozen in fear.

"Hope it changes its mind," replied Garcia, trying very hard not to move his lips as he spoke.

It wasn't to be, as the mastrichon roared and lunged at them. They scattered as the huge claws crushed the ground they had been lying on only a second earlier. Arya scrambled to her feet, charging Essence at her fingertips. The beast noticed this, however, and turned as if to charge at her but was distracted by small bolts of light hitting it in the face courtesy of Garcia.

"You're going to make it mad!" yelled Arya as it turned away from her and toward the bandit.

"I promise you it'll eat us even if it isn't mad!" he hollered back, diving to his left to avoid being speared on the end of one of the massive tusks.

"What should I do?" yelled Josh, as Garcia sprinted away from the creature.

"Protect Arya!"

"I just need a few more seconds!" she called out, a great ball of white Essence now having formed between her hands. "Get it to turn toward us!"

Josh spun around looking for anything to get the mastrichon's attention. Picking a rock up off the ground, he did the only thing he could think of and hurled it as hard as he could at the creature, striking it firmly on the head.

"Nice throw, mate!" yelled Garcia, as the beast skidded to a halt and immediately spun to face Josh.

A huge blast of energy erupted from Arya's outstretched hands—an incredible jet of Essence that rocketed from her like a comet and slammed into the mastrichon. The creature was lifted clean off its feet and crashed to the ground, tearing up the earth in massive chunks as it skidded to a halt.

"Good job!" called out Garcia, giving her the thumbs-up.

Josh turned to compliment Arya but saw she had collapsed to one knee and was holding her side in agony. He started to run over when a horrifying howl came from behind him. He turned to see the tremendous beast struggle to its feet—sticky, maroon blood dripping from its body where the Essence had burned a hole in it. Without hesitation, it charged at Arya, who could barely look up to see the attack coming.

There was nothing else for it. Josh dove at Arya to shove her out of the way just as the mastrichon reached them, catching him on the tusks and sending him flying through the air. The world spun around in a mad blur and a moment later he slammed hard to the ground, a sickening crack sounding as his head hit the hard surface of the flats.

In the brief instant before he lost consciousness, Josh swore he saw figures clad in shining silver speeding toward the beast, Garcia hunkered over Arya trying to protect her.

When he came to, he didn't have to open his eyes to know it was dark out. Without any hesitation or care to his own well-being, he sat straight up and looked around, only to see he was inside a tent, and Garcia was sitting next to him, looking startled.

"Easy there," he said, taking a deep breath. "You scared me half to death."

"What's going on?" asked Josh. "Where's Arya? Is she alive? What happened to the—"

He cut himself off as a wave of pain rolled through his head, causing him to wince.

"Lie back down," Garcia ordered. Josh groaned as he returned to a prone position, noticing he was on a cot. "Arya's fine. A little exhausted, but otherwise fine, she's in the cot next to you."

Josh turned to his left and saw Arya on her side, smiling bemusedly at him.

"Hi," she said playfully.

"Er, hi," replied Josh sheepishly.

"The mastrichon is dead," said Garcia.

"What...how?"

"Ah, you're up," said a familiar voice, walking inside the tent. "Good."

Josh lifted his head and was stunned to see Marilyn Fairbanks walking toward him, golden hair flowing freely behind her, armor tarnished with what appeared to be the dark red viscous blood of the slain beast. She gave Garcia a look.

"I'll leave you three at it, then," he said, rising to his feet and leaving them alone.

"What happened?" asked Josh after the thief had left.

"We arrived just in time to see your landing," she said without a hint of a smile, sitting in the chair that Garcia had vacated.

"We?"

"My squad and I," she explained, tossing her long blond hair over her shoulder. "And it was a good thing too, because otherwise all three of you would be dead."

"How'd you kill it?"

"Arya did most of the work," said Marilyn, turning toward her. "Although don't ever let me catch you using up that much Essence in one charge again, understand?"

Arya nodded, but didn't say anything.

"I'm serious," she chided. "You almost exceeded *my* Restraint Order, and you nearly killed yourself doing it."

"How?" asked Josh.

"The body works like a funnel for channeling Essence when you're charging it up like I did," said Arya. "The most external points of the body are where it empties—the fingers and toes."

"Correct," commented Marilyn. Arya nodded.

"The problem is that if you overcharge too much, you drain some Essence out of your own body," she continued. "I overdid it. I would've died if you hadn't pushed me out of the way."

"It was nothing," muttered Josh, his cheeks turning slightly pink.

"Once Arya had exposed a weak point, the rest was easy," said Marilyn.

"So what happened to me?" asked Josh.

"You cracked your skull pretty badly," she replied. "Like I said, our timing was perfect. You wouldn't have survived that injury for another five minutes without aid."

Josh looked over at Arya who, to his surprise, looked away.

"What happened to the thing?" asked Josh.

"We'll send it back to Danthian to be harvested," replied Marilyn. "I'm sure you know that mastrichons are quite valuable if most of the creature is preserved."

"You make it sound like we were purposely hunting it instead of just trying to survive," said Josh, raising an eyebrow.

"Which brings about the curious question of why you were down here in the first place," she countered. Josh looked away, unwilling to say anything. "Arya told me everything, you know."

Josh glanced at Arya, who nodded in response.

"Then why are you asking me?"

"I want to hear what you have to say," replied Marilyn. "For all intents and purposes, you're fugitives, so I'd like a good reason to not turn you in."

"I'm here because Arya's here," answered Josh. "I owe her and her father my life, so as long as there's something I can do to help, I'll do it."

Marilyn considered him carefully for a few moments.

"Well, that's as good a reason as any, I suppose," she said flatly. "And if I was the only person to have seen you, it would've been fairly easy to let you go on your way."

"You're not going to bring us back to Danthian?" asked Arya, sitting up.

"By order, that is what I'm required to do," she said monotonously. Josh and Arya opened their mouths to protest, but she held up a hand to silence them. "However, you two are injured and cannot possibly be expected to ride in your current conditions. I estimate that you both will be fit to ride by morning and so will be allowed to rest until then. *But if you were to escape before that*, well, there wouldn't be anything I could do about it, would there?"

Neither Josh nor Arya said anything as Marilyn stood up and walked to the entrance of the tent.

"Your horses are tied just a few feet behind you," she said thoughtfully. "I would also suggest you head a few miles southwest before turning toward the Deadlands. You may find something of interest there."

"Mary," said Arya. "How did you find us?"

Marilyn regarded both of them carefully for a few moments before smiling for the first time that evening.

"Isaac Matheson cares about both of you deeply," she replied. "When I went to make sure he was all right after the fire at Kendrall, he expressed deep concern that you were both in over your heads, and I assured him I would do whatever I could to protect you. Speaking of which…"

Josh and Arya watched as she pulled an envelope from somewhere within her armor and held it up.

"This envelope is addressed to my personal mailbox in the tower," she explained. "Only I can access it, and I check it three times a day. When the time comes, if you want my help, write where you need me to be on the outside, then use Essence to send it off. I'll be with you no more than two days after."

Arya took the envelope from Marilyn in stunned silence. She turned to leave when Arya spoke up.

"Marilyn," she whispered, looking as if she was holding back tears. "Why are you doing this?" The archon turned and looked at her, a hint of regret etched on her face.

"Because once upon a time, your mother did the same for me."

And she turned and left.

Arya sighed and looked up, sniffling briefly before Garcia rejoined them.

"So what's the plan?" he asked, sitting down.

"We're to escape," said Arya.

"How are we going to manage that?"

"She's left our horses behind the tent," explained Josh. "And I'm assuming that somewhere southwest of here there's an Essence spring?"

"Yes. If we leave now, we'd be at the Deadlands before sunup."

"You two need your rest," said Garcia. "Sleep for a couple hours, I'll wake you."

"There's no point," argued Arya. "Josh and I have been sleeping since midday. The sooner we leave the better."

"What do you think, Joshie boy?"

"I agree with her," he answered. "And to be quite honest, I'm not keen on staying in these flats any longer than necessary after what's happened."

Garcia shook his head and sighed, looking back and forth between the two of them.

"All right," he said standing up. He walked to the back of the tent and drew a knife from his belt, making a cut vertically along the canvas. "Let's go."

Josh and Arya scrambled out of their cots and stepped through the slit in the tent that Garcia was holding open for them. He quickly followed and before long, they were untying their horses from the stake in the ground.

"Come on," whispered Arya urgently. "Before anyone sees us."

The three of them mounted and wasted no time in riding off away from the camp. Josh glanced over his shoulder and was glad to see an absence of pursuers or alarms being raised.

"We made it," he called out. "No one's following."

"We're heading the right direction," said Arya, looking at the stars to navigate. "The spring should be a few miles ahead."

Indeed, the words were barely out of her mouth when a soft blue glow appeared on the horizon, pulsating gently every few moments. The light grew brighter as they drew closer, blossoming into a great white aurora. Reaching the source of it, Josh had to shield his eyes as they dismounted, and his mouth opened in awe as he began to grow accustomed to the light.

Where the solid, silver ground of the flats ended, a small, glimmering pool of iridescent light blue liquid began, so pure and clean that Josh could see directly down to the bottom when he knelt next to it.

"This is Essence at its purest?" he asked. He made to touch it, but Arya quickly grabbed his arm.

"And most concentrated," she replied, kneeling down beside him. "Too much of a good thing, you know." Josh nodded and withdrew his hand.

"How do you plan on gathering it up?" asked Garcia.

"Hand me that jar, will you?" she asked, pointing to a large glass container tied with one of the satchels. Garcia undid the knot and passed it to her, watching just as intently as Josh.

Arya placed the jar on the ground in front of her and pulled the archonic pendant out from inside her shirt. Silently, she closed her eyes and placed both of her hands over the metal disk. Josh and Garcia watched as a silver stream of Essence began to emanate from under her hands and branch out toward the pool. As soon it touched the surface, the bright blue liquid jumped up and began racing against Arya's stream toward her body. She quickly placed her hands inside the jar and let the blue liquid funnel into it for a few moments before siphoning the silver Essence inside as well.

"Stand back," she instructed. Garcia and Josh retreated a few steps as she fastened the lid tightly. "I hope this works."

Her fingertips glowed white for an instant before she pressed them against the surface of the jar. There was a tremendous burst of energy from the container and a loud blast that sounded like a firecracker going off. When Josh finally turned back to Arya, he saw a bright, white flame flickering inside the container.

"And there you have it," she said, handing it to Garcia. Josh looked curiously at the pendant around her neck, which was glowing faintly. "We'll need at least a dozen more, so let's get to it."

It only took a half hour to make the others, and before long they were saddled up and on the move again, though this time at a noticeably slower pace.

"You okay?" Josh asked Arya, riding beside her.

"I'm just exhausted," she said weakly. "I'll rest when we get to the Deadlands."

"I'm not too sure, but it seems to me like you made those Sparks by draining your own Essence," he said thoughtfully.

"You're very observant," she replied, breathing heavily. "I'll be fine."

"You shouldn't have made so many after what happened earlier," he argued. "You could die, right?"

"Yes," she said, nodding. "But somehow I get the feeling that no matter how hard I push myself, you'll be around to help me."

Josh sighed and smiled weakly.

"I don't like seeing you in pain," he admitted. "I don't like seeing anyone in pain."

"You can't save everyone," said Arya. "I've learned that over the years."

"I'm not trying to save everyone," he replied. "I know that, I'm a realist. But I can do everything to save the people I care about, and you've been just as good a friend to me as anyone else in my life. Maybe even better."

"Thank you, Joshua."

"Oy, you two!" yelled Garcia from ahead of them. "Keep up, will ya?"

"Arya needs a break," said Josh, riding up to him. "She's knackered out from making all the Sparks."

Garcia sighed and looked to the horizon, where the clean dark blue sky of the flats turned into a stormy black far in the distance.

"I'd reckon we're about four or five hours away from the Deadlands at full pace," he said. "And I strongly suggest we be there before morning, lest the search parties find us."

"When's morning?" asked Josh.

"Six hours, tops."

"So we'll rest for an hour," he said. "That sound good to you, Arya?"

He turned when there was no response and smiled slightly when her horse trotted up to him, its rider soundly asleep on its back.

"No point in stopping if she's already out," said Garcia. He waved his hand in the air gently, and the strands of Essence that floated from his fingertips flew toward Arya and picked her gently up off her horse, and placed her behind Josh a moment later.

"There is no way I'm competent enough to ride full speed with her," Josh said as he felt Arya shift and rest her head on his back.

"So we'll go half speed," replied Garcia, tethering Arya's horse to his own. "It's better than not moving at all."

"And if another mastrichon shows up?"

"Either our fair archon will hear it and come save us again," pondered Garcia, "or we're toast."

"Great," muttered Josh. "Lead the way, then."

They rode in silence, the clip-clop of the horses' hooves on the hard ground the only sounds of their progress. Sometime along the trip, Arya's hands had found their way around Josh's waist, and he leaned back into her slightly, feeling exhausted himself.

Finally, just as the sky was starting to turn pink, the ground under the black clouds came into view, and Josh marveled at the sight before him.

It was obviously called the Deadlands for a reason. The air was dark and polluted. The great black clouds covered the land completely, leaving no gaps for sunlight to sneak through and sending occasional bolts of lightning in random directions. Tepid winds blew at them, causing the dead bushes and trees still standing to sway violently. Far to the north, Josh could barely make out what looked to be a long mass of trees eclipsed in darkness—the forest of Andromar.

"Let's set up near that patch of foliage," said Garcia, pointing to a spot of bushes shadowed by a dead oak.

They quickly set up camp. Garcia floated Arya off Josh's horse and onto a blanket on the ground as Josh set up shelter.

"Glad to have a break," said Garcia, sitting down. He paused for a moment, tapping his finger against his cheek thoughtfully. "I've never been here before."

"Is there anything out there to attack us that I should know about?" asked Josh.

"Not that I know of," he replied. "But we'll still need to be careful."

"How come?"

"This man, Necanshin, there's a reason he was banished here."

"Well, he's responsible for turning the land into this, isn't he?"

"That's what we were all told," said Garcia thoughtfully. "But I get the feeling there's more to it than that."

"Why?"

"I heard something interesting from the archon I knew," he replied. "He said that even though Essence could be used for such destructive purposes, it could never destroy itself."

"What do you mean?"

"Well, you don't see any Essence floating about here like everywhere else, do you?"

"No," replied Josh, shaking his head.

"That means there was something else. Something I'm not sure I want to know about."

"It can't be that bad, can it?"

"Trust me, Joshua," said Garcia solemnly. "It can always be that bad."

Chapter Nine: The Exiled

The dawn light made way for a dreary, gray morning. The rumbling of thunder sounded in the distance every so often, the sun never once peeking through the thick, dark clouds.

Joshua was sitting on the ground with his legs crossed, trying very hard to empty his mind, when Arya stirred. He looked over and saw her staring up at him, bleary-eyed.

"Hello," he said warmly.

"Hi."

"Feel better?"

"I do," she replied, sitting up. She looked around and seemed mildly surprised to see her surroundings. "We're in the Deadlands?"

"You fell asleep on your horse," explained Josh with a lopsided smile. "You rode here with me."

"I did?"

"Apparently my back is quite comfortable," mused Josh lightheartedly.

"Sorry," she said sheepishly. "But a little sleep does wonders for one's energy. Where's Garcia?"

A loud whistle came from above, and they looked up to see Garcia perched atop the dead oak, waving at them.

"Keeping lookout," replied Josh, shrugging.

"Twit," she muttered with a chuckle.

"I heard that!"

"Well, come down here so we can be on our way!" she yelled up at him.

"All right, keep your shirt on."

Arya sighed as he clamored down the tree, jumping to the ground a moment later.

"See anything interesting?" asked Josh.

"Nothing, really," he replied. "Just more of this for miles."

"That's a good thing," said Arya, packing up her horse. "I'd be worried if there was anything else in this wasteland."

"Where exactly is this man's prison?" asked Josh, climbing onto his mount.

"In the center of these barrens," replied Garcia. "I guess the logic was to keep him as far away from Essence as possible."

"Right. How long do you think it'll take us?"

"We should be there sometime tomorrow," answered Arya as they started to ride. "Hopefully."

"I don't get it," said Garcia. "How does one man destroy this much?"

"I couldn't tell you," she replied. "If I knew, somehow I don't think I'd be going to him for help."

"Will he help us?" asked Josh.

"Who knows? I've never met him. I've heard stories that while he's a bit arrogant, he always had good intentions."

"I'd think this place would show otherwise," muttered Garcia.

"Nevertheless, if we're to prevent this war, we need his help."

"Did your parents know him?" asked Josh. "If you don't mind me asking, of course."

"I don't mind," replied Arya, biting her lip thoughtfully. "My father did. Not very well, but I believe they met a few times."

"Did he ever speak about him?"

"After the war, my father and Isaac were talking about it at the bar one night. They were very drunk, as usual, and when I arrived to take father home, I overheard him saying something about how Desmarthe had claimed that he was innocent—that the blast that leveled these lands wasn't his fault."

"Did he elaborate on it?"

"No. Some of the people in the bar weren't too happy that my father hinted at Necanshin's innocence—they'd lost family or friends in the explosion, you see—so I took him out of there and back to the farm to sober him up. He didn't speak of it again after that."

"Did you ever ask him about it?" asked Garcia.

"I never had reason to," she replied. "Especially after my mother died, the less we could talk about war, the better."

To the relief of the three riders, the journey into the heart of the Deadlands occurred with a much-needed lack of interruption. Midday came and went, and soon Josh found himself sitting on the ground next to Arya and Garcia, readying for supper.

"What have we got?" asked Arya as Garcia rummaged through one of the satchels.

"Looks like some rinds…and those berries you found a few days back."

"Are they still edible?" asked Josh, peering inside the sack as Garcia passed it to him.

"Can't see why not," he replied with a shrug. "If you get sick, we'll know not to eat them."

"Funny," replied Josh, popping a few in his mouth. "Taste fine."

"Good," said Arya, pulling out one of the Essence Sparks and breaking off a few twigs from a nearby bush.

"Wha's tha' fer?" asked Garcia, chewing loudly.

"A small fire wouldn't hurt," she replied. "It'd be nice to have a hot meal."

"I'm all for that," agreed Josh.

"Pity that Mary didn't leave us any of the mastrichon," said Garcia, swallowing. "The meat's delicious."

"I wouldn't have guessed that," remarked Josh.

"Wouldn't expect such a foul-smelling beast to be palatable, right?" asked Garcia with a sly laugh. "I know."

"I haven't had it myself," chimed in Arya as a few drops of Essence jumped out of the jar and ignited the sticks. "But I've heard it is quite good."

"Well, I'm not in any hurry to go hunt one down and find out, so this'll do just fine," said Josh, holding one of the rinds out over the flame.

"Too right, my boy," said Garcia, clapping Josh on the shoulder.

They ate in silence for a few moments before Josh leaned back against one of the satchels and looked at Arya.

"Hmm?" she asked.

"I've been wondering," he said.

"'Bout what?" asked Garcia.

"How big this planet actually is. I mean, you said yourself there are other provinces out there, right?"

Arya nodded. "I did. But we have almost no contact with them. I don't think there are very many people here who know anything about the outside world."

"That's why I'm curious. We've definitely ridden a long way, but where I'm from, that'd just be a fraction of going around the world."

"I once knew a lad who'd been outside our borders," commented Garcia, stroking his thin beard in thought.

"Where?" asked Arya.

"Teradon. It's the province that borders us to the south," he explained when Josh gave him a puzzled look.

"How on earth did he get there?" asked Arya.

"Blackwind Pass. It's a small spot in the mountains that can be traversed if you're brave enough."

"That's the pass I told you about," said Arya to Josh with a nod.

"Most people would never try—it's prime housing for mastrichons, and there've even been rumors of them breeding there, but he went for it and lived to tell the tale."

"Why would he risk such a thing?"

"He wanted to see the world," said Garcia appreciatively. "Some people are fueled by adventure, after all."

"What was it like?" asked Josh.

"He said it was a lot like here. Essence everywhere, a lot of farmland, nothing special."

"So what other provinces are there?" inquired Josh.

"Aside from us, Mafaelia, and Teradon, I don't know any others," he answered.

"Me neither," added Arya. "You have to understand, the only ways in or out of Lumenaria are the two ways I told you about—Blackwind Pass in the south, and the chasm in the east. Both are home to very dangerous creatures that, for the most part, only archons can deal with. Not to mention the terrain itself can kill you if you don't watch your step."

"I've heard of some boats sailing through the shallows to get to other lands," said Garcia thoughtfully.

"You'd be hard up to find a mariner who'd do it just for adventure, though," pointed out Arya.

"True."

"Oh well," said Josh with a shrug. "Would've been nice to see more of the world before I had to leave."

"You've got a long way to go before you can leave," said Garcia with a mischievous smile.

"I'm not complaining," said Josh, returning the smile.

"We should probably camp here tonight," replied Arya, gazing up at the dark, billowing clouds. "It looks like it may rain, and we don't want to get caught in that."

"It always looks like it might rain here," Josh pointed out.

"The air's heavier than it was earlier," she explained. "And we can't afford to use up Essence drying out clothes or warming people up."

"I agree," said Garcia, nodding. "Let's call it a night and get an early start tomorrow."

They were lying down under their standard makeshift tent, bundled up in blankets, when the steady, rhythmic beat of raindrops began to sound above them, mixing brusquely with Garcia's snores.

"I've always liked the rain," whispered Arya, her back to Josh.

"You knew I was awake?" he asked.

"I do now."

"Well done."

She rolled over and turned to face him.

"I can't sleep," she confessed.

"Worried something might come after us?"

"No," she said, frowning slightly. "I just feel guilty because I know my father wouldn't want me doing this. He'd want me to take care of everyone in Kendrall and not put myself in danger."

"You don't think that he'd be mad, do you?"

"I don't know what to think. He was always full of surprises. Once, he came home with a beautiful necklace from one of the shops in Kendrall for me." She reached into her shirt and pulled out a simple, silver chain necklace with a small charm hanging from it. "I'd seen it a few weeks earlier while we were getting supplies in town and had spent a good five minutes fawning over it before we moved on."

"It's beautiful," said Josh, admiring it.

"I miss him terribly," she admitted, her voice catching slightly.

"It's like you said," replied Josh, covered her hand with his. "He's always with you."

Arya said nothing; she only nodded and wiped at her eyes.

"And if it makes any difference, I think he'd feel just as much admiration for you as I do."

"Thanks," she said, blushing. "You're a good man, Joshua Cooper."

Day broke late, and coupled with breakfast after waking, it was nearly midday when they began travel again.

The journey was exceedingly boring. Although they continued to ride hard, Josh found himself struggling to pay attention. Multiple times he was nearly unseated as his mind wandered to the multitude of items weighing upon it.

They continued without eating, and by the time the sun began to wane—a dark yellowish tinge creeping into the clouds up from the horizon—the focus of all three riders was starting to grow short. Finally, after an eternity, a short granite structure came into view—the only sign of life they'd seen since leaving the salt flats.

"Is that it?" asked Josh, as they rode forward.

"I would expect so," replied Arya. "There's no reason for anything else to be out here."

"It's smaller than I expected."

"It's mostly underground," said Arya. "More secure, I suppose."

The structure was, in fact, just a solid block of stone with a staircase carved into the side, leading down under the murky barrens.

"There's nowhere to leave the horses," said Garcia.

"They'll behave," replied Arya, dismounting and patting her steed on the nose. "Won't you?" The horse whinnied at her. "See?"

Garcia raised his eyebrows but said nothing and jumped to the ground.

They stepped cautiously onto the staircase, loose pebbles jumping down into the depths with each step taken. After twenty feet or so, the stairs began curling into a spiral. They descended carefully—darkness overcame their vision not too far in.

"I can't see a damn thing," grunted Garcia from in front.

"Just feel around for the wall," said Arya. "There's bound to be some light eventually."

"Eventually" was nearly ten minutes later of stumbling through the blackness, when a faint flicker of light began to illuminate the passageway.

"I guess we're almost there," grunted Josh as torches mounted on wall brackets started appearing.

"When we get there, let me do the talking," said Arya.

"Why you?" asked Garcia.

"Because I know a bit about him, and I'll surely be more tactful than you will."

"Fine, fine," muttered Garcia, waving her off.

At last, the stairs straightened out and ended, a flat, dank hall greeting them. A great set of steel bars partitioned off the end of the corridor, creating a cell.

"Here we go," breathed Arya, stepping forward.

As they approached, Josh could see that the "cell" actually looked fairly comfortable. Two bookcases were standing along the left wall, filled to the top with volumes of all varieties. A bed with a nice wooden frame was in the corner, and along the back was a bathtub and toilet. On the right was a small kitchen sink and stove, with some foods and spices sitting on a small table next to them. Lastly, there was an armchair in the middle, occupied by an older, skinny man with a long silver goatee. He was wearing a dark blue robe, was completely bald, and sported a pair of sandals that looked to be made of mastrichon leather.

"Is that you, Jhyris?" he asked in a raspy voice without looking up from the book he was reading.

"No," replied Arya, stepping in front of the bars.

The man looked up and they were met with a pair of cold, silver eyes. He raised an eyebrow at the three of them, a mixture of surprise and annoyance etched on his face.

"So…are you some people who've come to threaten me for killing their loved ones all those years ago?" he asked, setting his book on the bed. "Because if you are, you should know that you're not the first, and you won't be the last."

"We want your help."

He laughed out loud.

"Help? Hah. This crude cellar is just as devoid of Essence as the surface. And even if I could help you, why would I?"

"Because you feel that you made a mistake but were wrongfully punished for it." He looked at Arya appraisingly. "Because you want to prove your worth to the people who hate you, and because I think that deep down, you love this country and would do anything to protect it."

"Who are you?" he asked after a moment.

"This is Garcia Theron and Joshua Cooper," she replied. "And my name is Arya Tremayne."

"Tremayne, you say?" he asked, perhaps almost slightly impressed. "The daughter of Wester and Rae?"

Arya nodded, and for the first time since they'd seen him, the frown that seemed to be permanently etched on his face disappeared.

"My name is Necanshin Desmarthe, the Vanquisher," he said with a smile that revealed his yellowing teeth.

"Pleased to meet you," said Josh respectfully.

"Aye, me as well," added Garcia.

"How is your father?" he asked, returning his attention to Arya. "Still running about in drunken cheer every night?"

"He's dead," replied Arya flatly. "For about a week now."

Necanshin raised an eyebrow at this. "I'm sorry to hear that," he replied sincerely. "Wester was a good man."

"You knew him?"

"Once upon a time, before the war."

Arya waited to see if he would continue, but it was apparent from the following silence that Necanshin was unwilling to disclose any more information.

"We need your help," she repeated after a few moments.

"And what can I possibly do for you from in here?" he asked, more curious than impatient.

"We need to go into the forest," said Arya. Necanshin let out a loud snort. "I know you did it, and I was hoping you might impart some knowledge on the issue."

"If I was going to consider this, I'd need to know your motives for wanting to waltz into that forsaken wood."

"Another war is about to begin in Lumenaria. I have to do what I can to stop it."

"Elaborate," he said after a moment, folding his hands in his lap and reclining in his chair.

"There was an explosion during a kingball match," she explained. "Only a few lived—my father gave his life to save Josh and me. While the archons were busy there, two renegade students from the academy named Kristopher and Mareth Rothwyn broke out Tyran Nazerf and six others, and we think they're going into the forest to try and destroy the seal that's holding Seras Falrider."

"And you want my help so you can run all willy-nilly into the woods and get yourself killed by Seras's second-in-command and two extremely powerful academy students, if not Seras himself?" asked Necanshin, skeptically.

"Yes," replied Arya firmly, not even blinking.

"Well, if you want my help, then you'll have to get me out of here."

"How are we supposed to do that?" she asked.

"That's not my problem, is it?"

"You can't just tell us what we need to do to survive?" asked Arya, somewhat desperately.

"It's not a matter of telling," Necanshin replied with a snort. "If I'm not with you when you go into that forest, you'll all be quite unable to defend yourselves when the unfriendly beasties come hunting."

"All right, well, how did the archons get you in that cell?" asked Garcia. "You must know how this place is set up."

"I was bound and gagged when they did it," said Necanshin. "I was alone until one of my apprentices came and helped me undo the ropes that were binding me."

"Well, there's got to be some kind of door or a lock," said Garcia, looking around at the bars.

"We can use Essence to find it," a hesitant Arya said after a moment. She knelt down, pulled a jar containing an Essence Spark from one of the sacks, and opened it.

Josh watched as strands of Essence floated from the jar and around the outside of the cell serenely. He stole a quick glance at Necanshin and was moderately unsurprised to see the retired warrior looking longingly at what he'd been deprived of for so many years.

"There," she said, pointing as the threads of light gathered along the base of the right wall. They walked over to the spot as the Essence began to swirl and take shape.

"A shovel?" asked Garcia as Arya reached out and took it from the air.

"What else would I use?" she asked, as if it were the most obvious thing in the world.

Garcia shrugged as she began to dig, a loud clang resounding in the cave a few moments later. They knelt down as Arya uncovered a black metal box with two keyholes in it. One was surrounded by various glowing runes, the other plain.

"Figures," muttered Arya, siphoning off more Essence from the jar and forming a key. She placed the key inside the lock surrounded by runes and turned it, a loud click following. "Well, that's one."

"What about the other?" asked Josh.

"Essence can't unlock it," she replied, standing up. "It was forged with anti-Essence metal. Only a real key can open it."

"Lucky for you, I'm around," said Garcia with a wink, pulling a couple tools from his belt.

"You can pick it?" asked Josh.

"What good's a thief who can't pick locks?" replied Garcia in an affronted tone, inserting the tools into the keyhole.

"Wait," said Arya, stopping him.

"Hmm?"

She turned towards Necanshin. "If we let you out, what are you going to do when we're finished?"

"Well, that will depend on the manner of our victory," he replied.

"I can't expect you to return here, but if we make it through this, you go away, and you don't come back."

Necanshin regarded her carefully for a moment. "As you wish, Lady Tremayne."

Garcia looked up at Arya, who in turn glanced at Josh, who could do nothing but shrug. Garcia refocused his attention on the lock, shifting the tools about inside the small box.

"Should be right about...there."

A second click sounded, followed by a loud rumble and a series of clanks, as if gears and levers were turning and falling into place. A great tremor shook the ground, and dirt and rocks fell from the ceiling as the bars began to rise, disappearing into the roof of the cave.

"You're a motley bunch, aren't you?" asked Necanshin once the bars were completely raised, not having moved from the chair he'd been spectating from.

"We'll be whatever we have to be," said Arya heavily.

"Quite. You know, they'll execute you for this."

"We're, um, already wanted for other things," said Josh sheepishly.

"Is that so?" asked Necanshin, finally rising to his feet. "Good."

"Good?" asked Garcia.

"The best partners are the ones with nothing to lose," he said walking by them. "That's your first lesson."

"We have horses outside," said Arya as they followed him.

"Excellent."

They walked in silence, Necanshin leading the climb up the dark stairs. Josh thought the man's pace was a bit strained—as if he wanted nothing better than to bound up to freedom two steps at a time but refused to do something so undignified.

A few minutes later, the blackness of the stairwell began to fade. The faint glow of the surface thankfully allowed them just enough light to see their feet as they trudged on.

They emerged from the tomb a moment later, stepping out onto the barren plain. Necanshin looked up and took a deep breath, closing his eyes as he did so.

"It has been too long since I've breathed fresh air," he said exhaling peacefully. "If for nothing else, I thank you for letting me taste it again before my time in this world is up."

"You can repay us by helping to prevent a war," said Arya, readying the horses. Necanshin didn't respond—he just continued to look out at the land that had contained his prison for so long. Out of the corner of his eye, Josh saw Arya withdraw the letter that Marilyn had given her.

"What's that?" asked Necanshin, his back still turned.

Arya jumped, surprised that he'd seen her.

"A letter to a friend," she replied. "She'll help us in the forest."

"Ah," said Necanshin, turning and eyeing her carefully. "What makes you think she can survive in the forest?"

"She's an archon."

Josh expected some sort of dissent from their new addition to the group, but none was forthcoming.

"I see."

"She said to use Essence," muttered Arya to herself, unscrewing the lid of one of the Sparks.

"Give me the letter," said Necanshin with a sigh, holding his hand out impatiently.

Neither Arya nor Necanshin moved an inch as they stood staring at each other. Josh and Garcia looked back and forth between them as if they were watching a tennis match.

"What do you want with it?"

"You're not an archon. I can send that letter off much faster than you can. If you want your friend to arrive in time to help, give it here."

Arya stared at him silently for a bit before speaking.

"We need to write where she's to meet us on the outside."

"Well, hand it over and I'll take care of it."

Still, Arya made no move.

"Look," said Necanshin impatiently. "If you can't trust me enough to take care of that for you, then you had no business breaking me out in the first place."

"You'll forgive me if I'm a bit skeptical that you have no qualms with letting an active archon—someone who is sworn to arrest you for escaping—join our party."

"My dear girl, do you think for even a fraction of a second that if I could be overpowered by a single archon, I would be of any use to you whatsoever?"

Arya remained silent for a moment and then sighed. Distaste crossing her features, she handed him the letter.

"And some of your Essence as well, please."

Garcia looked at Arya, who pursed her lips and nodded. Reaching into one of the satchels tied to the horses, he removed one of the Sparks and handed it to Necanshin.

"A nice bit of craftsmanship," he commented, admiring the letter while opening the jar. "Not all archons could've created something of this quality."

"Why?" asked Arya.

"It's got an Essence signature scribed into it," he said, molding the Essence into a weblike sphere encasing the letter. "When mail is sent through normal channels, Essence is used to send it directly from the post box to the mail office."

"I know that already," huffed Arya.

"This letter has been modified in a way similar to that, but instead of the mail office, it will go directly to the recipient." He finished with the Essence and tossed the empty jar back to Garcia, the letter now floating above his outstretched palm. "A special workaround, written right into the very paper. Fairly ingenious, if you ask me."

He flicked his hand up slightly, and the letter rocketed skyward, screaming off like a firework in the direction of Danthian.

"Now that wasn't so bad, was it?"

"We'll see," said Arya, mounting her horse.

"Erm, I just noticed," commented Garcia. "There're four of us and only three horses. Who's going to walk?"

"Joshua can ride with me," she replied. "If you don't mind?"

"It's not like I haven't done it before," he said with a shrug.

"We should be off," said Necanshin, mounting a horse. "The sooner we get to Andromar, the better."

"We'll need to sleep at some point," said Garcia, saddling up and riding over to him.

"If you're serious about this, you'll survive without rest for a night," said Necanshin, as Josh and Arya joined them. "Besides, you can sleep when you're dead."

Chapter Ten: The Edge of Madness

The ride out of the Deadlands didn't take long. Josh managed to doze off a couple times while riding with Arya, but it was always short-lived, as the rough bouncing would wake him sooner rather than later.

Even though it was impossible to tell the exact time of day while in the Deadlands, it was just as night was beginning to fall that a dark shadow appeared on the horizon, the clouds finally disappearing ahead.

"Is that it?" he asked Arya.

"Yeah," she replied with a yawn. "Andromar."

"Want me to take the reins for the rest of the way?"

"We're almost there. I can hold out until then."

Necanshin had other ideas. As they approached the edge of the forest, he made a sharp right turn. Instead of riding into the black shadows of the trees, they found themselves alongside them.

"Where are we going?" called out Garcia.

"Somewhere to rest and wait for your young princess's friend," he called back.

Fortunately, it was only a few minutes later when a great, ruined tower appeared on the horizon, guarding a dark split in the mountains beyond. Arriving at the base of it, their new leader dismounted and surveyed the wrecked structure with an expression of distaste, while Garcia, Arya, and Josh caught up with him.

"Thul'Azar?" asked Garcia. "We're staying here?"

"Would you prefer the hard rock of my prison?" countered Necanshin, annoyed. "There'll still be some old cots in here to sleep on."

"Let's have a go at them, then, shall we?" asked Josh, helping Arya off the horse.

"Come along."

The ex-archon led them into the tower, which despite being ruined, had a rather roomy, oddly peaceful interior. It took him all of two minutes to find the quarters where the guards had slept, and both Arya and Garcia fell onto the cots, asleep before their heads touched the pillows.

"Lightweights," scoffed Necanshin, stalking out of the room with Josh in tow.

"What is this place?" asked Josh, following him back outside to the horses, where he gathered the reins and led them inside.

"It's an old watchtower that guards the chasm leading to Mafaelia."

"Why's it here?"

"Well," he began, unpacking some of the supplies, "in the old days, people were paranoid about outsiders. This province is so unusually isolated from the rest of the world that people here assumed their way of life to be special, that Essence was unique to this region...and they didn't want to be disturbed."

"So towers were built to protect the entrances?"

"Indeed. There's another tower to the south, guarding the pass through the mountains."

"Oh."

"You should get some sleep," said Necanshin. "I'll wake you when your friend shows up."

"How do I know you won't leave?" asked Josh. Necanshin sighed and looked him up and down.

"You're not from around here, are you?"

"How'd you guess that?"

"Foreigners aren't hard to spot when you've seen as much of this world as I have." Josh said nothing. "So…you're like Luther?"

Josh nodded. "Except I can't use Essence."

"That's to be expected," said Necanshin. "Luther and his brother are the only foreigners who've ever been able to do it, after all."

"Why is that?"

"Who knows?" he said uncaringly, kneeling next to a small circle of stones. "They were both here for a long time. That probably has something to do with it."

"Right," said Josh dejectedly.

"You look like you just accidentally dropped your birthday present down the village well."

Josh snorted at that.

"What drives you to learn so badly?" asked Necanshin igniting a small fire in the pit. "Surely you must want to get home?"

Josh nodded. "I do. But I owe Arya my life. I promised to help her with this."

"And you feel that if you can use Essence, you'll be able to help her more effectively, hmm?" he asked perceptively. "Is that the only reason?"

"Why wouldn't it be?" asked Josh, confused.

Necanshin paused and looked at him for a moment.

"The princess is quite attractive, isn't she?"

Josh raised an eyebrow at the older man and then turned his gaze away.

"She is," he said quietly. "But she's just a friend."

"Hmm. Quite," remarked Necanshin. "You want to know a trick about Essence, then?"

Josh nodded, still not looking at him.

"I don't know what others have told you about how it works or how you go about using it," he said, "but there's one thing you need to know."

"What?" asked Josh, glancing sideways at the ex-archon.

"You can't force it to work for you," he said in a soft voice. "You have to let yourself work for *it*."

"What does that even mean?"

Necanshin said nothing; he just winked at Josh and continued about his business.

"You should rest. The next few days are going to be hell."

"Compared to what the last few have been?"

"Your friend—the thief—told me about the mastrichon on our way here," he said evasively. "Tell me, did that beast shake your courage at all?"

"It was a bit scary, yeah."

"Listen to me closely, boy," said Necanshin, leaning over so close that his goatee was nearly poking Josh in the mouth. "Mastrichons are a joke. Caught my first one when I was twenty, and I did it by myself."

"What's your point?" asked Josh strongly, though inside he felt very intimidated by the fact that had just been revealed to him.

"There are far greater horrors than you can possibly imagine in that forest. Nether is twisted and chaotic. It's unnatural."

"I thought it was just the opposite of Essence," said Josh. "That Essence was life, and Nether was death—"

"A common misconception," interrupted Necanshin. "Only a few know the truth."

"Which is?"

"Nether is tainted, evil. There is nothing natural about it for it is, in fact, a cancer of this world."

"So it's corrupted Essence?"

"Indeed," he said, nodding almost imperceptibly. "Much like its counterpart, it too can restore and complete life—but in a much more sadistic manner."

"I don't follow," said Josh, shaking his head.

"Think of it like this, lad. You say that Essence reflects life?" Josh nodded. "Nether isn't death. It's the *un*-death."

Josh had retired after his conversation, accepting for the time being that he would just have to trust Necanshin to remain in their company. Not having had a soft place to sleep for several days, the comfort of fabric—opposed to the cold, hard ground—lulled him into sleep moments after he'd rested his head.

He awoke some time later from a dreamless sleep to the quiet chatter of Arya and Garcia.

"Should we wake him?"

"Nah, let him rest, it's been a long couple of days."

"Guys?" asked Josh, blinking.

"Looks like he's up, anyway," said Garcia. He was standing in front of a cracked mirror and using a rather large field knife to shave his scruffy facial hair.

"How are you feeling?" asked Arya. She'd tied her hair off into a ponytail and Josh couldn't help but remember Necanshin's comment about her appearance during their conversation.

"Better," he replied, flushing slightly.

"What are you all red in the face about?" she asked, chuckling.

"Nothing," he replied evasively. "How long have I been out?"

"About fourteen hours," said Garcia.

"We're expecting Mary soon," added Arya. "It's been almost two days."

"Do you know what we'll do once she arrives?"

"Not a clue," said Arya, shaking her head. "He still won't tell us."

"He's a bit dodgy like that," said Josh, sitting up. "Do we have anything to eat?"

"I found an edible plant growing on the slope of the mountain," drawled Necanshin, stalking into the room with a basket in his hand. "It's not bad, unless it's just as dodgy as I am?"

"I didn't mean it in a bad way," defended Josh, holding up his hands.

"I'm aware," droned Necanshin, offering the basket to Josh. "Your friend is less than an hour away," he added, turning to Arya.

"How do you know?"

"I've been around archons long enough to know when one's coming," he replied. "I could smell that armor fifty miles away."

"Right," replied Arya, rolling her eyes slightly.

"Make yourselves ready to leave the moment she gets here. Not a second to waste, after all."

And he wandered off without another word.

"Do you ever get the feeling that he's just doing this to amuse himself?" asked Garcia, still focused on not cutting himself with the knife.

"I don't really think we'll ever know," replied Arya, shaking her head disdainfully.

"Have either of you got an idea of what's in store for us?" asked Josh as he began to help pack up the supplies.

"In terms of what?" asked Garcia.

"Like, how we're supposed to deal with going into the forest."

"Nope."

"I wouldn't worry about it," said Arya gently, tying up one of the satchels. "Necanshin's done it before. I'm sure we'll be all right."

"Yeah, but to be fair, the man is absurdly powerful."

"Did something happen?" asked Arya. "You hadn't been expressing any kind of unease before this."

"I talked to him after you both fell asleep," confessed Josh. "He told me some things about Nether…"

"Like what?" prompted Arya after Josh trailed off.

"I don't know, maybe I'm just being paranoid," he said dismissively. "But I get the feeling there's going to be some really bad things in there."

"There are," said Arya solemnly. "I've heard rumors—"

"Things coming back from the dead," interrupted Garcia. "Those kinds of rumors?"

Arya turned and gave Garcia a look that would have silenced a lion.

"Something like that," she replied in a tone that suggested she was quite annoyed he had the audacity to even suggest such a thing.

"It's true, then?" asked Josh. "Things really come back from the dead in there?"

"Nothing can come back from the dead," said Arya in a strained voice, now looking as if she regretted bringing the subject up at all. "It's more as if things don't die. Instead, they pass from 'alive' into this really warped and mutilated state of existence."

"I'd rather face a pack of mastrichons than go through that," commented Garcia offhandedly.

"Damn it, Theron!" yelled Arya, eyes flaring. Both Josh and Garcia started, causing the latter to nick himself with the blade.

"Owwww!" he whined rather loudly. "What'd you have to go and yell at me for?"

"Stop being such a drama queen," she scoffed, shaking her head and throwing a towel at him. "And stop trying to scare Joshua."

"Oh, lay off. He's a tough lad."

"It's fine," reassured Josh, putting his hand on Arya's arm. "I'm not really that worried."

She softened instantly and turned to face him.

"I'm sorry," she said quietly. "I guess I'm the one who's a bit tense."

"Why?" asked Josh, nearly laughing. "You're probably almost as powerful as Necanshin."

"I'm nowhere near as powerful as he is," she replied seriously. "The only thing that makes it remotely comparable is this."

She withdrew the silver pendant from around her neck and held it gently in her hands.

"What exactly is it?" asked Josh. "I meant to ask but, you know…"

"We've been a bit busy," she said with a sympathetic smile, which prompted a nod from Josh. "It's the royal seal of Lumenaria."

She held it up for him to see. Inscribed on the surface was a great bird whose wings were spread in a graceful circle up over its head, the wingtips nearly touching at the top. A double helix was carved around the edge, and various small runes were carved into the metal where there was free space.

"I thought the sword and rose was the seal," questioned Josh. "Like what's on the money."

"That's just the crest of Danthian. The seal is only used for special things, like the archonic pendants."

"Oh. What does it represent?"

"The bird is a phoenix," she explained. "A keeper of the natural cycle."

"Natural cycle?"

"Life and death—which is what the helices symbolize."

"So what does it do?"

In response, Arya took one of the Essence Sparks and pulled a few light blue strands from it. Swirling them about in the air, she let them descend gently into her outstretched palm, and a moment later a great blast of white energy erupted from her hand, up and out of the ruined ceiling.

"Whoa."

"Essence, like anything else, has impurities," she said. "This pendant has been smelted in such a way that allows the bearer to remove most of them— which in turn makes the Essence used much more powerful."

"Which is also why you need one to make Sparks," added Garcia, using the towel Arya had thrown at him to dry his face.

Josh opened his mouth to reply, but was cut off when Necanshin stormed into the room looking quite displeased.

"I can sympathize with you two being all lovey-dovey, but can you refrain from showing off anymore, lest you inform absolutely everything in that infernal abyss of a forest of our current location?"

"Sorry," apologized Arya, her cheeks turning a shade of red that resembled a stop sign.

He turned on his heel and stalked out without another word, his cloak billowing out behind him.

"What's he doing out there, anyway?" asked Garcia, using some Essence to patch up the cut on his chin.

"I dunno," said Josh, glancing out of their quarters. He could see the top of Necanshin's bald head barely peeking above his hunched shoulders, muttering something to himself.

"Let's have a look, shall we?" suggested Garcia.

The three of them walked over to him quietly. They were a few feet away when he glanced over his shoulder at them.

"What?"

"You've been keeping to yourself," said Arya. "How come?"

"I'm preparing myself," he replied, returning his focus to something in his hands.

"For what?" asked Josh, trying to glean what Necanshin was so intently staring at.

He was holding one of the jars that had contained an Essence Spark they'd long since used. Inside was a black flame, just like the one Josh had seen in Luther's laboratory, and Necanshin was siphoning off strands of it into his body through his fingers.

"Nether?" breathed Arya venomously, backing away slightly. "What the hell are you doing with that?"

"If I'm to take care of you when we go into the forest, I'd better be good and toughened up for the task," he snarled.

"You're building a resistance to it?" asked Garcia.

"Yes," he replied. "And it's quite unpleasant, so if you don't mind, I'd like to carry on in peace until your friend arrives."

They turned and walked hesitantly back to the quarters, where both Josh's and Garcia's eyes fell to Arya, asking for answers.

"It makes sense," she muttered, sitting down on her cot. "The only way to not be overpowered by Nether is to get used to its poison."

"What'll he have us do, then?" asked Josh.

"Who knows?" she replied flatly. "At this point, I don't think it's relevant."

"Why do you say that?"

"He's filtering that…that filth into his body," she said sadly. "Doing something like that could kill him if he's not careful. If he's willing to give his life for this, we have to be ready to do the same."

"Your friend's here," they heard him call out from the next room.

"Time to move," she said, looking at them carefully. Josh let out an anxious sigh and nodded, feeling rather like a freshman on the first day of high school.

"Let's go," said Garcia, grabbing his things and leading the way out toward Necanshin.

"Are you going to be okay?" asked Arya concernedly.

"I'll be all right. I'm just a bit nervous."

"It's a good thing."

Josh looked at her strangely. "Why?"

"Because it means you're human," she replied. "And more importantly, you understand what you're getting yourself into."

"I don't know about that second part," he replied with a dry laugh, picking up two of the satchels and slinging them over his shoulder.

"You'll find out quickly, then," she said with a reassuring smile, grabbing her share of the luggage.

"Ladies first."

She smiled weakly and walked out of the room, Josh following closely. They arrived outside of the tower to find Garcia saddling the horses, with Necanshin nowhere in sight.

"Where is he?" asked Arya. Garcia nodded skyward, and Josh looked up to see Necanshin perched on top of the ruined tower, looking out over the forest with an expression on his face as if there was nothing in the world more boring.

"Ahoy there!"

They turned to see two riders on horses galloping toward them—a grinning Marilyn Fairbanks, blond hair flowing out gallantly behind her, and another, younger girl who Josh didn't recognize.

"Whoa!" she called out to her horse, pulling back on the reins as they reached the tower.

"Mary," said Arya with a broad smile, jogging forward and embracing the older woman in a hug as she leapt off her horse.

"This is my apprentice, Hannah Wentworth," she replied, introducing the younger girl. Hannah dismounted her horse and nodded politely to them. She had short, shoulder-length brown hair and soft green eyes, but her most unique feature was a long, thin scar that went from just above her right eyebrow, down over her eye, and onto her cheek. She was about as tall as Arya and looked only slightly older. "You'll forgive her, she's rather shy."

"It's all right," said Arya, nodding in greeting.

"So where is your new partner-in-crime?" she asked.

In response, Necanshin leapt from the top of the tower and sped toward the ground, floating the last few feet quite gently before his sandals touched the earth.

"Necanshin Desmarthe, at your service, milady," he said acidly with a mock bow.

"You really are just as much a show-off as everyone says," said Marilyn with a disapproving frown.

"My dear woman, the academy has really lowered its standards of quality if you thought that was impressive."

"Indeed."

"There is no time to waste," he said, picking up a couple satchels. "We should be off."

"What were you doing up there?" asked Garcia, pointing skyward.

"I was trying to get a measure of which direction we should be heading once we go inside," came the reply. "After all, you don't want to go wandering around in there aimlessly, do you?"

He was met with silence and nodded. "I thought not."

"What exactly are you going to have us do?" asked Marilyn, returning to her mount.

"Nether poisons a person by overpowering the Essence in the body," he replied. "But Essence can adapt to the evils of its opposite, much as it can adapt to anything else. So," he continued, clapping his hands together, "we're going to go into the forest—perhaps about a mile or so—and sit tight for a few hours. If no one looks like they're about to die, we'll keep going in small increments like that until we've reached our destination. Assuming there are no problems, then the fun will really start."

"That seems incredibly time-consuming," remarked Josh.

"If you plan on living through this, you'd best believe me when I say it's the only way. Even the Rothwyn twins had to go through something similar."

"That doesn't really make me feel better," he replied. Necanshin glanced sideways at him, and for a split second Josh thought he saw a trace of a smile, but a moment later it was gone, and Necanshin had walked forward off in the direction of the forest.

"We're not taking the horses?" asked Marilyn.

"You'll find that animals are a lot less resilient to Nether compared to humans," he said. "From here, we walk."

"Grab your things, then," said Marilyn softly to Hannah.

They quickly placed food and water on the ground for the horses to consume while they were gone, no one daring to try breaking the tension that had risen.

Necanshin said nothing further. Once they were done, he set off in the direction of the dark, tall trees and the blackness that lay beyond them. Garcia followed, Josh and Arya behind him, with Mary and Hannah bringing up the rear.

They walked in silence for a minute, as that was all it took to reach the edge of the wood. Necanshin stopped in front of the first tree and looked around it cautiously, as if checking for booby traps. He appeared satisfied and took a step into the shadows, which eclipsed his person almost instantly. Garcia followed silently, and Josh paused at the base of the great trees, all easily taller than the sphere he'd seen his one and only match of kingball played in.

"You'll be okay," said Arya, resting a hand on his shoulder. "Trust me."

"You haven't led me wrong yet," he replied with a rueful smile, taking a step into the darkness.

It was as if someone had injected his veins with ice. There was no light in this place. All warmth and shreds of life had been replaced by death and darkness. Josh had never felt more alone.

He heard Arya shiver as she followed him into the forest.

"Ugh," she groaned.

"I couldn't agree more," said Marilyn, joining them.

"I never thought it would be like this," said Arya.

"I don't think one can really prepare for what we're going to experience in here," replied the older woman.

"How about your apprentice?" asked Arya. "Will she be all right?"

"Hannah's quite tough," reassured Marilyn.

"What's her story, anyway?" asked Arya quietly. "You didn't tell me you'd be bringing anyone else."

Marilyn sighed. "She's another war child. A bit of a prodigy…not unlike yourself."

Arya smiled and blushed a little, although the tinge in her cheeks was subdued undoubtedly because of their surroundings.

"I tried to convince her not to come, but she was adamant," explained Mary. "She'll do anything to prevent another war from coming to Lumenaria."

About ten minutes passed in uncomfortable silence, a strong sense of nausea growing on Josh with each passing step. The surrounding darkness only became thicker, until it reached the point where they each had to carry an Essence Spark in order to see at all. Finally, as they reached a small clearing, Necanshin called a halt and began to set up some shelter.

"We'll rest here," he said. "Everyone feeling okay?"

"I've been better," muttered Garcia. Josh thought he looked a bit pale.

"Everyone else?"

They all nodded, though Josh's nausea was starting to really affect him, and he sat down so as not to lose what little he'd eaten that day.

Arya and Marilyn went off to start a small fire in the clearing, while Josh opted to lie against a tree and rest, willing the urge to vomit away.

"Are you okay?" a soft voice from his left asked.

He opened his eyes in surprise to see Hannah crouched next to him, concern etched on her face.

"I think I'll live," he replied, resting his arm on his forehead. "But I don't feel so good."

"It should pass in time," she said, sitting down next to him. "I expect it to be worse for you because you're not from here."

"You know a lot about me, apparently."

"Lady Fairbanks was telling me about you," replied Hannah. "About how you stayed with Arya to help her even though you didn't have to."

"She saved my life," said Josh with a shrug. "And her father died to protect us. I owe them both."

"Just because a person owes someone, doesn't mean they make good on it," she replied.

"What about you?" asked Josh. "How did you become Marilyn's apprentice?"

"I was assigned to her by the academy," she replied.

"You're a bit young to be doing fieldwork, aren't you?"

"I'm nineteen. There have been many younger than I who've died in battle."

"It's still a young age, though, right?"

"It is," she said with a nod. "But I don't mind."

"Why not?"

Hannah didn't say anything; she only looked away.

"I'm sorry," said Josh. "I don't mean to pry."

"I have no family," she said softly, barely above a whisper. "They were taken from me during the last war."

"I…I'm sorry."

"It's all right."

"What about Marilyn?"

"She's wonderful," replied Hannah. "But it's not the same as having a mother and father…or brothers and sisters."

"I wouldn't really know," he confessed. "My parents don't get on all that well."

"Don't take them for granted," she said. "They may not show it, but they love you."

"You're the second person to say that to me," said Josh, a smile playing on his lips.

"It's good advice," she replied, the corners of her mouth turning upwards ever so slightly.

"If you don't mind, can I ask you…" He hesitated.

"My scar?" she asked. "It happened when my parents died."

"Oh."

"It's all right," she said, and it was obvious she didn't mind sharing the story. "There was a fire in my house. A metal beam crashed from the ceiling and struck me in the face."

"How old were you?"

"Nine. After my parents died, the academy picked me up and inserted me into the system."

"Marilyn said you were very talented," he commented.

"As a result of the accident," said Hannah with a nod. "The beam that hit me was infused with Essence—some of it discharged, and as a result I have a higher capacity for it than most people."

Josh glanced at her, and to his surprise saw that her scar was shimmering slightly.

"Do you enjoy it, being an archon?"

"Oh, I'm not an archon yet. I still have much to learn."

"But do you enjoy what you do?"

"I…I've never really thought about it," she replied. "For me, there isn't any other option. My family wasn't wealthy, and the academy accepted me when I would've had nowhere else to go. I owe it to them."

"Seems to me like you're unhappy," said Josh plainly.

"This is what I choose to do with my life," replied Hannah, turning away.

Josh frowned at his own candor and apologized. "Sorry. I didn't mean to offend."

Hannah sighed and stood up.

"I know. I'm going to help the others."

And she walked away without so much as a second glance. No sooner had she left than Marilyn came over and sat down next to Josh.

"She likes you," she commented. Josh craned his neck forward and looked at her with a raised eyebrow.

"What makes you say that?"

"Well, as I'm sure you noticed, she almost never talks to anyone."

"Yeah, that had me wondering."

"She was teased a lot when she was younger, so she doesn't speak much. I think you not being from around here nor completely understanding our world appeals to her."

"I can relate," said Josh.

"How so?"

"Where I'm from, most people aren't all that friendly," he explained. "So being here, it's a nice little change. Everyone's been really kind for the most part…well, almost everyone," he corrected, an image of Derecks Whitemane flashing through his head.

"I see," said Marilyn, getting up. "You know, I think our worlds aren't all that different."

"Oh?"

"There will always be bad people and good people, and nothing we do will ever change that."

"That's true," agreed Josh. "But I've always felt that the more people you help, the fewer bad people there'll be in the future."

"It could take a long time for such a change to occur, you know."

"I never said it was instant," he said with a smile.

"Indeed," replied Marilyn, returning the smile. She wandered over to Garcia, who was being tended to by Necanshin and Arya—the latter patting a damp cloth on his forehead. Marilyn squeezed her shoulder and took the cloth, taking over for her. Arya wiped her hands on her pants and walked over to Josh.

"Aren't I popular today," he remarked as she sat down.

"Hmm?"

"You're the third person to chat me up in the past ten minutes."

"Mary and who?"

"Hannah," he replied, nodding in the direction of the brunette who was preparing some food to eat for the group.

"Oh," said Arya, taken aback. "She talked to you?"

"Yeah, I was surprised too."

"What did you talk about?"

"Mostly about her," he replied. "I asked her how she got the scar."

"Let me guess, a burn from Essence-rich metal?"

"You don't miss a beat, do you?"

"Well, someone in my position picks up on a lot of things," she admitted. "She's very gifted from what Mary tells me."

"I think she's unhappy."

"How come?" asked Arya curiously.

"She just comes off like that, I suppose," he replied with a sigh. "I shouldn't pry, it's not my business."

"In any case, you should get some rest. It's going to get much worse from here on out, or so our ex-archon tells me."

A rustling from high above caused both of them to jump slightly. Necanshin and Marilyn whipped around at the noise.

"Quiet," the former hissed, opening the jar housing the Essence Spark he was holding. They were all silent for several minutes. Each of them was trying to gauge the situation, but the billowing darkness only allowed their range of sight to extend to the trees nearest the clearing. The campfire cast flickering shadows against the trunks, and each slight movement of the flame caused their eyes to dart toward it. Finally, after an interminable amount of time, Necanshin capped the jar and returned to his business, each of the others taking this as a sign they were safe for the time being.

"I don't know how I'm going to be able to sleep now," joked Josh. "This is like living in a horror film."

"What's a film?" asked Arya.

"It's a great moving picture up on a screen," he said, waxing nostalgic. "Like a play, but it's not in real life."

"Doesn't that take some of the glamour away from it?"

"You'd think so, but some of the things the people who make the movies can do are unreal," said Josh. "Special effects, they're called."

"What are they?"

"Well, for example, I've heard that they can take a dozen people and—using computers—make it look like there are two hundred thousand."

"Really?" asked Arya, shocked. "Wow. All we have here are plays and kingball."

"I'd like to see another match sometime," said Josh. "Under better circumstances, you know."

"I know," she said as Josh let out a huge yawn. "You really should try to sleep."

"I almost don't want to," he said. "I want to be on my guard and all that."

"It's okay," she said shuffling over so their shoulders were touching. "I promise, nothing will happen to you."

"And what about you?" he asked, unconsciously leaning his head on her shoulder. "What if you need protecting?"

"I'll wake you, then," she said with a gentle smile. "Sound good?"

Whether it sounded good or not remained unanswered, as Josh had already drifted to sleep.

Chapter Eleven: Deathborne

In the next day, the group journeyed farther into the forest, the darkness growing thicker with each step they took. They had yet to encounter anything unfriendly, but Necanshin pointed out that it was only a matter of time—the farther one ventured into the trees, the more bloodthirsty and unholy the beasts were, both in quality and quantity.

An unearthly chill had arisen from seemingly nowhere, and they were cold as well as tired, in a foul mood, and in Garcia's case, sick.

They had taken another break to allow Necanshin to tend to the bandit. Josh glanced over from his spot near the campfire, where he was seated next to the three women. Necanshin was next to Garcia, and by the dim flicker of light, Josh could see that not only had all the color drained from the bandit's face, but it had left some of his facial hair as well.

"What the hell?" he remarked, as Necanshin gave Garcia a damp cloth.

"It's the Nether," said Marilyn grimly. "It's draining his life away."

"Will he live?" asked Josh.

"You should ask Necanshin," she replied. "He knows more about it than I do."

"How come it's affecting Garcia more than the rest of us?"

"I guess his body isn't as resilient," she replied morosely. "That's the cold truth of it."

Josh shook his head and stared into the fire. The warm red and orange flames were the only source of heat they'd had since their entry into the wood. His eyelids were getting heavy and he was about to nod off when a sudden movement just beyond the nearest tree caught his eye.

"I just saw something," he whispered worriedly.

"Where?" asked Arya, immediately pulling three Essence Sparks from a satchel and handing them out.

"Just past the tree there."

"What'd you say?" asked Necanshin, coming over quickly.

"I just saw movement beyond that tree," said Josh, pointing.

"Stay put," he said firmly. He furnished a Spark from within his robe and strode off in the direction that Josh had indicated.

Necanshin stopped at the tree and glanced behind it, unscrewing the lid of the jar as he did so. After a moment, he looked in the air and around some of the other trees before turning and walking back toward them.

"You're sure you saw something?" he asked Josh impatiently, standing next to him. "We haven't got time for false alarms."

"I know what I saw," retorted Josh. "It was like…like a shadow scurried from that tree over to the left."

"Well, we'll just have to be on our guard. I think if there had been something it would've attacked us, but—"

A terrified cry rang out from behind the five of them, and they spun around to see Garcia lying on his back, trying to shield himself from a massive creature with silver and black fur. It had hulking, humanlike arms and the legs of a bull. Upon realizing it had been discovered, it turned to look at them. They were greeted with three warped and malformed faces staring at them, all on its single head. Six black and glinting eyes, three distorted noses, and three mouths—all contorted and twisted with fangs and teeth bared. A low growl came from each while viscous, brown saliva dribbled off the creature's chins and onto the forest floor. Looking closely, Josh could see a deathly black mist emanating from and surrounding the creature, falling silently to the dirt below.

"Guys?" asked Josh, his eyes wide, not daring to blink or look away for even a fraction of a second.

The beast let out a tremendous sound that echoed throughout the area, making the blood pound in Josh's ears. No sooner had that happened, than it spun at them and launched itself in the air, flying toward the group with claws bared.

In an instant, a huge jet of white light erupted from Josh's left and exploded into the creature. It went flying backward and slammed into a nearby tree, howling in agony as the stench of burning flesh filled the air.

Garcia scrambled to them as Necanshin stalked over to the slain beast, a disgusting hissing coming from its corpse. There was a gaping hole in its chest where the blast had hit, and a sticky black liquid was pouring onto the ground from inside it.

"What...what is it?" asked Arya, her mouth open in horror.

"Who knows?" said Necanshin without a shred of emotion. "Something that wandered in here and got eaten up by the environment, no doubt."

"You mean that thing used to be normal?" asked Josh.

"That's what happens in here, boy," said Necanshin. "We need to move. We'll have created quite a noise and we don't want anything else showing up."

"What about Theron?" asked Marilyn.

"He'll start feeling better soon enough," replied Necanshin, packing some pots and pans up hurriedly. "That creature had probably been siphoning Nether into him since our first stop."

"You knew?" asked Arya, shocked.

"I was never going to let it get out of hand," said Necanshin. The others in the group looked at him angrily, and Garcia had an expression on his face that suggested he would've liked to clock the ex-archon. "The thing about the residents here is that you never know how smart they are."

"What is that supposed to mean?" asked Arya, crossing her arms.

"If it knew I was on to it, that thing might've picked a worse time to kill him." He pointed at Garcia. "We needed it off our backs if we're to continue on, and you're raving if you think I was going to go hunting some unknown monstrosity on my own in here."

They all looked at each other skeptically, but as there was no dissent voiced, each went about gathering their things quickly. Although none of them were too pleased with Necanshin's behavior, it was agreed that another visitor would be most unwelcome.

They had just finished packing when Necanshin stood up suddenly, eyes wide and alert, looking around carefully.

"What is it?" asked Josh.

"We're in trouble."

Josh was about to open his mouth to ask how Necanshin could know such a thing but never got the chance. The older man shoved a sack into his chest, and in a remarkable act of strength, lifted Garcia off the ground and over his shoulders.

"Follow me," he ordered to them. The words hadn't escaped his mouth when a clicking hiss permeated the air from somewhere nearby. "Whatever you do, don't fall behind."

And he set off at a dead run into the trees.

For a split second the others were too stunned to react, and then Arya tore after Necanshin, seizing Josh around the wrist and wrenching him forward.

"What the hell is chasing us?" he yelled, Marilyn and Hannah hot on their heels and something hot on theirs. "And how the hell are we supposed to outrun it?"

"I don't know!" she yelled back. "Just keep running!"

About a minute of frantic chase passed. Twice Josh stumbled over large tree roots and Arya had to expend Essence to pull him to his feet without losing pace.

Suddenly Necanshin stopped and turned, waving them on.

"Keep going!" he barked at them as they ran by. "There's a clearing a couple hundred feet ahead, stop and wait there for me!"

"How do you know that?" yelled Arya over her shoulder, his figure engulfed by the blackness seconds later.

"Just do it!"

It took them less than a minute to reach the clearing. Hannah and Marilyn jogged up a second later, breathing heavily.

"Where the hell is he?" asked Marilyn, resting her hands on her knees.

"I don't know," said Arya, as several loud explosions sounded a little way away. "Having fun, apparently."

"This is not the time to joke around," replied Marilyn. "I wonder if we should go help."

"Um," said Josh, staring ahead. "Arya?"

"What is it?" she asked, turning to him.

"What's that?"

He was pointing at a dim, red light emanating from a car-sized hole in the ground in front of them. Lying next to it was a shriveled, blackened corpse.

"I...I don't know."

"Good," said a voice from behind them in the darkness, and Necanshin came out a moment later, looking like he had just returned from his morning jog. "You all made it."

"What happened back there?"

"We attracted some guests," he replied. He set Garcia down against a tree, the color having drained from the thief's face.

"If I never come back here, it'll be too soon," he muttered, barely able to find the words.

"Nothing I couldn't handle, fortunately," continued Necanshin, removing a flask from his hip and taking a long pull from it.

"What is that?" asked Arya, pointing at the small crater.

Necanshin glanced over her shoulder and let out a grunt of disapproval before walking past them to investigate it.

"Hmph," was all the noise that came from him as he crouched next to the body, obviously more interested in that than the light.

"So what's going on?" asked Marilyn.

"Well," he began thoughtfully, "there's good news, bad news, and, in all likelihood, very bad news."

"Go on, then," urged Josh.

"The good news is that we're exactly where we're supposed to be," he explained, pointing at the crater. "That's the seal of Seras Falrider."

"What?" breathed Hannah, and they all turned to look at her. "You never told me he was still alive."

"I'm sorry," said Marilyn softly. "I didn't find out until recently, and I didn't want to tell you unless I was one hundred percent sure it was true."

Hannah said nothing, but anger was etched on her face, and Josh could tell that she was fighting back tears.

"The bad news," continued Necanshin, "is that he's not in there."

"What?" said Arya in a murderous tone, gritting her teeth.

"And the really bad news is that he's right there," he droned on, pointing at the charred body next to him as if having expected her reaction.

Arya had leveled her index finger at Necanshin—her mouth open to say something else—but had frozen at those words. Josh thought he might've laughed if the situation hadn't been so serious.

"I don't understand," said Arya. "If that's him, where are Nazerf and all the others that broke out of Synax?"

"Where are the Rothwyn twins?" added Marilyn, prompting a nod from Arya.

"You can have a look at this bastard while I go and snoop around for a moment," said Necanshin, motioning at the corpse. "And hopefully I'll be able to answer that for you."

He walked off a short distance and began searching for something unknown to the rest of them. The three women knelt down around the blackened, shriveled body. Pain and fear was carved into its face, as if something horrid had befallen this man right before he died.

"What the hell happened?" asked Josh.

"He's been depleted," said Marilyn quietly, appraising the body.

"Explain to me what that means again?"

"It means someone drained the Essence…or Nether…from his body," said Arya, standing up and looking away. "And naturally, the more powerful a person is, the greater the gain from depleting them."

"Hence why it's really bad news," said Marilyn, also standing as Necanshin reentered the clearing.

"Nazerf and the other six who escaped are about thirty feet that way," he said, pointing over his shoulder. "All the same as him," he added, nudging Seras's body with his foot.

"And the Rothwyn twins are nowhere to be found," said Garcia. It wasn't a question.

"Indeed not," said Necanshin. "Which means we should assume they are both much more powerful than Seras ever was."

"What now?" asked Arya.

Necanshin began muttering to himself, but Josh paid no attention. His focus was on Hannah, who was still kneeling over Seras's malformed body, her mouth hanging open slightly.

"Are you okay?" he asked gently, crouching next to her.

"This man was responsible for leaving me an orphan," she replied softly. "To find out he was alive, only to see him dead again…it's very surreal."

"I understand."

"For so long I've wanted to cause him the same pain he caused me."

"I'm not sure that'd be possible," said Josh thoughtfully. Hannah looked at him inquisitively. "From what I've heard, he was a real bastard." He shook his head. "I think that anyone who could do such awful things would be incapable of love, which means he'd never be able to feel the same kind of pain you did."

"I'm not sure if that makes me feel better."

"I think it just means that you're a better person than he was, and you shouldn't let your hatred consume you."

She regarded him carefully for a few moments, then turned and wrapped her arms around him tightly, resting her chin on his shoulder.

"Thank you," she whispered.

"Erm...anytime," he replied awkwardly, returning the hug.

"Ahem."

They broke apart to see Garcia and Marilyn smiling bemusedly. Arya stood next to them, her arms crossed and lips pursed. Necanshin had resumed his normal expression of boredom.

"I was saying we should start heading back for the horses," he said, twirling his goatee around his fingers. "There's no reason to be here anymore."

"You don't think Mareth and Kristopher are still in the forest?" asked Josh.

"It's unlikely. This had to be their goal in breaking out the others—they wanted Seras's power for themselves."

"But why bother with the jailbreak?" asked Garcia. "If their goal was just Seras, that is."

"Likely they didn't know where he was, or they needed help to break the seal."

"Or they just wanted to keep the archons distracted," said Marilyn. "Danthian has been a mess lately with all the investigations."

"True," replied Necanshin with a thoughtful nod.

"So less chat, more leaving this place, then," said Garcia, who Josh noticed was back on his feet and looking healthier.

Marilyn nodded. "I agree. We need to get back to civilization and make sure nothing's happened."

A tremendous screech suddenly sounded somewhere to their right, causing all of them to look in that direction as lids quickly came off jars that contained Sparks.

"Hmm," muttered Necanshin. "Smart creepers."

"What are you talking about?" asked Arya, whipping around to face him.

"Well, that little chase we had earlier?" he asked. "There were about a dozen...things after us."

"And?"

"I couldn't really kill all of them," he said, frustrated. "Maybe you'd like to give it a try?"

"Less arguing, more leaving," urged Garcia, motioning that they should exit the clearing sooner rather than later.

"I'm with him," agreed Josh, heading over to the thief.

"How far into the forest are we?" asked Marilyn as they finally got on the move.

"About five miles," called out Necanshin. "A nice good run, if you ask me."

"Let's get to it," said Arya, taking a few deep breaths. Necanshin didn't wait; he immediately ran off, leaving them to follow.

"I don't know about you," said Josh, following Arya as she chased after the older man. "But I don't know if I can run that far."

"I think, Joshua, if you want to survive, you'll manage," she said in between breaths. She opened a jar and weaved the Essence in midair while running. A moment later a few of the strands converged and were absorbed into Josh's chest.

"I hope," he breathed, suddenly feeling invigorated.

Despite the boost, after twenty minutes of jumping over tree roots Josh wasn't sure how much longer he could last. He was drawing breath with every stride he took, his lungs unable to hold more oxygen than that.

"Arya," he wheezed, forcing himself on. "I'm running...out...of air—"

"Don't talk!" she called, and it was obvious she was struggling too. "Just keep going!"

And suddenly they were stopped, Necanshin having halted in front of them. Josh collapsed to the dirt, hyperventilating, unable to stand a moment longer. Arya sat down roughly, landing with a thud, and breathing just as heavily.

Marilyn and Hannah caught up, and though both were breathing hard, neither appeared on the verge of falling down. They quickly used more Sparks to reenergize the group, and while it helped a bit, Josh was still blinking spots out of his eyes.

"You two are out of shape," said Marilyn, taking a few deep breaths.

"Quiet," hissed Necanshin, looking around.

They were still in the forest, no shreds of light permeating the darkness yet.

"Why did we stop?" asked Arya, breathing hard between her words.

"We've nowhere to go," he replied.

Josh raised his head from the forest floor and looked up. He suddenly felt a great, evil presence surrounding them, just out of eyesight beyond the darkness.

"What is that?" he wheezed, unable to conjure more volume from his voice.

"More creatures?" asked Marilyn.

"No," said Necanshin. "Something...else."

And then something appeared beyond the trees in front of them. Josh felt his blood run cold as he looked at this creature.

It was a woman...well, womanlike in any case. Its body was feminine enough, save for a rotting chunk missing from the creature's right shoulder. The face was very similar to the body—the left side was that of a normal young woman, but the right was corroded and deformed. Black tendrils flowed from the top of her head where hair should have been. Sprouting from her back were eight long insect-like legs, the tips of which were silver and sharp as daggers. Her eyes, just like every other creature they'd encountered in the forest, were jet black.

"No," breathed Arya, eyes wide. "It can't be."

"What is it?" asked Josh, struggling to a kneeling base. Arya said nothing. She rose shakily to her feet, holding on to his shoulder for balance.

The creature began advancing on them with long, fluid strides that left no motion or energy wasted. Necanshin stood in front of them, a Spark at the ready. For the first time since he'd joined them, Josh saw a flicker of fear pass across the man's face.

The creature let out a low hiss and bared its teeth—yellow and decaying, and a trickle of black saliva ran from the corner of its mouth.

"Arya Tremayne, get back here!" commanded Marilyn in a panicked tone as Arya advanced to the front of the pack, stepping around Necanshin.

"What are you doing?" he asked in a condescending tone of voice.

She ignored them, continuing her wary but determined gait toward the creature. Its expression had changed—it seemed somewhat surprised but whether it was from Arya's unabashed advance or something else, Josh didn't know.

"Um…people?" asked Garcia, facing behind them.

"What?" asked Josh.

"There's, um, things."

"What?" asked Marilyn, not turning.

"Big, unfriendly things."

"What are you talking about?" she asked, finally tearing her gaze away from Arya. Josh also looked away and did a double take as suddenly they found themselves surrounded by at least a dozen very big and unfriendly-looking creatures, all with a misty, black aura.

Arya looked around and saw this. Quickly, she returned her gaze to the Nether woman who still appeared to be weighing the situation.

"I know you can understand me," said Arya. "Please, help us."

The creature let out a low hiss as the other beasts surrounding the group began to close in on their helpless prey.

"It's me…it's Arya…"

The creature's expression became strained, as if it was trying to do something foreign in nature.

"Arya?" asked Josh, his shoulders pressed against Marilyn's and Hannah's, with Garcia and Necanshin closing off the other side of the circle they'd created. "If you're going to do something, do it faster."

The words had barely escaped his mouth when the monster nearest to him—a catlike beast with yellow fangs and silver claws—launched itself into the air and at the group. Josh instinctively raised his arms over his head to defend himself, when he suddenly heard a very loud clicking noise and a piercing screech from the creature that had been attacking them. He cautiously looked through his arms to see the beast thrashing on the ground nearby, a great, silver spike embedded in its chest.

He spun around to see the female creature pointing a bare insect-leg at the cat, the tip of which having been what impaled the thing. He stared on in shock as a second later the dagger regenerated on the end of her limb.

They each looked at the insect woman, which was snarling madly, as if trying to resist some unknown power. Finally, it made eye contact with Arya and in a quick, small gesture nodded over its shoulder.

"Let's go," said Arya, not missing a beat. "Now."

"Yeah," said a frantic Josh. "Let's."

They tore past, and it rounded on the remaining creatures. As they sprinted off, screeches of pain and agony echoed behind them continuously until they were out of earshot.

And finally, the darkness began to fade into a dull gray, and then a lighter gray, and finally, after an eternity of running, they broke through the last trees and stumbled out onto the ground. It was midday, gray clouds floating peacefully in the sky above them.

"We made it," huffed Marilyn, sitting down.

Josh had fallen again, unable to stand any longer. He cracked his eyes open and was greeted with a pair of sandals standing in front of him. Looking up, he saw Necanshin leaning down, handing him a small flask of water.

"Drink up," he said. "You did well."

"Thanks. What happened back there?" he asked between gulps.

"You should ask your friend."

Josh looked over his shoulder and saw Arya sitting a little way away with her back to the group, hugging her knees to her chest.

"Go," said Marilyn. "I think I know what happened, but you should be the one to talk to her."

"Why?"

"Please, Joshua," she answered, looking away.

Josh watched her as she walked over to Hannah and they began talking in hushed tones. Sighing, he struggled to his feet and limped over to Arya, willing his muscles to not cramp.

She said nothing as he sat down next to her.

"Arya?"

He looked at her and to his surprise, saw tears forming in her eyes. She sniffled and looked away, blinking rapidly.

"What is it?" he asked, covering her hand with his. "What's wrong?"

"Do you remember," she said shakily, "when you first showed up, you asked me how many people appear here from other worlds?"

"Of course," he said with a nod.

"And I told you that the only other person I'd met who wasn't from here was a girl named Tanya?"

"Yeah?"

"That...that creature..."

Josh's eyes widened as the realization of what she was implying hit him.

"You...you're telling me that...that thing, the woman, that was her?"

She buried her face in her knees, nodding almost imperceptibly.

"I thought you said she was killed?"

"That's what I thought," she choked out. "But I guess something else happened."

"How could you not have found out?" asked Josh. "Unless someone lied to you?"

"It was my mother, why would she have lied?"

And suddenly it occurred to Josh why Marilyn had been hesitant to discuss this with Arya.

"You knew," he said, turning around to look at the archon. She'd been watching them from a distance for a minute and looked away shamefully at the accusation.

"I did," she replied softly.

"What?" asked Arya, rounding on her. "How...how did you know?"

"Both your parents knew, and your mother asked me to keep it from you. She knew how much you loved Tanya and how much it would've broken your heart to hear her true fate."

"I think it would've hurt less than it does now!" she cried exasperatedly. "She's been a Deathborne for all these years, and none of you tried to help her?"

"We wanted to, so dearly," explained Marilyn. "But you can't go running into the forest for something like that. It could've taken us months to find her, and there's no guarantee anyone would've even reached that point alive."

"I would've done it," said Arya through gritted teeth.

"And that's why your mother didn't tell you." Marilyn looked away and turned back toward Garcia and Necanshin, who were muttering animatedly about something.

"What's a Deathborne?" asked Josh, returning his attention to Arya. She was looking down at the ground, playing with a loose rock with her fingers.

"Humans who neither get killed by Nether or adapt become assimilated by it. They turn into terrible creatures like what you saw back there. Terrifying, powerful, and completely bloodthirsty."

"Well, not completely," said Josh. Arya raised an inquisitive eyebrow at him. "You got through to her. Some part of her is still there."

"I'd almost rather it weren't," she said, sniffling. "Can you imagine being imprisoned in that body, in that forest?"

"I don't want to imagine it."

"I can't let this stand. None of this is right."

"No, it isn't," said Josh. "But one thing at a time. We still have a province to save."

"I know. I'm not sure what I could do, anyway."

"When we save the world, you can work something out."

"I hate to break up this beautiful moment," said Necanshin, sauntering over to them, "but we have business to take care of."

"He's right," added Garcia, joining them. "We have to get back to Ageria and make sure it's safe."

"And Hannah and I have to return to the academy and appraise the other archons of the situation," said Marilyn. "If the Rothwyn twins haven't destroyed it already, that is."

"Do your best to leave me out of the proceedings," asked Garcia.

"I'll be delicate with what I say," she reassured.

"Regardless of who does what," said Arya, rising to her feet. "We have to get moving first."

"Agreed," said Garcia, readying their mounts.

"Let's go," said Marilyn. "If we ride hard we can be back in Danthian within two days."

Josh saddled up behind Arya, just as they'd been doing since their party had grown.

"Do you get the feeling that something terrible is about to happen?" she asked quietly as the others climbed onto their horses.

"Worse than what's happened already?"

Arya nodded in response.

"I get the feeling something isn't right," he said.

"What do you mean?"

"I don't know…none of this makes much sense."

"You're right," she replied. "We need to be prepared for anything."

Josh wrapped his arms around her waist, but as he did so he brushed the medallion around her neck with his hand. For a brief instant, a warm, energetic sensation rippled through his body from where his fingers had made contact, but a second later it was gone. Arya glanced at him over her shoulder, a curious expression on her face.

"Sorry," he blushed. "It was an accident."

"You felt it, didn't you?"

"How'd you know?" he asked.

"I felt a small change in the Essence around us. Granted, there's almost none of it out here, but still."

"It's gone now," he said.

"You might end up figuring this whole thing out just in time," she said softly.

"Oy, you two!" yelled Garcia. Marilyn, Hannah, and Necanshin had already ridden off, and were quickly becoming small specks in the distance. "Pay attention or you're going to get left behind!"

"Let's get moving," said Josh, avoiding Arya's previous statement.

"As you wish, Joshua," she replied. She bucked the reins and the horse sped off after Garcia's, dark clouds building on the horizon.

Chapter Twelve:
The Labyrinth of Tannoral

The group rode along the perimeter of the forest for twenty hours straight. They used the last of the Sparks to rejuvenate themselves, and just as the riders were about to collapse from exhaustion, the endless array of solid, gray clouds broke. Splashes of sunshine began to show here and there, and Essence became visible in the surrounding air again. As soon as grass began to reappear underfoot, they reached a large, ruined tower—newly ruined by the looks of it—behind which a great wall twenty-five feet tall extended out and into the distance.

"What happened here?" asked Josh as the riders grouped up in front of the razed building.

"This is part of a wall which separates the Veran Hills from the forest. It also encloses Synax," said Arya. "This is the southern watchtower."

"You mean *was*," said Garcia.

"This isn't good," said Marilyn worriedly. "We passed here on our way to you, and there were at least two dozen guards active and in full battle dress."

"What do you think happened to them?" asked Arya.

"Should we go in and see if we can find out what happened?" suggested Josh.

"No," interjected Necanshin. "We have no time."

"Why not?" argued Marilyn. "If there are survivors in there—"

"Then they'll be picked up by archons if and when we prevent those two men from destroying our country."

"He's right," said Arya, barely above a whisper. "If it's like this here, imagine what other places could be like. Places like Danthian."

"We should make haste," said Marilyn. "We're still just under a day from Kendrall."

"There's a village a couple hours from here that might be able to help," said Garcia.

"The only thing we need to know is how far the destruction has spread," said Necanshin determinedly. "Our job is to get back to Danthian. Nothing else."

"Let's go, then," said Marilyn, spurring her horse on and tearing off toward the west.

They rode along the base of the great wall for an hour before it veered north, the great fields of Ageria lying before them. Glancing back at it as they rode past, Josh noticed a black column of smoke rising in the distance.

"What's that?" he asked Arya, pointing at it.

"The prison," she replied, deflated.

"We're riding headfirst into war, aren't we?"

"If not, we're all that's left to stop it," she answered, looking determinedly straight ahead.

Josh said nothing. He only sighed and rested his forehead against her shoulder.

"Joshua, I would never fault you if you want out of this now, while we're still reasonably safe."

He looked up and saw Arya glancing at him over her shoulder. Smiling sadly, he reached out and covered her hand with his.

"I promised you, I'm here until the end. Besides, where would I go?"

"I just don't want you doing this out of some misplaced sense of duty to me and my father."

"I'm not," he assured her. "I'm doing this because I want to, because your land deserves better than Mareth and Kristopher Rothwyn, and because I couldn't bear the thought of someone dying who has done so much for me."

"Thank you," she replied after a moment, leaning back into him slightly. "If you stick around long enough, it's going to be me who ends up owing you."

"I think we're still quite a long ways from that."

"We may have a problem!" yelled Garcia from a little bit in front of them. Josh and Arya looked up and saw him pointing at the horizon, where dark, billowing clouds were beginning to take shape very rapidly.

Necanshin, Marilyn, and Hannah dropped back to the three of them, and slowed so they could all hear each other speak.

"What do you suppose it is?" asked Marilyn. "It's forming too fast to just be a normal storm."

"Logic would suggest it's something other than nature," drawled Necanshin.

"So what do we do about it?" asked Josh.

"Going around will take too long. We'll have to brave it."

"How bad can it be, yeah?" asked Garcia.

"Why you would say something like that, I'll never know," said Marilyn, turning forward, whipping her reins, and speeding off with Hannah and Necanshin in close pursuit.

"You get the feeling they're forming their own little group?" mentioned Garcia as he, Josh, and Arya quickened to catch them.

"Archons stick together," said Arya. "Even if they're ex-archons."

The clouds grew more ominous, periodic flashes of lightning illuminating their black depths for a moment here and there.

Finally, rain began to fall lightly. Josh made to brush away a droplet that had landed on his cheek, when a painful burning sensation started to emanate from where the liquid had made contact.

"What the hell?" he complained, rubbing at it fiercely.

"What's wrong?" asked Arya, turning around. A drop of rain hit her arm, and she nearly lost control of the horse as a great red splotch appeared where it had landed.

Ahead of them, a great dome had appeared above the three archons to shield them from the acidic downpour.

"Take the reins," commanded Arya through gritted teeth. Josh didn't even question it, he grabbed the leather straps from her and she quickly conjured up a shield large enough to protect them.

Garcia had caught up with the archons—who had slowed so that they could all regroup—and he too had red and pink marks on his arms and face.

"We'll need to stick together from here out," said Necanshin, who looked to be sustaining the shield without any effort. "This will probably only get worse."

The words hadn't even left his mouth when a great, arcing bolt of red lighting erupted from the clouds and landed a few hundred feet from where they were.

"Let's go, people!"

They all rushed off after Necanshin, riding with his hand in the air to maintain the shield. Josh was still trying to figure out a way to quell the burning but was having no luck.

"Try to stop thinking about it," said Arya. "You'll only make it worse."

"Easier said than done."

"Heads up!" yelled Marilyn from in front of them.

They both looked up to see a tremendous, fiery boulder come rocketing from the heavens and land directly in their path. Necanshin barely swerved in time to avoid it as more began to hurtle down from the sky.

"We can't stay out here!" yelled Marilyn. "Even your shield can't stop them all!"

"We have to continue!" called out Necanshin.

"There's another way!" yelled Garcia, pointing to a small hill off to their right. "That's an entrance to Tannoral over there!"

Necanshin seemed displeased with the detour, but it appeared that despite his skill with Essence, he was growing weary with how much was being used. Without a word, he veered off in the direction of the hill, a great boulder resting to the side of it.

As they approached, Garcia extended his hand toward the boulder. A flash of white light erupted from his palm and struck the rock. Instead of exploding, vaporizing, or any number of other things Josh expected it to do, it merely rose up in the air, exposing a vast cave.

"Everyone in!" yelled Garcia, as another fiery meteor missed him by only a few feet.

They galloped into the opening at full speed, and the boulder landed with a great 'thud' behind them once Josh and Arya had ridden inside.

The cave was actually a tunnel, as Josh quickly learned when he noticed that none of the horses had broken stride. It was very well lit; hundreds of bracket-mounted torches lined the walls of the ever expanding passageway, which was quickly growing to the point where one could fit a large trailer truck inside.

"Where are we?" asked Josh.

"Tannoral," replied Arya. "The underworld labyrinth of thieves."

"I thought Garcia said it wasn't as big as all that."

"It must've slipped his mind."

"You'll forgive me for not wanting to divulge the greatest secret of my trade to someone from the royal line!" he yelled back at them, having heard their words.

"Where will this take us?" asked Marilyn, still riding at full speed.

"All the way to Danthian!"

"You're joking."

"Not at all, although—" He was cut off as Necanshin's horse clipped a thin wire and a flurry of arrows went screaming by inches from his head. "There are booby traps."

"You ride up front, then!" yelled Necanshin furiously. "I'm not dying today, and certainly not for the likes of an inattentive thief!"

"What the hell is this place?" shrieked Marilyn as her horse set off another trap and nearly fell into the collapsing hole that had appeared.

"It's designed to keep unwanted people in," he explained, reaching the front. "Forever!"

"Isn't that lovely!" yelled Arya sarcastically. "You know where you're going, right?"

"I haven't been this far east in the tunnels before!"

Josh and Arya shared a worried look.

"Don't worry, I know what to look for! Just follow my horse's path exactly!"

They did, although it certainly wasn't the easiest task in the world. For hours they dodged traps, having close calls many times.

The tunnels twisted and turned, descending ever deeper into the ground, but despite the distance they were covering, they had yet to see any other forms of life.

"I thought there were supposed to be large cities down here!" yelled Arya.

"There are!" shouted back Garcia. "We're going around! I thought it'd be better to draw as little attention to ourselves as possible!"

Josh wasn't sure, but he could've sworn he saw Necanshin mouth to Marilyn, *He's learning.*

And then they were stopped, a six-way junction sitting before them. Garcia was staring blankly at the mouths of each tunnel, clearly with no clue as to which yielded the correct path.

"So, which way?" asked Necanshin, hopping off his horse.

"I've no idea. I've never seen this place in my life."

They each dismounted, trying to find some clue as to the proper direction.

"Well, this didn't turn out to be very effective," muttered Josh twenty minutes later.

"Better late than dead," replied Arya.

"Give it a rest you two," grumbled Garcia, who was examining the nearest aperture. "There have got to be some markings signifying which way is which…"

"Quiet," hissed Necanshin, holding his hand up. They stood in silence for a bit, and then suddenly, from the tunnel nearest Josh and Arya, the echoing of footsteps sounded clearly in the air.

"Hide!" whispered Marilyn urgently. They each grabbed their horses and ducked into the mouths of the other tunnels, crouching in the shadows.

The footsteps drew closer, and after a minute, a cloaked figure appeared from the passageway nearest Josh. His face was obscured by the hood he wore, and his arms were crossed inside the sleeves of his robe. He was alone.

They watched in silence as he continued on without stopping, moving down the corridor nearest Garcia.

"A patrol?" asked Marilyn quietly, once the person was out of earshot.

"No thief would wear something like that," replied Garcia disdainfully.

"In that case, perhaps it would be prudent to follow," suggested Necanshin, already stalking off in the direction the person went.

"What about the horses?" asked Arya.

"We'll stay and watch them," said Marilyn, putting a hand on Hannah's shoulder.

"Make sure you stay hidden," said Garcia. "There's no one down here who'll be friendly to archons."

"I understand."

"Let's go, and keep it quiet," said Necanshin, annoyed at having to slow his gait so they could catch up.

They jogged to close the distance, and within a few minutes they saw the figure again, walking stoically far ahead of them.

"It doesn't make sense," whispered Garcia. "We should be miles away from the nearest city. What the hell is a patrol doing out here by himself?"

"We are following him so we can find that out. Now keep it down," spat Necanshin, his voice barely above a whisper.

"You said you've never been here before?" asked Arya.

"No, none of this looks familiar."

"What part of 'stop talking' did you not understand?" breathed the ex-archon. Arya rolled her eyes but said nothing.

They followed until the figure reached a four-way intersection where another cloaked person was waiting. The first man reached the second, and they began talking in hushed tones.

Arya nudged Necanshin and pointed at the two men. He nodded in response and twirled about some Essence in his fingertips. He placed a hand to his ear, and a moment later a thin wisp of Essence trailed from his ear out into the clearing. "Nothing, again," he repeated to them, his voice barely audible. "There's never anyone down here these days. Lord Mareth made sure all the thieves were scattered into hiding in the other passageways."

Josh, Arya, and Garcia all gaped at each other at hearing this.

"My rounds are over, I'm going to report to the others. I'll talk to you later, then. Good-bye."

They watched as the second figure left through the passage on their right, while the first walked through a tiny arch that was only large enough for one person to enter at a time.

"So the Rothwyn twins are hiding down here," said Arya after several minutes.

"It appears so," said Necanshin, the trail of Essence dissolving back into the air.

"Down that tunnel?"

"Probably," said Garcia. "See there?" He pointed at two large zeroes painted above the arch. "That tells us this particular tunnel is special."

"What do you mean?" asked Josh.

"All the tunnels down here have markings to help identify their respective destinations. Usually some kind of lettering is used, but in some cases, the number zero is used to signify a dead end."

"So this is one of those tunnels?" asked Arya.

"In theory."

"What do you mean 'in theory'?" asked Necanshin impatiently.

"Well, a double zero is somewhat special."

"What does that mean?" asked Josh.

"It means that there's a very dangerous reason this tunnel has no exit," said Garcia seriously. "An enter-at-your-own-risk type of deal."

"We're following him," said Necanshin. "So I hope you have an idea of what we'll be up against."

"In all likelihood, a Nether fissure."

"Wonderful," droned Arya as they ventured out into the intersection.

It was lit by a metal chandelier hanging from the ceiling, six candles in holsters around the black steel. Josh glanced at the other passageways as they walked by; sure enough there was an M over the one the other sentry had departed through, and an H over the last tunnel.

"So why couldn't you figure out where to go back there?" asked Arya, as they filed into the tiny tunnel.

"Those passages aren't marked. It must've been overlooked."

"Seems pretty important to be overlooked," she said.

"There was probably an emergency. Undesirables getting too close to one of the nearby entrances, trouble in one of the cities—it could've been many things."

"Pay attention," whispered Necanshin, who was now stooping so as not to hit his head. "And be quiet, I hear voices."

They continued on, the echoes of distant conversation wafting through the constricting passageway. Finally, it opened up into a huge cavern with stalactites hanging from the ceiling. A great pit lay before them, at least fifty feet deep, with a ladder leading down into it.

Quietly, they approached the edge, lying down once they could see over the precipice. All four pairs of eyes widened at the sight that lay before them.

A great pool of what looked like liquid silver was shimmering in the ground below. Gathered next to it, Mareth and Kristopher Rothwyn—along with at least a dozen other hooded figures—were standing around a wooden table, a great map of Lumenaria spread out on it. Crates and sacks of supplies were strewn about them.

Josh glanced over at his companions, all of whom were wearing looks of shock on their faces—even the normally stoic and bitter ex-archon.

"What is it?" whispered Josh.

"It's Essence *and* Nether?" breathed Arya.

"It's not possible," whispered Necanshin. "The two are naturally incompatible. There must be something else, something forcing the mix to keep it stable."

"Shh, listen," hushed Garcia.

"Everything is in place?" asked Mareth, his voice echoing throughout the cavern.

"Yes, my lord," one of the cloaked figures replied. "With the bandits scattering to the remote corners of Tannoral, the path to Danthian is clear."

"The march will be unimpeded, then," said Kristopher. "The archons will never know what hit them."

"Right," muttered Mareth.

"My lord, if it's not too bold, may I ask how you plan to storm the capital?"

"You doubt our abilities?" asked Kristopher.

"Not at all, sir, but if I may, you are but two against an army of dozens, if not hundreds. There is no denying your power, but at some point the numbers will overwhelm you, will they not?"

"Perhaps it's time to create our army, then," said Mareth, grabbing one of the nearby sacks and opening it.

A quiet hiss came from Necanshin as Mareth extracted the same orb with blue and orange flames that he'd used at the bandit camp. He held it at arm's length and it floated peacefully off his hand.

Suddenly, the flames inside it began to swirl rapidly, as if a small tornado had just formed inside the orb. The wisps of fire on the crystaline surface grew and jumped into the air, evaporating just as quickly as they'd formed.

"Look," whispered Arya, nudging Josh.

The silver liquid in the pool was also beginning to swirl, a small vortex having appeared. Mareth floated the orb over to the edge so that the flames jumping from it were almost touching the liquid.

"What's he doing?" asked Garcia.

"Shut up and watch or you'll get us caught," hissed Necanshin.

They looked on as one of the trails of fire finally touched the surface of the pool. A bright arc of red lightning erupted from the orb and struck the silver liquid, and a great bubble began to form on the surface, as if air was trying to escape.

Josh watched in horror as the bubble burst, and a dark, silver beast with glowing red eyes splashed out of the murky liquid and landed on the ground next to Mareth.

With every flame that touched the pool, more creatures spawned, each heeling at Mareth's side as they escaped from the liquid silver.

"Let's go," said Necanshin, pulling them away from the pit. "We've seen enough."

"What the hell happened back there?" asked Garcia, once they had reached the intersection and were heading back toward Marilyn and Hannah.

"That artifact Mareth was holding is called the Orb of the World," explained Necanshin. "It's one of four, maybe five relics from the first war."

"What is it, exactly?" asked Arya.

"Supposedly, a long time ago, Nether was—for lack of a better term—less tainted," he said. "It was orange instead of black."

"And the blue is Essence?" asked Josh.

"Quite so. There are stories that the Nether Wraiths were defeated by some unique weapons which retained the most powerful properties of both elements, and that orb is one of them."

"What were those monsters?"

"I can't say for certain. What's likely is that with their amplified power from all the people they've depleted, the Rothwyn twins were able to use the purer form of Nether to fuse together Essence and the more-impure Nether that exists today. With a mixture like that, it wouldn't be hard to use the orb and bring some supernatural monsters to life."

"So they bred an army," said Arya with a defeated expression. "Just like Seras."

"It appears that way."

"What do we do about it?"

"I'm not sure," he muttered.

They reached the large intersection and found Marilyn and Hannah crouched in one of the nearby tunnels with the horses.

"Glad to see you made it back," said Marilyn, standing up. "Is there any news?"

"Nothing good, I'm afraid," said Garcia.

"The Rothwyn twins," said Necanshin. "And they have the Orb of the World."

"What?" asked Marilyn skeptically, though concern crossed her features.

"They're creating an army from some kind of Essence and Nether mixture," he continued, "and they're going to storm Danthian."

"Well, we have to stop them," said Hannah. The others all turned and looked at her, surprised to hear her speak.

"I agree," said Marilyn. "But saying and doing are two different things."

"If we can destroy the orb, their army should vanish, and then we can fight them ourselves."

"How do you plan on doing that?" asked Arya.

"We'll need to set up an ambush," said Necanshin. "The orb will have to be in an open spot, so it can provide power to the creatures directly. If the timing is right, we might be able to capture the twins and take down everyone else without much of a fight."

"And where exactly do you plan on doing this?" asked Arya. "These tunnels run all the way to Danthian—"

"Here," said Garcia, who had, unbeknownst to the group, removed a large piece of parchment from one of his satchels and spread it out on the floor. "See here, the tunnel that leads to Danthian bottlenecks right before the exit. If we can beat them there, we can set up in spots that will blindside them."

"You have a map?" yelled Arya.

"Lower your voice," hissed Necanshin.

"If you had a map, why didn't you look at it before?"

"Wouldn't have done any good," he answered. "We're too far from the cities to be on it, but I have a feeling that this tunnel here"—he pointed at a spot on the parchment—"isn't too far away."

"How do we get ahead of them?" asked Marilyn.

"Here," he said, pointing at the map again. "There's a series of small tunnels near City Four that will act as a shortcut. The twins will be unable to use them because they have a lot of men, so we should beat them by a bit if we go now and don't stop."

"We're still at least a full day from Danthian, maybe more," said Arya. "We haven't slept in almost two days, and we need to get there with enough energy to fight. How is this going to work?"

"What do you think?" Marilyn asked Necanshin.

In response, he withdrew a jar from his robe containing an Essence Spark. Without speaking, he siphoned the Essence out of the jar and funneled it into Marilyn, Hannah, Arya, and Garcia.

"That should hold you for a while," he replied, discarding the container.

"You were holding out on us?" asked Arya venomously, her eyes narrowing.

"We needed to save some for an emergency," he replied. "Would any of you have been able to refrain from using it before now?"

"None for me?" asked Josh, trying to shift the focus.

"You don't use Essence to fight, and you can sleep on the way there," he replied. "We have no time to waste. If they get into Danthian, there is no way we'll be able prevent outside casualties."

"Do you think this'll work?" asked Arya, who seemed to have calmed down for the time being. "We're outnumbered pretty badly."

"If you do exactly what I say, when I say it, we'll have a chance," said Necanshin, apparently satisfied with the renewed energy of the four he gave Essence to. "We should leave now. The more time we have to prepare the better our odds will be."

"Lead the way, thief," said Marilyn.

"Yes ma'am," he said with a nod, saddling up and galloping off down a nearby tunnel.

"What do you think?" asked Joshua once he and Arya were mounted and following the others.

"I don't know what to think," she replied. "I think that we're going to have to fight pretty damn hard if we want to live through this."

"I'm a bit nervous," he confessed.

"Me too," she said with a laugh.

"You don't look it."

"I do an okay job of keeping my emotions in check," replied Arya. "But it doesn't matter how I feel. I've got to be at my best, so now is no time for fear."

Joshua said nothing. He merely rested his forehead against her back as they rode through the cold tunnels, hurtling toward an inevitable conflict that seemed likely to decide the fate of the entire province.

Chapter Thirteen: Black Fire

The hours passed in a tired haze for Josh. They didn't stop once, and when they finally reached their destination, he was asleep and had to be prodded awake by Arya.

"You sleep a lot, you know," she said with an amused smile as he groggily shook himself in an effort to regain his senses.

"I'm not used to getting this little sleep," replied Josh. "Are we there?"

"We are."

The others had already begun wandering around the tunnel, looking for any irregularities in the terrain that they could use to their advantage. About five minutes passed in near silence while the three archons whispered amongst themselves, before Necanshin called them all over to the edge of the tunnel—a narrow archway ten feet high and four across.

"All right," he said brusquely. "The situation is not quite as favorable as our esteemed burglar led us to believe."

"I never said it'd be perfect," defended Garcia. "I just said it'd give us a chance."

"And a chance is all we'll have," he replied. "The exit is too narrow to capitalize fully on the fact that they'll be bottlenecked."

"What do we do?" asked Arya.

"We're going to have to hope that the Rothwyn twins are paranoid," he muttered.

"What does that mean?"

"If the twins are at the front of their army, we'll have no chance," explained Marilyn. "Mareth has the orb, and if we can't destroy the orb, we all die."

"Why not just get rid of it first and foremost?" asked Garcia. "If they're leading the pack, just blast it away while they're in the open, right?"

"The whole point of us attacking them here and not where we found them is that the narrowness of the exit reduces their effective numbers," said Necanshin, pinching the bridge of his crooked nose in frustration. "Don't forget, there are six of us, and at least a couple dozen of them before their new friends."

"So what's the plan?"

"I was in the middle of telling you," he droned, rolling his eyes, "that since the tunnel is too narrow, we'll have to trap their army as best we can, assuming that the twins know to let someone else march in front."

"Why would they do that?" asked Josh.

"It's the tactically correct move to not go first or last," said Marilyn. "Generally, the more insulated you are from open space, the more protected you are."

"Correct," said Necanshin. "So assuming that the Rothwyn twins will be somewhere in the middle of the pack, I'll be hiding up there"—he pointed upward at an outcropping of rock that created a corner where he could effectively hide from view—"and when the time is right, I'll do everything in my power to make sure the orb is destroyed."

"Hannah and I will be in the tunnel to attack from the front," said Marilyn. "If we're overcome, she'll run to the exit and sound the alarm."

"I'll be attacking from the top, assuming I don't die in the effort to destroy the orb," said Necanshin. "You three will be hiding in the back and will attack once the battle starts."

"Where exactly do you want us to hide?" asked Arya.

"Here," he said, tossing them two large black blankets. "Hide against the wall under those. You won't be seen."

"All right."

"And I'll need your medallion," he added, looking pointedly at her. Arya's hand subconsciously went to her chest, where the medallion her father had left her was resting.

"Why?"

"Aside from the fact that the closer it is to the twins, the easier it'll be for them to sense it, I'll need it to have a chance of destroying the orb."

"It's okay," said Marilyn, looking at Arya softly. "I've already given him mine."

Arya bit her lower lip hesitantly, and undid the chain behind her neck. Holding the metal disc in her hand, she looked up at Necanshin.

"Will it be that hard to destroy?"

"Child, this thing has been in our world for as long as humans have. Nothing survives that long unless it's durable."

She sighed and tossed it to him. Necanshin caught it with an outstretched fist and fastened the chain around his neck, tucking it into his shirt.

"We don't know when they'll arrive, so we have to be in position and ready to go as soon as possible," he said.

"Right," said Garcia. Necanshin looked up, and Marilyn and Hannah turned and began to walk toward the exit. "Wait, um, what exactly do you want us to do?"

Necanshin turned and looked at him.

"Anything and everything."

They were all in position minutes later—Necanshin tucked safely away in the ceiling, Hannah and Marilyn at the exit, Garcia along the left-hand wall, and Josh and Arya along the right.

"How long do you think it'll be?" he whispered to her. She was lying on top of him so as to prevent them from sticking out too far into the tunnel, and it was a strange experience for Josh.

"As long as it takes," she replied. "Are you uncomfortable?"

"Not exactly," he said, and he was glad it was pitch black under the blanket so Arya couldn't see the tinge in his cheeks.

"Listen, Joshua, there's no guarantee any of us will get through this."

"I know. I'm not leaving."

"That's not what I was going to say," she said. "You've done so much more than I could have ever asked of you. You've been a good man and a greater friend, and no matter what happens here today, I will never forget what you've done for me."

"You say that like it's certain we're going to die."

She leaned forward so that her mouth was right next to his ear.

"I'm terrified," she confessed. He turned his head ever so slightly toward her. "The fate of the entire province rests with us, and if we fail, no one will know of my father's innocence. Or that Necanshin, despite being a complete ass, is a good man. Or that you, an outsider with no knowledge of Essence, played just as much a role as anyone else."

"Then we won't fail," answered Josh. "It's as simple as that."

"Joshua, it isn't that simple—"

"Yes it is," he interrupted. "The reason we can win this is because they fear failing. They know what it means if they do. Why do you think they depleted all those students and Seras?"

"You think they're scared?"

"It may seem like we have more to lose than they do, but it's never that simple," said Josh. "Because the truth is that they've invested their entire lives in this plan. Without it, they're nothing, and they know it."

"You know, you sound a bit like Necanshin," mused Arya.

"I have my moments," he replied, smiling slightly.

She leaned forward again and kissed him on the cheek.

"Thank you," she whispered. "For everything."

"Don't thank me quite yet," he replied, as a few nearby pebbles began to bounce around slightly on the ground. "They're here."

The low, rhythmic beat of footsteps permeated the air from behind them. Slowly, the beat grew louder, until the clanking and thundering of armored boots and heavy claws was mere feet from where they were lying. Josh felt his heart start to race as the first great, silver beast drew even with them and continued past, a seemingly endless line of claws behind it.

"Steady your heart," said Arya, so softly that even Josh barely heard it.

Josh did as she said, closing his eyes and willing himself to breathe deeply. As he did so, the footsteps slowed and quickly came to a halt. Josh glanced at Arya warily.

"My lord?" they heard someone ask.

"Something's wrong," came the reply, and it sounded like Mareth. "There's an unusual amount of Essence gathered here."

Josh's eyes widened in alarm, but Arya shook her head almost imperceptibly, telling to him remain calm.

"What should we do?" said the first voice.

There was silence for a moment before Mareth spoke again.

"We're not alone."

And then two things happened at once, very quickly. A great high-pitched noise surrounded them, followed nearly instantly by a tremendous comet of energy rocketing from Necanshin's position high above toward the enemy.

Josh waited for something...*anything*...but it never came. No explosion, no great collision. In fact, save for a soft, pulsing hum, there was complete silence. He lifted the corner of the blanket a fraction off the ground so as to see what was happening, and his eyes widened at the situation.

Flanked by two dozen cloaked figures and at least a hundred silver beasts, Mareth stood holding the Orb of the World—which was pulsing orange—in his hand, high above his head. A few inches above the orb was a great ball of white energy, floating peacefully as if suspended in space and time.

"You," spat Mareth, looking straight up at the figure of Necanshin, who was suspended in midair above the ball of Essence, having been frozen in time along with his attack. "When did they let you out?"

"When they found out that lunatics were busy siphoning off everyone who ever had talent," he replied calmly, though there was no mistaking the distaste in his voice.

"Whatever do you mean?" asked Kristopher, stepping forward.

"I suppose Seras Falrider just happened to shrivel up and die all by himself?"

A small smile played on the lips of Mareth.

"You've been busy."

"What do you want?" asked Necanshin. "Forget your games, what did you come here for?"

"What do we want," echoed Mareth with an impatient sigh, cocking his head slightly toward his twin. "What makes you think you could ever comprehend what we want?"

"Some misplaced sense of justice, then," said Necanshin. It wasn't a question.

"Justice, much like beauty, is in the eye of the beholder," answered Kristopher, his obsidian robe fluttering slightly behind him. "Is it just that two teenagers get forced to watch their parents burn in their own home? Or that those same teenagers were then by taken by force to serve the very government that failed to protect their family?"

"You cannot seriously pretend to hold the government responsible for the actions of rogues and vagrants," spat Necanshin.

"The Grand Arbiter has always known about Tannoral, yet he never found it necessary to cleanse our land of the filth that live down here."

"So, under your logic, I could blame your parents for spawning you two psychotic bastards, then?" sneered the ex-archon.

"You fool." Mareth's eyes shimmered black. "You have no idea what you're up against."

"Don't I?"

"You're no more special than any other bureaucrat sitting high on their horse up in the Citadel," jeered Kristopher. "All bark and no bite."

"And you two are just like any other mindless moron who's tried to take on the Throne," replied Necanshin, a hint of an evil smile on his face.

"How do you figure?"

"You waste time monologuing!" he exclaimed. In an instant, the stasis he had been held in shattered with an earsplitting bang. With a single deft move he raised his hand and fired a charge toward the Orb and the floating mass of Essence that was hovering just inches above it.

Josh saw the eyes of Mareth and Kristopher widen in horror for the brief instant before the charge hit the ball of energy. Josh barely had time to brace himself as a tremendous explosion shook the very walls of the cavern. Liquid Essence and Nether erupted from the broken orb, streaming all about the area and setting everything it touched ablaze in flames of blue and orange. Very quickly, each of the hundred, silver monsters roared in agony and exploded in bursts of silver, illuminating the tunnel sporadically much like fireworks in the night sky.

"NOW!" screamed Arya, throwing the blanket off her and Josh and releasing a bolt of Essence she'd built up in her hands at the nearest cloaked figure. It struck the person, but instead of blasting him backward, it burned straight through and hit three more before dissipating.

Suddenly blinding flashes of white and jets of black were flying around the cavern in all directions. Instinct taking over, Joshua sprinted forward and tackled the nearest cloaked figure, hurtling his fist into the side of the person's head over and over again until the body stilled underneath him. Quickly, he got up and looked around for another target and saw three cloaks advancing on Garcia, who was struggling to keep them off.

He tore forward and lowered his shoulder into the first one he reached, knocking the person into the other two, which gave the thief more than enough time to blast the three of them away from him and Josh.

"Thanks for that," he said with a grateful nod.

"Anytime," replied Josh, turning back toward the battle.

"Watch it!" yelled Garcia as Josh turned away, and he barely saw a huge black jet of Nether screaming at him from the left. Just as it was about to strike him, a bolt of white energy came from Arya and crashed into its path. The two opposing forces destroyed each other in a great explosion and sent Josh hurtling into the air and toward a stream of fiery Essence that was burning along the nearby wall.

He braced for impact, but it never came. His body relaxed as his momentum halted, and he saw Garcia flexing his arms, directing him gently to the ground.

"We're even!" he yelled with a wink, returning quickly to the battle.

Josh chuckled and ran back into the fray, but his laughter was short-lived. A sickening feeling entered his stomach as he saw Kristopher and Mareth standing in the center of the battle encased in a shimmering black bubble. Mareth's arms were straight out and his head was back, as if he was being crucified. The black glow coming from his body suggested he was powering the shield. Kristopher saw Josh running at him and gave him a lopsided grin before thrusting his palm outward.

Immediately Josh doubled over, gasping for air—the thrust, though invisible, had delivered a sensation much as if he'd been hit in the chest with a shovel. Struggling to a knee, he looked up and saw Kristopher raise his palm above his head, a dark red glow appearing above it a moment later.

"Shite," whispered Josh. He looked around and it appeared as if he was the only one who'd noticed—the last few hooded figures were falling, and each of his comrades were sinking all their energy into finishing the battle. "Ary—" He coughed hard and took a deep breath. "Arya!"

"Josh?" she yelled, dispatching her attacker and running over to him. "What's wrong?"

"Bomb," he coughed, nodding toward Kristopher.

"Oh hell."

And just like it had over a week earlier, a spiderwebbed ball of dark red energy formed above Kristopher's hands, pulsating softly.

"Necanshin!" yelled Arya, pointing at the light.

He glanced over at her and his gaze immediately shifted to where she was pointing. Growling, he threw his arm back and began gathering Essence in it— the brightness increasing from dark gray to blinding white much faster than Josh had ever seen before.

Necanshin raised his hand above his head and was about to level his palm at the twins, when the pulse went off and froze everything in suspended animation.

"A valiant effort," said Mareth, his voice echoing through the now still and quiet tunnel. "But one step behind, as you've been all along."

The Essence in the air began to converge on the ball of crimson just as it had at the kingball match, and the white energy in Necanshin's hand began to fade back to darkness.

"Good-bye."

"Not yet!" roared Necanshin, breaking from the suspension.

What happened next happened too fast for Josh to comprehend. Just as the last strands of Essence were pulled to Kristopher, Necanshin's entire being flashed white, and the resulting explosion was so massive that chunks of stone fell from the roof of the tunnel, and the ground shook violently. Josh and Arya cowered on the floor, covering their heads with their arms.

When at last the tremors had stopped, Josh looked up and saw Mareth through the ruins, sprinting off back toward where they'd come from. He quickly looked around and saw Garcia slumped against a nearby wall, blood trickling down his forehead and face. Hannah and Marilyn were lying motionless near the exit of the cave, and Necanshin was slumped over—but moving slightly—next to Kristopher, who had seemed to have lost a significant chunk of his body.

Arya quickly ran over to Necanshin. Kneeling next to him, she pressed her fingers to the side of his neck, but he swatted them away with his hand.

"Here," he groaned, blood running from his mouth. He yanked the two archon medallions from his neck and placed them in her hand. "Don't let him escape."

Arya nodded and sprang to her feet, sprinting off down the tunnel after Mareth.

"Arya!" yelled Josh, scrambling over to Necanshin. "Damn it."

"Go," he grunted. "There's nothing more you can do here." And he too went unconscious.

Letting out a frustrated groan, Josh climbed to his feet and took off after both of them.

He sprinted down the great tunnel, but didn't see any traces of Arya or Mareth before he reached the first intersection, six tunnels branching off the main one.

"Bollocks," he muttered, turning around, trying to figure out which way to go. He was about to run down the smallest tunnel when suddenly an explosion sounded to his left. Wasting no time, he sprinted in that direction, his breaths becoming shorter as he expended more oxygen with each step.

He'd run only a couple hundred feet when he saw Arya hunkered behind a fallen boulder, blood running down her left arm and looking very exhausted.

"Arya!"

"Get down!" she yelled at him.

He looked up just in time to see Mareth unleash a huge obsidian blast in his direction. Abandoning all pretense, he dove head first toward the rock that Arya was behind, the blast missing him by mere inches.

"What's going on?" he asked as another blast loosened stones around the area, sending them pelting down onto their heads.

"He's so powerful," she said weakly, a painful grimace on her face. "Anything I send at him he just deflects away."

"What should I do?"

"Joshua…"

"What should I do?" he yelled frantically.

"Run," she said, staring at him softly. "Run, and warn the city."

"I'm not leaving you here," he said, shaking his head.

"I can provide you cover enough to escape," she urged. "You'll only have a few seconds—"

"Stop," he interrupted, holding up his hand. "I'm-not-leaving."

"Damn it, Joshua!" she yelled as Mareth cackled behind them, sending another jet that shook the walls of the tunnel, the fire in the torches shaking violently.

"You can't hide forever, Miss Tremayne!" he called out with a maniacal laugh. "Think of how your father would be turning over in the grave my brother put him in if he saw you cowering in fear!"

"Don't you even mention my father!" she screamed, charging a blast of white Essence and firing it over the boulder. Josh peeked just over the top of the rock and saw Mareth deflect the streak of energy with a wave of his hand.

"Touched a nerve, have I?" he jeered. "Let me ease your suffering, then."

They had no time to react as a huge blast put a great crack in the boulder. It broke apart and crumbled to the ground, exposing them to Mareth, who was facing them with an outstretched hand that was engulfed in black fire.

"Too late for mercy, too late for forgiveness," he said with a sickening grin. "There is only time for fear."

"I will not die so easily to the likes of you," said Arya, shielding Josh with her good arm.

"Why talk so big when you can't back it up?" he asked with a high, cold voice, the fire around his hand growing in size.

"If I don't make it," she whispered to Josh, hiding her bad arm behind her back, "promise me you'll run."

He looked down at her hand and his eyes widened as he saw a black glow appear.

"Promise me," she urged, almost begging him.

"I…I promise," he whispered.

"To hell with you, meddlesome pests," said Mareth with a sneer, his obsidian cloak starting to flutter in a breeze that was picking up around him.

"You first," spat Arya.

She flung her hand forward, the charge of Nether releasing instantly at Mareth. He stared in shock at the sudden burst of black energy and could only use his arm to shield himself as the jet impacted cleanly, a great shockwave resulting from the colliding Nether.

Josh was knocked clear off his feet and landed hard against the wall behind him, crumpling to the ground as it continued to shake.

Finally, after a moment, the quaking passed, and he staggered to his feet, leaning against the wall for support.

"Arya?" he called out into the darkness—the blast had extinguished all the torches. He stumbled forward trying to find her, and after a few paces tripped over something. Kneeling down, he felt a soft fabric and squinted hard, trying to discern what it was. "Mareth's robe," he muttered, flinging it aside—and failing to notice the lack of a body accompanying the discarded garment.

A soft moan behind him made him whip around, and he scrambled on his hands and knees over to the source of the noise.

"Arya?" he asked softly.

"Joshua," she replied, her voice weak.

"I can't see anything," he said. "Are you hurt?"

Arya lifted her hand and a small stream of Essence trailed from her fingers to the nearest torch and lit it, casting an orangish glow over the two of them.

"Oh no," breathed Josh, his eyes widening in horror at the state she was in.

Her clothes were torn in numerous places, blood seeping through from deep wounds in her arms and torso. Painful, blackened burns littered her face and hands, as if someone had held an open flame directly to her skin. Her leg was bent at an awkward angle, and a small pool of blood was forming under her head. A sticky, black liquid was trickling from the corner of her mouth.

"The price for using Nether," she whispered, barely able to speak.

"What...what do I do?" asked Josh urgently, his voice laden with panic. "How do I help you?"

"You've already done so much," she said, her hand searching out his and closing around his fingers.

"No, Arya—"

"Give my parents' medallions to Isaac," she whispered.

"Don't die."

"Thank you..."

And her body stilled.

Josh knelt next to her in shocked silence. Silent, violent sobs wracked his body. He fell forward, tears streaming down his face, his forehead buried in her torso. He held on to her limp hand tightly, not allowing himself to let go.

"Come back..." he cried softly, his free hand balled into a fist and falling again and again against her chest in frustration.

And suddenly, he felt a strange warmth he'd never experienced before in his life. A warmth that started at his core and spread to the tips of his fingers and toes. He opened his eyes slightly and saw the Essence in the air nearby swirling around him, converging toward where he was lying with Arya.

There was no explanation for it, no words to describe what he understood in that moment. There was no more doubt, no hesitation—the Essence around him would respond to his will, and his will was decided.

Sitting up, he breathed deeply and placed his hands over her heart, pouring the energy and Essence from the air into healing Arya's wounds and restoring her life.

It's rather like a freefall, he thought to himself, as the power he felt began to surge and pour from his fingertips into Arya's body. The rush just continued to mount, the energy amplifying with every passing second, until at last he opened his eyes and saw his entire body glowing the purest white.

With one tremendous push, he concentrated all his efforts on focusing the healing energies into the lifeless girl before him, and instantly the white glow funneled down his arms, out his hands, and into Arya.

He swayed uneasily on the spot, and realized that perhaps he'd overly expended his own life's Essence.

The sound of armor clanking against the stone floor sounded in the distance—archons coming for them, no doubt—but it was of no consequence to Joshua. He felt his consciousness slipping, and briefly saw Arya's eyes flutter open the tiniest bit before falling into darkness.

Chapter Fourteen: Redemption

It was peaceful. A quiet, painless floating black with no fears or worries, and only the sound of Josh's breathing to interrupt time.

"Ye did well, lad."

And Wester's voice, apparently.

"Wester?"

"Aye."

"Why can't I see you?"

"No one kin see through death, lad."

"So I'm dead, then?"

"Ye don' listen very well, do ye?" he said with a laugh. "Yer not dead, hence why ye can'na see me."

"Where am I?"

"I've no idea," he said with a chuckle. "But ye've dun well."

"I did what I could," replied Josh.

"And it's been more than enuff. I'm glad tha' ye lived through tha' blast, Joshua Cooper. I'm very proud of both ye and Ari. And tha' thief o' yours too."

"Thank you, sir."

"Wester, lad, Wester."

"Right."

"Tell Ari I love her, will ye?"

"Of course," answered Josh.

"Thanks. Now then, I think ye'd better be gettin' back to reality."

"This…you aren't real?"

"Real is only what ye make it to be. How could what I say change tha' at all?" he said kindly, the echoing voice fading into the darkness.

Josh wondered briefly what Wester meant by that but felt himself growing very tired quite rapidly and lost consciousness again before he had time to think about it.

A soft white light woke him, briefly darkening periodically in small flickers. Blinking his eyes open, Josh saw that it was the curtains fluttering gently in the guest quarters back on the farm in Kendrall.

Much like the first time he'd awoken in the room, it was empty, although this time there were voices coming from the main room of the cottage.

He closed his eyes and rested against the pillow, too tired and sore to move. The door opened and he squinted tentatively, not sure he was ready to be discovered awake quite yet.

Unfortunately, the woman that entered was the nurse who had tended to Isaac earlier, and the one thing Josh knew about nurses was that they always seemed to notice every single detail of the patients they cared for.

"You're awake," she said softly, hurrying over to him. "I'll fetch you some tea right away."

"Wait," croaked Josh, surprising himself at how hoarse he sounded. "Jocelyn, right?"

"Yes, milord," she replied, bowing slightly.

"Um, Josh is fine," he said, taken aback at being addressed like that. "Is Arya all right?"

"Her Highness is fine," replied Jocelyn with a smile.

"Highness?"

"A lot has happened in the three days you've been unconscious, Josh."

"Such as?" he prompted when she didn't continue.

"'Tis not my place to say."

"Right," he said. "Is she here?"

"Aye, she is."

"Could she bring the tea, please?" he asked. "I'd...I'd like to see her if possible."

"Of course," said the nurse, standing and heading over to the door. "Um, if it's not too rude?"

"Hmm?"

"The tale of your journey has already spread throughout the province," she said reverently. "You and the others are already heroes to the people."

"Thank you," replied Josh after a moment.

"I'll just go bring Her Highness, milord."

From the moment the door closed, a loud commotion reached Josh's ears. The sound of chairs scraping against the floor and feet stamping toward his room quickly filled the air but was silenced a moment later. He could hear Jocelyn saying something to the people outside, but couldn't discern any words through the closed door. Finally, after a moment, the door opened.

She was wearing a simple yellow sundress with the archonic pendant hanging around her neck, and her brown hair was flowing freely over her shoulders. However beautiful she was, though, it was simply seeing Arya alive and well that made Josh smile.

"You're up," she said simply, sitting down next to him on the bed.

"You too," he replied, still smiling.

"Here," she said, handing a Josh mug of the hot tea that he hated. "You knew it was coming."

"Is that supposed to make me feel better?" he asked with a chuckle, before touching the cup to his lips and draining it in one go.

"Not in the slightest."

"Good," he replied in disgust, his face scrunching up at the taste of the liquid. "Because it didn't."

They sat in silence for a moment, both content to have some semblance of peace at last. Josh looked up and saw her staring at him with a look he'd never seen before in his life—as if she'd never been happier to regret something.

"What is it?"

"In the short amount of time I've been alive, I've never met anyone quite like you, Joshua Cooper."

"Your father was a pretty remarkable man—"

"I didn't say he wasn't or that you were better than him," she interjected, "but you are still someone I consider myself blessed to have known."

"No one's ever said anything like that to me before," replied Josh after a moment.

"I'm surprised," said Arya, keeping a straight face. "You don't go around saving the lives of young women back home?"

"Not on a daily basis," he replied coyly. They each laughed briefly, smiles still etched on their faces. "So, I hear I've missed quite a bit."

"An understatement," she said with a nod, pursing her lips slightly.

"What happened?"

"Do you remember anything?"

"No," said Josh, shaking his head. "I saw you stir a bit before I blacked out, but nothing else."

"I awoke, of course," said Arya, sighing. "I remember opening my eyes and wondering why I wasn't dead, and then I saw you lying there and immediately knew what'd happened."

"I guess I can use Essence now," he said chuckling. He held his hand out and watched as the sparkles in the air drifted peacefully toward his fingers.

"Apparently," she said, smiling. "The entire royal guard showed up about ten seconds after that."

"How'd they find us?"

"You can't have a battle that big right under the capital and expect no one will notice," she quipped. "They saved everyone."

"Everyone?" asked Josh. It suddenly occurred to him that he'd completely forgotten about the others, not to mention the twins. "What happened to them?"

"Garcia, Marilyn, and Hannah were all inches from death, but they brought them back just like you. Necanshin is, of course, a true warrior, and the moment they poured some Essence into him he healed right up and sprang to life like a daisy." Josh laughed at that.

"What about Kristopher and Mareth?"

Arya bit her lower lip and turned away slightly, not allowing her gaze to meet his entirely.

"Arya?"

"Kristopher is quite dead," she said after a moment. "I don't know exactly what happened, but Necanshin did something to the shield that the twins were using so that Kristopher was exposed to the blast, and well, I've heard it wasn't pretty."

"And Mareth?"

"No one knows," she replied, shaking her head. "His robe and the charms and relics he was carrying to enhance his power were found next to you and me...but there was no sign of him."

"What do you think happened?"

"I have no idea. Maybe he was vaporized in the blast when the Nether collided, maybe something else happened."

Josh said nothing, but his face showed doubt.

"Only time will tell," she said. "Besides, if he did survive, he has nowhere to hide without the orb and his possessions."

"I guess you're right," said Josh. "So what happened after that?"

"It was rather funny, actually. Derecks came storming into the hospital room again like he had before, threatening us with treason charges and the death penalty—"

"What?" he exclaimed.

"Let me finish," she said smiling and holding her hand up. "He's going off on his tirade, when all of a sudden Grand Arbiter Gainsburgh walks in and puts an end to his ranting."

"The Grand Arbiter's returned?"

"He told me afterward that his timing was 'most fortuitous,'" replied Arya with a laugh. "He's cleared us of all charges."

"Really?" asked Josh, a wave of relief washing over him. "What about Garcia and Necanshin?"

"Garcia is getting off but has been warned to avoid acts of banditry from now on or his old offenses will come back to haunt him. Necanshin...well, he's a trickier situation."

"Why?"

"Because he's too powerful for his own good," replied Arya simply. "Luther came down during the discussion to hear some of the parts of the battle, and even *he* says that no one should've been able to destroy the orb."

"So what'll happen?"

"That's up to Lord Gainsburgh, and him alone, but it's likely Necanshin will, at the very least, be freed from his prison."

"Ah."

"Anyway, word spread fast of what happened. Rumors, mostly. The people here who lost their homes needed a good story to cheer them up, I suppose," she continued. "The rumors were, of course, completely ridiculous, so the Grand Arbiter made a public statement concerning what really transpired."

"So that's why the nurse called me 'milord' just now?"

Arya nodded. "Without a doubt. You're just as big a hero as I am."

"Yeah, tell me a bit about that," he asked curiously. "Jocelyn was calling you Her Highness?"

"My lineage isn't a secret," she replied with a shrug. "I think after what's happened, more people are inclined to refer to me by my official title rather than a friendly name."

"I hope you won't be too upset if I still call you Arya then."

"Not in the least," she replied, smiling. "In any case, though, there are a few people who'd like to see you."

"Oh?"

"I believe that's our cue," said Garcia, barging through the door with Isaac, Marilyn, Hannah, Luther, and another man Josh didn't know who was dressed in red and gold clothes that were far more regal than he had yet seen.

"I suppose you'll tell me you weren't eavesdropping this time, either?" asked Arya in a disapproving tone.

"Darling, I'm a thief," he replied, holding his hands up in defense. "It's my business to be sneaky."

"I guess I can forgive you this one time," she said trying to not smile.

"How are you, Joshua?" asked Marilyn.

"Sore, tired, relieved. Take your pick," he answered with a laugh.

"As a young man who just helped save the world should be," said the man he didn't know. "We haven't had the pleasure of being introduced. My name is Byron Gainsburgh."

"The Grand Arbiter, sir," replied Josh, extending his hand.

"Only those I give orders to call me 'sir'," he said as he shook Josh's hand. "You may call me Byron." Josh nodded. "As our fair princess has no doubt mentioned, you have been cleared of any charges that may have been levied upon you."

"She did mention it," replied Josh. "Thank you."

"It was the least I could do, seeing how you all protected my land while I was taken ill," answered Byron. "Sadly, even the leaders of men are vulnerable to sickness."

"Mortals are prone to ailment," said Arya sagely. "Such illness proves you are fit to lead mortals, my lord."

"Logic was always a gift your mother loved to taunt me with," he said laughing.

"So what happened with Synax and that horrid storm?" asked Josh.

"Synax was razed to the ground," said Gainsburgh without a hint of regret.

"And it is my opinion that the twins did us a favor in that regard. The building was old, decrepit, and a constant drain on the treasury because it was so far from Danthian. Now we can build anew, something much more modern and less costly to maintain."

"What about the people inside?"

"They escaped in time," said the Grand Arbiter. "There were a few archons present that were able to maintain order. As for the storm you mentioned, it did put quite a damper on the rebuilding efforts of various towns and villages throughout this land that Mareth and Kristopher had already destroyed."

"And Kendrall?"

Gainsburgh frowned. "Quite a few residences were burned down, and it saddens me to say that there were casualties, but we are a resilient race and will bounce back stronger."

Josh nodded solemnly, unsure how to respond.

"I am afraid that my time here grows short—there is still much for me to attend to in the capital."

"Of course," said Josh, moving to get up.

"Sit, my boy," interjected Byron gently. "You will always be welcome in my land. You can show me the courtesy of standing when you return here in good health, if you ever choose to do so."

"I'm not sure about that yet," replied Josh with an uneasy chuckle.

"Well, whatever you choose in the future, I wish you the best in all your endeavors."

"Thank you. Oh, Byron?"

"Hmm?"

"What'll become of Necanshin?"

The Grand Arbiter regarded Joshua carefully for a moment.

"What would you have me do with him?" he countered.

"Erm…well, we wouldn't have been able to accomplish anything without him," said Josh. "Prison doesn't seem fair, even if he is a bit of an arse."

Gainsburgh snorted amusedly at this.

"Your wisdom is beyond your age," he replied. "As it so happens, I ran into an old friend while I was recovering in Mafaelia who knows the Vanquisher quite well and agreed to take custody of him."

"He can keep him under control?" asked Garcia skeptically.

Byron smiled. "I doubt it. But *she* does have a bit of temper, and even I don't care to get on her bad side."

"I'm glad to hear it," said Josh bemusedly.

"Now then, I must take my leave."

They nodded to each other as Byron turned. Marilyn and Hannah saluted him by bringing their right hands to their left shoulders as he passed, and he nodded at them, too, before leaving.

"I like him," commented Josh, once the Grand Arbiter had gone.

"Quite a bit more than Derecks Whitemane, eh?" said Luther with a grin, nudging his shoulder.

"That's a bit of an understatement," he replied, laughing.

"We're going to go get ready," said Marilyn. "We'll be outside if you need us."

"All right," replied Arya as they left, Hannah sending Josh a soft smile as she followed her mentor out through the door.

"Get ready for what?" asked Josh.

Luther, Garcia, and Arya looked at each other for a moment before Arya turned to Josh.

"We're having Father's funeral today," she explained.

"Oh..." said Josh, at a loss for words.

"I know you just woke up and all, but it'd mean a lot to me if you could be there," said Arya, fidgeting a bit.

"Of course," he said without hesitation. "Where is it?"

"Behind the cottage," she replied. "In about twenty minutes, actually."

"Definitely," affirmed Josh.

"Why don't you two go on and get ready so I can have a chat with Joshua for a few moments?" said Luther, smiling at them.

"Sure," said Arya. "We'll be out back. Join us whenever you're ready."

"You've had quite an adventure, my boy," he said cheerfully once they were alone, sitting where Arya had been.

"To say the least," scoffed Josh lightheartedly.

"I'd rather like to hear what happened between Arya and Mareth from you," he said.

"Why me?"

"You saw it firsthand from an outside perspective, and Nether is something I've been researching extensively, after all."

"It wasn't like anything I've seen before," said Josh thoughtfully. "It wasn't an explosion. It was more like the two streams of Nether couldn't interact."

"How do you mean?"

"Like...all right, you know when you have two magnets?" said Josh, remembering something he'd read in his science text. "If you put the magnets together with the same poles aligned, they'll force themselves apart."

"I see what you mean," said Luther, understanding. "So you're saying that Arya's and Mareth's Nethers were incompatible?"

Josh nodded. "Something like that. When they collided, there was this huge pulse of energy that knocked everything around. I went flying into the side of the tunnel and the torches went out."

"And then you found our young princess," finished Luther.

"I found Mareth's cloak first," remembered Josh. "But I didn't pay it any attention because I was looking for Arya."

"Yes, Mareth's worldly possessions were all found next to the both of you, but he was nowhere to be seen."

"Do you know what happened?"

"I haven't the foggiest," replied Luther sadly. "Nether has still not been researched extensively enough to be understood completely."

"Is it possible that he lived?"

"Anything is possible, Joshua, as I'm sure you've found out," he replied with a smile. "You were transported two hundred million light-years across the universe in the blink of an eye, you helped save a province from certain anarchy, and you learned to use Essence."

"Yeah. How'd that happen, anyway?"

"I did tell you that strong emotional events can trigger Essential reactions," explained Luther. "Losing Arya—someone you obviously care a great deal about—was clearly something you were unwilling to let happen."

"But why is it that now I can use it without any effort?"

"Because you've felt what it's like," came the answer, and Josh thought he saw a tinge of regret in the old man's eyes. "Like riding a bicycle."

"I suppose," said Josh. "Oh, why was it that Arya could use Nether in the first place?"

"You all could have, I think," said Luther thoughtfully. "Going into the forest and having its poison penetrate your bodies was probably more than enough to give you the capacity for using it. Now, take a few minutes and get ready." He swirled the Essence in the air about, and a moment later a clean pair of pants and shirt came floating in through the door. "Freshen up, make sure your legs aren't too wobbly, then come join us out back."

"Will do," he replied with a nod. "Oh, Luther?"

"Yes, lad?"

"You said that time passes at the same speed all over the universe, right?"

"I've not encountered anything to make me think otherwise."

"So that means I've been missing for almost three weeks back home?"

"I'd say that's very likely."

Josh bit his lower lip and sighed.

"When do you think you might be able to send me back?" he asked.

"I had a feeling you'd want to go home," answered Luther gently. "I brought everything we need with me. You can go whenever you want."

Josh nodded and pursed his lips in thought.

"Is it easy to come back?"

"Nothing's easy," replied Luther evasively. "But if you try hard enough, I'm sure you'll find a way."

"All right."

"I'll see you outside."

Luther left, and Josh changed into the fresh clothes that he'd been brought. He sat back down on the bed hard and put his head in his hands.

It wasn't that he really wanted go home—home meant his parents arguing and the same, dull routine every day—but he knew he had to. It wasn't fair to make the people who cared about him think he'd run away for good, or worse. But at the same time he'd felt more at home in Lumenaria than he ever had in Salisbury.

Putting such melancholic thoughts from his head, he stood and walked to the door. He found the dining room empty, save for Garcia who was sitting at the table, waiting for him.

"They wanted me to wait for you just in case you needed help," he said, standing. "You seem to be doing fine, though."

"You too," said Josh with a nod. "How're you feeling?"

"Never better," replied the thief with a smile. "You probably didn't hear from Arya, but the GA is going to formally recognize Tannoral as a city."

"He's quite a remarkable person," said Josh thoughtfully. "That's excellent news."

Garcia nodded. "It's a huge step toward getting rid of crime."

"You're saying you won't miss riding about the land, holding up merchants for their wares?"

"I wouldn't go that far," he replied coyly. "But I can understand the need for peace and order as much as the next guy. After all, it was the thief I called captain many years ago who orphaned the twins in the first place and caused all of this."

"Right," remembered Josh.

"Now, then, we have our respects to pay," said Garcia, nodding at the back door. "You know," he continued as they started walking, "I didn't know Wester too well, but to protect you, Arya, and Isaac from an explosion like the one in the tunnels, he must've been one hell of a man."

"You knew Wester?" asked Josh, turning to face Garcia properly.

"Yes, but don't tell Arya," he replied with a nervous laugh, running a hand through his long, black hair. "Before I was a thief, I fought in the military. Wester was the one who taught me the trick of thinking about the worst possible outcome."

"*He* was the archon you knew?"

"He was my commanding officer and was one hell of a guy."

"He certainly was," said Josh, gazing out one of the nearby windows. "Imagine what we would think if we'd known him for as long as Isaac or Luther."

"Too right, you are," agreed Garcia, lowering his voice as they reached the door. "Quiet now, I think they're about to start."

He opened the door and Josh's jaw dropped slightly at the sight.

At least ten thousand people were gathered in the field behind the farmhouse, some having brought chairs, most sitting on blankets. They were all facing a stage far in the distance where Josh could barely make out Arya, Isaac, and Marilyn sitting along with three or four others he didn't know next to a beautiful oaken casket. There was absolute silence among the entire crowd.

"Arya said to go around to the front," whispered Garcia.

"It'll take us ten minutes just to get up there," muttered Josh, his eyebrows still raised in shock.

"Better late than never. Come on."

They made their way around the crowd to a small section in the front where about fifty white wooden chairs had been set up. On the way they passed several faces Josh had seen before in the village and the capital—including

McPhearson, the town drunk and Hodge, the guard who'd let them into Danthian. When they reached the front, Josh saw a large coffin-sized hole in the ground in front of the chairs, and a few feet past that, the stage.

Hannah and Necanshin were sitting next to two vacant chairs, and Josh followed Garcia as he made his way over to them. A few rows behind the empty seats, he saw Arlen, the tailor, sitting quietly and looking extremely worn.

"You did well, lad," said the ex-archon as Josh sat down. It was the first time he'd ever addressed him in such a friendly manner.

"Thanks," replied Josh, nodding gratefully. "What happened to you?"

"I've still got a bit of fight in me, apparently," answered Necanshin, a hint of a smile playing on his lips.

"You seem a lot more relaxed."

"I'm looking forward to never setting foot in the Deadlands again, if I can help it."

"I've been wondering," said Josh hesitantly. "What actually happened there?"

Necanshin turned and looked at him carefully before sighing.

"The forest used to extend much farther south, and the flats farther east," he said pensively. "Seras had been gathering up massive amounts of Nether for something. No one except him really knew what it was for. I wasn't willing to take any chances."

"So you destroyed it?"

"Yes," replied Necanshin. "His base was at the edge of the flats, on the border between the mountains and the forest. I snuck in by myself one night and was scared by what I saw. It wasn't just monsters he was breeding in there. He was using prisoners and warping them into Deathborne like the creature that we saw in the forest—the one Arya knew. He had his generals pitting them against each other like dogs to weed out the weak, and all the while this tremendous pool of Nether was sitting behind it, untouched."

"So you destroyed it," repeated Josh.

"I'd have been a fool not to," said Necanshin. "You've seen what happens when Nether and Essence collide. I got spotted and overcharged my own Essence in panic. I wouldn't change a thing about it…except maybe no one believing the story."

"Speaking of not many people liking you, I'm a little surprised to see you here."

"Wester Tremayne was a wonderful friend and ally of mine," he replied seriously. "His passing is truly a great loss for the world, just as Rae's was."

"I would've liked to meet Arya's mother," mused Josh.

"She was just as wonderful and caring as you imagine." Josh noticed for the first time since he met him that Necanshin looked quite aged. "But enough for now, the service is about to begin."

Josh watched as Arya stood, gathered some Essence in her hand, and pressed it to her neck.

"Everyone," she said softly, though her voice was amplified at least a hundred times over. "Thank you all for coming today. I know that if he was here to see it, my father would be thankful for each and every one of you.

"Many of you—in fact, almost all of you—knew him as the archon and war hero Wester Tremayne. A man who was, in part, responsible for winning the last great war, a man who protected this land with every fiber in his being. But only a handful knew him as the loving father and husband that he was, so I would like to share that part of him with you.

"My parents moved to this farm shortly before I was born, and from the earliest memories I have of him, my father always put his family before everything else. He taught me everything I know; how to use Essence, how to work the fields, how to be a good person. Even after my mother died, and he began to drink more frequently and heavily, he was still always there for me— the only thing that changed was that every once in a while, I'd have to be there for him.

"Most of you know how he died, but for those who don't, he was killed during the explosion at the kingball stadium over a week ago. My father died saving my life and the lives of two other people who have been there for me when I needed them most, one of whom he barely even knew." She gave Josh a small sad smile as she said this. "He always placed the safety and welfare of others as his highest priority, and he upheld that belief until the very end.

"I have but one thing to ask: that when you speak of him, you do so with the respect and kindness that he earned from this life for being a hero. Not just in war, but in everyday life, as well."

She turned to face the coffin and placed her hands on it. Bending over, she touched her lips gently to the oak. Josh watched sadly as he heard muffled sobs and sniffles coming from all directions. When she was finished saying her good-byes, Luther, Marilyn, and Isaac stood and joined her, each embracing her gently for a moment before walking down off the stage.

"What's going on?" Josh asked Garcia.

"Arya will stay on until everyone's left, then we'll bury him," he replied as Arya sat back down.

"We?"

"Yeah, she wanted us with her and the others when they lowered him into the ground."

"Oh."

"It'll probably be a while before everyone manages to head out. People will want to pay their respects and all. You should go up there and keep her company."

"Er, it's not really my place—"

"He's right," interjected Necanshin stoically. "Solitude is a terrible thing, after all."

Josh paused to look at the ex-archon for a moment, and Necanshin gave him a lopsided smile that held an unmistakable amount of irony. "All right," said Josh, getting up and walking around to the side of the stage.

"Never thought I'd see you agree with me so easily about something, old man," said Garcia with a sideways glance.

"There's always a first for everything, thief," replied Necanshin cleverly.

Josh hesitated at the stairs of the stage. Looking at Arya, he wondered if he really should intrude, but she spotted him and motioned for him to join her before he could think about it.

"That was a wonderful speech," he said, sitting next to her beside the casket. "It would have made him proud."

"I'm glad you think so," she said, looking away slightly. "I know he would never have wanted anything from me, but I always wanted to make him proud."

"You know," said Josh, putting a hand on her shoulder. "He is."

"What do you mean?" asked Arya, looking at him.

"I think I talked to him while I was unconscious," he answered. "He wanted me to tell you he was proud of you...of all of us."

"I'm a little jealous that you had the chance to speak to him," she said. "I wish I could have."

"I'm not even sure it was real."

"Real is only what you make it to be," she pointed out.

Josh smiled. "He said the exact same thing. I still have no idea what it means."

"Think of it like this," she said, staring into the distance. "Say I wanted to start a fire. I'd need flint, but what if I didn't have any?"

She turned her hand over and a few sparkles of Essence floated into her palm, forming into a small flint a moment later.

"The flint is real now," she explained. "I wanted it to be real, so it became real. The same thing is true with speaking to loved ones who have passed on. If you want it to be real, it is."

"I would love it if it was that simple, but we don't have Essence or conversations with the deceased where I come from."

"Maybe not, but you have willpower, and that's just as good."

"You know, I never thought about it like that."

The mass of people slowly began to dwindle, many coming up to the stage to express their sympathies to Arya. Josh received a few curious glances here and there from people who couldn't associate his face with his name, but after Arya introduced him they were just as polite and respectful, a few even bowing to him.

At last, hours later, the final attendees had departed, leaving Isaac, Luther, Marilyn, Hannah, Garcia, Josh, and Necanshin on the stage with the sole survivor of the Tremayne line.

"Ready?" asked Isaac, placing a hand on her shoulder.

"As ready as I'll ever be."

They all stood next to Arya as her hands began to glow a pale white. Josh watched in awe as the coffin floated off the stage, hovering slightly in the air. She directed the casket above the hole in the ground and gently lowered it. When it was safely in the earth, dirt began to fill the hole from seemingly nowhere, until all that remained was a bare patch of new soil.

"Could I have a moment?"

"Of course," said Isaac, turning and helping direct everyone back to the house.

Josh turned and looked at Arya as she walked down from the stage and removed the pendant from her neck, burying it in the fresh soil. He paused and watched for a moment as she knelt beside her father's grave. Regretfully, he turned back toward the cottage as he heard a choked sob come from his friend, who was, at long last, able to let her tears come forth.

Chapter Fifteen:
The Other Side of the Door

When Arya returned to the house, her eyes were red and puffy, but she held her head high and greeted them with a smile.

"Come with me, Joshua?" she asked, after they had all comforted her in turn.

"Um, sure."

"We'll be back in a little bit," she said to the others. They nodded as she walked up the spiral staircase in the corner, Josh close behind.

He followed her up to the roof. The sun was just starting to set, the horizon a vivid pink.

"I imagine you'll be leaving soon," she said somewhat distantly.

"Very soon," replied Josh with a hint of regret. "Luther's brought everything he needs to send me back."

"I don't blame you for wanting to go home," said Arya. "You must miss it terribly."

"I don't know," he replied hesitantly. "Anyone can have a house, but it takes love to make it a home."

"You still doubt your parents' love for you?"

"No, just for each other," he said with a sigh. "It's just not warm and comfortable. I always feel like I'd rather be somewhere else."

"Do you really wish that?"

"I really wish they'd get along," admitted Josh. "I have a few scattered memories of us actually acting like a happy family. I miss that."

"I'm sure you'll have that someday."

"I hope so," he said. "Oh, by the way, I owe you something."

"You don't owe me anything—" began Arya, but he held up a hand.

"Trust me for a moment," he said with a smile. Arya nodded curiously as Josh held out his palm much like she had on the first night he'd been in Lumenaria. Comprehension and a smile dawned on her face as the sparkles in the air began to swirl about in his hand, and a moment later a silver animal had appeared, glistening just like the horse she had given to him.

"It's beautiful," she whispered in awe. "What is it?"

"It's a unicorn," he explained. "A mythical creature that's in fairy tales from my home."

"Thank you," she said softly, hugging him tightly.

"You're welcome," said Josh, returning the embrace. "I promised I'd return the favor, didn't I?"

"You are, if nothing else, a man of your word," said Arya, not ready to let go. They stood like that for a few moments, not content to completely say their good-byes just yet. "Do you think you'll ever return?" she asked, looking at him.

"I can't predict the future," he said. "I think it's unlikely that I'll not want to."

"I'm glad to hear that."

"Luther said that time passes at the same rate here as it does back home, which means I've been missing for nearly three weeks," said Josh. "I need to go."

"I understand," replied Arya sadly. "Let's go, then."

They walked back inside the cottage and down the stairs, where Luther had moved the tub from the corner of the room out to the kitchen floor and filled it with water.

"What's all this?" asked Josh.

"I figured you were saying your good-byes, so I took the liberty of getting set up to send you back to England," he replied. "If you're not leaving, I can take it down, it's no trouble."

"No, no," said Josh. "It's time."

"It's been wonderful having you here, lad," said Isaac, hugging Josh tightly. "Take care of yourself, hear?"

"Of course...and fix that losing streak," he said with a grin.

Isaac grumbled at him but laughed, mussing up his hair.

"You're a hell of a guy, Joshua," said Marilyn, smiling and shaking his hand.

"Thanks."

"Be well," said Hannah softly from behind her. Josh smiled at her and nodded, and he swore there was a slight blush in her cheeks as he did so.

"My boy!" exclaimed Garcia cheerfully. "I will tell grand stories of you to all the little bandits in Tannoral. There won't be a child in our province who doesn't know your name by the time you get back."

"I don't know if that's something I really want," joked Josh playfully. "But thanks."

"For you, anything," said Garcia appreciatively.

"Joshua."

Everyone turned and looked at Necanshin, who had gone serious. Josh's eyes widened as the old man extended his right hand, while his left was stroking his silver goatee.

"You may not have been able to use Essence until the end," he said, as Josh shook his hand. "But your heart was equal to any warrior I've fought alongside before, and for that, you will always have my respect."

"You too," replied Josh gratefully. "You're a hell of a fighter. You put on a real show the entire time."

"I know," said Necanshin with a smile. "I was there."

"You about ready, lad?" asked Luther, who had produced a painting of an old water closet from his robe.

"The painting from your laboratory?" asked Josh, recognizing it.

"Indeed," affirmed Luther. "Your destination."

"All right, so what do I do?"

"Just get in," said Luther with a smile. "I'll do the rest."

Josh nodded and took a deep breath, stepping into the basin and sitting in the water.

"It's cold," he said, shivering slightly.

Luther laughed lightly. "You'll live. For the record, Joshua? You did quite a job while you were here."

"Thanks."

"Wait," said Arya, quickly darting into the guest room and coming back out a moment later with the horse she had made for him on the first day he'd been there. "Don't forget this."

He nodded and took it from her, smiling in thanks. Arya leaned over the tub and kissed Josh on the cheek.

"You're still a wonderful man, Joshua Cooper," she said. "I'll miss you."

Josh looked up at her and smiled sadly.

"No matter what happens, I'll never forget this world, or you."

"Ready, son?" asked Luther, leaning the painting against the front of the basin.

"Let's do it," said Josh with a resolute nod.

His heart began to race as Luther removed the drainage stopper and the water began to funnel away. Josh watched as the man's hands began to glow, turning white in only a few moments.

"Say hi to my brother for me, will you?" asked Luther, winking. Josh didn't have a chance to respond as Luther plunged his hands into the tub.

The bottom dropped out from underneath Josh, and instantly he was racing through a tunnel of vibrant, scattered colors, speeding toward a growing light ahead.

And suddenly it was all over. Josh landed hard with a thud in a black room. From what sounded to be the next room over, he heard a familiar voice muttering something.

"Hello?" he called out. There was a loud crash from outside, as if the beholder of the voice had been startled and dropped something. Quick footsteps sounded, approaching where Josh was still sitting. A moment later a door to his left was thrown open, light flooding the room and blinding him.

"Joshua Cooper," the voice breathed, barely above a whisper. "Is that really you?"

Josh's eyes began adjusting to the light, and his jaw dropped when he figured out who was staring at him.

"Ned?" he asked in shock. Sure enough, it was the shopkeeper from the local apothecary.

"Well, this explains quite a bit," said the old man, helping Joshua to his feet. As he stood, he saw a painting hanging above the tub he'd landed in that looked eerily similar to Luther's laboratory.

"You're Luther's brother?" he asked, astounded.

"Yes, but don't go advertising that," he said, ushering him out of the bathroom.

"Is this where you live?" asked Josh, looking around at the flat. It had a sofa, a television, and some stairs leading down to somewhere.

"Yes, yes," replied Ned. "Come on downstairs." He led him down the stairs and through a door at the bottom that led to the store—the same door that sported the DO NOT ENTER sign. "Don't tell people about Luther," he reiterated. "It wouldn't do to have to lie to people when they ask me where he is or what he does."

"I suppose not," mused Joshua, still feeling that the situation was a bit surreal.

"Now then," said Ned, coming around to the front of the store, "we don't have all the time for you to tell me everything that happened, so try and sum it up for me, yeah?"

So Josh briefly described the events that happened for the two weeks and some odd days he'd been in Lumenaria—from meeting everyone, to the kingball match, the journey to the forest, and the battle with the Rothwyn twins.

"I met Wester once," said Ned with a sigh. "I'm sure you heard that my brother and I fought a war in Lumenaria many a year ago. Wester was stationed with the unit one camp over from us."

"It seems like a pretty small world there," commented Josh.

"Oh, it's quite a bit larger than what you saw," replied Ned with a wink, not offering any further information. "But Wester was a good enough man. I'm sad to hear he's passed on."

"Yeah. So what's been going on here while I've been gone?"

"Wouldn't you believe it, you made the news," said Ned with a chuckle, pointing at a stack of newspapers on the counter. Josh went over to read the headlines and blanched when he saw SEARCH CALLED OFF FOR BOY AND SHIP CAPTAIN plastered on the front page.

"Oh hell," he muttered, flipping to the page with the story on it. "The three-week long search for seventeen-year-old Joshua Cooper and forty-eight year-old fishing boat captain Thomas Patrey was called off early this morning after Her Majesty's Coast Guard rescue workers were unable to find any traces of the two males or the ship they'd departed on," he read aloud. "It is believed that the boat was capsized during the violent storm that invaded the English Channel, causing rogue waves and whirlpools—an extremely unusual event for a body of water not in the open ocean. Thomas Patrey is not survived by any family, and Joshua Cooper's parents could not be reached for comment."

"So you see," Ned pointed out, "you should probably hurry on home."

"Right," agreed Joshua, jogging toward the door. "Oh…um, Ned?"

"Yes, lad?"

"I saw a picture of Luther's laboratory in that room." Ned nodded in response. "Is it possible to use it to return to Lumenaria?"

"I've never tried, nor do I plan to," he answered. "And you'd need Essence, which, as you can see, isn't in large supply around these parts of the universe."

"Couldn't one use the Essence in their own body?"

"There isn't enough," answered Ned, shaking his head. "You'd kill yourself before you made it over there."

"Right," said Josh, dismayed. "I'll come back soon so I can tell you the rest of the story."

"I look forward to hearing it."

Much as the last time Josh had left his store, Ned watched the young man depart with a sideways glance; only this time his eyes skirted to a small box tucked away underneath the counter before he returned to his duties.

Josh realized as he jogged home that his sprints through the forest and Tannoral had made him more apt to running—he barely felt exhaustion as he ran the short distance from the shop to his house, ignoring the curious glances he received from passersby.

A few minutes later he arrived at his front step, breathing not nearly as hard as he expected, and knocked twice.

When no response came, he looked around the side of the house for the family car. He saw it parked silently in the driveway, and his brow furrowed as he knocked again loudly.

"God damn it, I've told you people to leave us alone!" yelled his father from somewhere inside. "We're not ready to give you an interview. Let us mourn our son in peace."

"I'm not from the news agency," called Josh nonchalantly, as if coming home to parents who thought you were dead was the most normal thing in the world.

From the inside of the house, Josh heard footsteps and the sound of the door being unlocked, his father flinging it open a moment later.

"Now look here—"

Jacob Cooper froze, his jaw hanging open and his breathing growing shaky.

"I'm home," said Josh with a smile.

His father took one great step forward and threw his arms around Josh, crying heavily.

"My boy," he whispered, overcome with emotion.

"Who is it, Jacob?" asked his mother, walking into the hall with a teacup and saucer. She stopped when she saw Josh and his father on the stoop. The dishes fell from her hands and shattered on the wooden floor.

"Joshua?" she asked, her voice breaking.

"It's him, Annie," said his father, waving her over. "He's come home."

"Oh my God," she cried, running over to Josh and wrapping him in a hug much like his father's. "It's really you."

"It's really me," grunted Josh, struggling to breathe.

"Where have you been?" she asked, pulling back and looking him over to see if he was genuinely all right.

"I don't know if you'd believe me," he said with a chuckle.

"We have all the time in the world," said Jacob, ushering him inside. "Why don't you try us?"

So Josh led his parents into the sitting room and told them the entire story, start to finish, not leaving out a single detail. Neither of them interrupted once, though whether it was from intrigue or disbelief, Josh couldn't tell.

"And then I woke up in Ned's bathroom," he said, smiling at the irony of it all. "Turns out, he was Luther's brother all along. After that, I came right home."

"Joshua," said his father, impressed, "that is one hell of a story, but it is rather hard to believe."

"I'll show you, then," he said simply, getting up from the maroon recliner he'd been relaxing in and shuffling over to the hall where the pieces of the broken teacup and saucer were still scattered about the floor. Jacob and Annie followed him into the hall looking at each other inquisitively. Josh glanced over his shoulder at them to make sure they were watching and then looked down at the floor, concentrating on wanting the cup and saucer to be repaired more than anything else.

He heard gasps come from both of his parents as the tips of his fingers glowed a soft white. The fragments of the dishes began to shudder and move slightly, realigning themselves and sealing the cracks. When he was finished, he bent down to pick up the saucer. As he lifted the dish, the piece he was holding cracked off, and the rest of the saucer fell back to the ground and shattered again.

"Er, yeah," he chuckled nervously, turning around to face his parents. "I'm still not quite that good at it."

"I don't believe it," breathed his mother, holding on to his father for support. "How can this be possible?"

"I remember I was having a conversation with Luther while he was teaching me how to use Essence," explained Josh. "I said the exact same thing. He looked at me and replied, 'No matter how unlikely anything may seem, one must always remember that the odds are much worse for something as extraordinary as life to exist.'"

"That's a pretty good line," replied Jacob appreciatively, ruffling his son's hair. "So this Luther is Ned-down-at-the-apothecary's brother?"

"Yeah," answered Josh. "I didn't really tell Ned the whole story. He showed me the papers where it said I was gone for good and figured I should get home."

"We should have him over for dinner sometime," suggested Annie.

Jacob smiled. "I agree. I'd love to hear more about this land."

"Me too," said Josh, pleasantly surprised at the fact that his parents seemed to be getting along. "So, um, fill me in. What day of the week is it?"

"Been gone that long?" asked his father, laughing.

"Just been through a lot," he countered, smiling.

"Wednesday," he answered cheerfully.

"I guess I've got to go to school tomorrow?" he asked with a hint of distaste.

"You must be quite a bit behind on your work," said Annie ruefully. "And in any case, I'm sure all your mates will want to know you're alive and well…especially that Tricia." Josh and Jacob looked at her as if she'd gone mad, but a huge grin spread on her face and she started laughing. "I'm only having you on. Honestly, you two…"

"Yeah, well, I can't exactly tell them the story, now, can I?" said Josh, with skepticism. "They'd think I'd gone mad."

"You could show them," suggested his father.

"I'd like to keep that a secret," said Josh seriously. "I don't want that much attention, to be honest."

"I don't blame you at all, son," said Jacob with a nod, wrapping his arm around Josh's shoulder. "Let's go fabricate you a believable story, then."

The "believable" story involved Josh floating around at sea for over a week and a half before drifting back to shore and walking all the way back to Salisbury. It was far-fetched, but—as his father had pointed out—more plausible than the truth.

There wasn't a single person in school the next day—student and teacher alike—who didn't point and whisper as Josh passed in the hall. After all, it's not every day that someone you know comes back from the dead.

It took about a week for the hysteria to die down. Even after that, there were still curious people who would ask Josh to tell them the story of how he lived. It wasn't something he minded—at the very least it allowed him to keep the truth for himself.

Ned joined Josh and his parents for dinner at least once a week after that. It turned out that he'd been in Lumenaria for much longer than Luther had let on, and he had quite a variety of stories to share with them.

Finally, June came around and, with it, summer holidays. Much like it had been on the day that Josh found his way into a different world, the afternoon was warm and breezy when the final bell of academic year rang. The students all rushed outside to bask in their now extended freedom, and once again, Josh stood just outside the doors unbuttoning his collar while letting the cool air wash over him.

"Oy! Joshiekins!"

He looked over and saw the same group of students playing cards on the grass.

"Come on and join us!"

Josh chuckled to himself as he walked over to the five boys, each of whom greeted him in turn as he arrived.

"What're you lot playing, Roy?" he asked, directing his question to the heavy boy with a mop of red hair.

"Gin," came the reply. "Five pence a point."

"I thought poker was the game of choice," mused Josh. A cheer went up as he sat down next to them, all eager to have him join in their fun.

"We vary it up every now and then. You know Carl, Henry, John, and Frank," said Roy.

"Yeah," said Josh, nodding in greeting. "How're you all doing?"

"Never better," replied John. "School's out for summer, after all."

"Let's not lie to each other," quipped Josh as Carl dealt the cards. "You lot have been skiving classes for this card game all year." This was met with laughs and cheers.

"Oy, not all year. Can't play in the snow, after all," the red-head replied, grinning.

"Oh, stop trying to cover your arse, Roy," said John.

"Yeah, we all know you'd need a tent to cover it."

"Very clever," deadpanned Roy, swatting at Henry, who had made the remark.

They played cards for about an hour, and Josh ended up losing about a pound in the end, but it was well spent. He couldn't remember the last time he'd enjoyed himself so much.

The walk home was the same as it'd always been—homeless men curled up on cardboard boxes, stray dogs barking at him, and car horns blaring at each other. It didn't bother him as much as it used to. Instead of wanting to get out of the rough part of town as quickly as possible, he would take in the surroundings and even toss a bum a few pence every now and then.

He was in a good mood from the card game and the end of school, so he made a detour from his normal route to head into town to see Ned.

"Joshua!" exclaimed the shopkeeper as the bell jingled to signify the door opening. "This is a pleasant surprise."

Josh walked over to Ned and shook his hand. "You know," he commented, looking around the shop. "How is it that you're still in business? I never see anyone in here."

"Most people do their shopping on the weekends or after they're done with work," replied Ned sagely. "Not in the middle of the day."

Josh laughed. "True."

"Speaking of work, are you interested in having a job this summer?"

"Heh, I just got out of school, Ned. Let me relax for a week and I'll get back to you."

"Fair enough," replied the older man, smiling. "What brings you around today?"

"What brings me around any day?" countered Josh.

"Lumenaria," answered Ned astutely.

"I was thinking about that story you told me last week when you and Luther were in the mines in the Endless Rise," said Josh. "You were telling me about eternium."

"Right, well, eternium is one of the metals that archon armor is made out of," explained Ned. "It's refined from raw form and infused with Essence and various crystals that you can find in the mines. It's extremely strong and increases the wearer's power greatly."

"Yeah," said Josh, nodding. "Tell me more about those crystals."

"The ones from the mines?" asked Ned. "My brother could tell you more about them than I could, but from what I understand, Essence crystallizes in those mines. You can even find rocks with veins of solid Essence running through them, so as you can imagine the crystals have quite a bit of value."

"Right," said Josh, thinking deeply.

"Why do you ask?"

"Do you remember how there was the captain of the fishing boat who was taking me across the channel?"

"Of course."

"I was wondering if you'd ever seen or met him while you were in Lumenaria," said Josh. "Or if you knew where he might've got one of those crystals."

"I didn't recognize the name or the face when I saw it in the paper," replied Ned, shaking his head. "Lumenaria isn't the only province with Essence, you know."

"You think maybe he wound up in one of the other provinces?" asked Josh.

"As I'm sure you've heard many times by now, Mr. Cooper, just about anything is possible in this universe."

"Yeah."

"Was there anything else?"

"I know I'm trying to get in shape, but I think the start of summer merits a Mars bar, don't you?"

"If you're spending money in my shop, anything you want is merited," said Ned, winking.

"I'll see you on Monday for dinner, then?" asked Josh, walking over to the door once he'd paid.

"Of course," replied the shopkeeper, smiling warmly.

Josh nodded in thanks and stepped outside. The sun was casting a warm, yellowish glow on the pavement. He looked up at the sky and wondered what had happened to the man who showed him kindness and hospitality on that night over two months ago.

Making up his mind in an instant, he pulled his mobile phone out of his pocket and dialed a number.

"Hello?" came the feminine voice on the other end.

"Hey, Mom, it's me."

"Oh, hello Joshua. What's going on?"

"I just wanted to let you know that I'm not going to be home for dinner tonight," he said.

"Where are you going?" she asked worriedly.

"I just have some business I need to take care of," he replied. "I promise it's perfectly safe."

"Joshua…"

"Mom, please just trust me."

The other line was silent for a few seconds before he heard a sigh.

"Be lucky, Joshua. Please just call if there's a problem."

"I will," he said, chuckling. "I'll see you later tonight."

"Bye, luv."

He hung up the phone, pleasantly surprised at the newfound trust with his parents. Without hesitating, he turned right, walking toward the bus stop.

It was nearly eight by the time he finally arrived in Southampton, the bus dropping him off at the port just like it had the last time. He walked over to where the *Iron Princess* had been moored, but as he expected, the water next to the pier was vacant.

Frowning, he looked around and saw the familiar MCCLEARY'S PUB AND GRILL sign flickering in the twilight. He headed over and pulled the door open, the same musty, dim atmosphere greeting his senses.

"Excuse me?" he asked, walking over to the bartender.

"Hey, I remember you," said the man, polishing a glass. "You're that kid who went missing a couple months ago. You were talkin' with Tom."

"Right," said Josh with a nod, pleased that the man remembered him. "I was actually wondering if you knew where he lived."

"Righ' down the street," replied the barkeep. "I can't recall which building, but he had an apartment about a block from here. Just take a left when you get outside."

"Thanks," said Josh with a grateful smile.

He exited the pub and headed left down the sidewalk. There were five apartment buildings in the next two blocks, and he didn't see Thomas Patrey listed as a resident in any of the first three.

He reached the stoop of the fourth building and glanced at the names next to the doorbells. He was about to turn away and go to the fifth when he saw TOM P. listed next to the buzzer marked 3A.

"Are you lost, son?"

Josh turned and saw an older woman carrying a bag of groceries standing behind him, obviously waiting to get inside.

"I'm sorry," he apologized, stepping out of the way.

"It's perfectly all right, dear," she replied, getting her key out and opening the door.

"I don't mean to intrude, but did Thomas Patrey live here?" he asked.

"He did," answered the woman with a nod. "Are you a friend?"

"Something like that."

"I'm sorry to tell you, but he went missing a couple months ago. No one's seen him since."

"I heard. I was just trying to find out more." The woman went to remove her key from the door and fumbled the bag slightly. Josh saw the groceries start to slip and deftly managed to catch the bag before it spilled onto the stoop.

"Oh my," she said, shaking her head. "Thank you so much."

"Not at all," he said, smiling warmly. "Let me carry this up for you."

"You don't mind? I've become terribly clumsy over the years."

"Of course not," said Josh, following the lady inside.

"My name's Martha," said the woman as they climbed the stairs to the third floor.

"I'm Joshua," he replied.

"Are…are you the boy who went missing with Tom?" she asked, staring at him carefully.

"Yeah," he admitted, rubbing the back of his neck with his free hand. "I always wondered what happened to him. He was really nice to me and I feel sort of responsible."

"Nonsense," dismissed Martha, shaking her head. "Tom would never have held you responsible for a freak storm like that."

"I know, but we were out there because he offered to take me."

"If he offered, then that was his business," she said as they reached the landing on the third floor. "You don't need to feel responsible at all for it. Good luck in your search," she said, smiling warmly as Josh handed her the groceries.

She left him on the landing and walked down the hall. He was about to turn back down the stairs when he saw a door that had a brass 3A nailed into it.

Determined to see if he could find any clues, he looked around to make sure he was alone before closing his hand around the doorknob. He felt the slight warmth of Essence form on his fingertips and he pushed it into the lock, hearing it click open a moment later. Taking one more quick glance down the hall, he opened the door and slipped inside.

The flat was small and cozy, more than enough for one man. There was a couch and television in the living room, a small kitchen with a counter that separated the two rooms, and two doors, one for the bedroom, the other most likely for the bathroom.

Instinctively, Josh headed for the bathroom. He opened the door and flicked the light switch on. The room was painted an ugly shade of green, the floor tiles were cracking and the shower curtain was dirty.

One thing caught Josh's eye, though. Hanging above the toilet was a painting of a large, open-air bath with the familiar glimmering grains of Essence scattered all around it.

He walked over to the artwork and stared up in awe at a place he'd never heard about, much less seen while in Lumenaria. Chuckling, he looked down and his eyes widened when he saw a small envelope sitting on the top of the toilet addressed in neat print: TO JOSHUA.

"No way," he whispered to himself, picking up the envelope and turning it over. There was a wax seal on the back of a sword crossed by two elegant feathers. Opening it, he pulled out the paper inside and read.

Joshua,

If you're reading this letter, you've undoubtedly made it home safe and sound, and for that I'm grateful. If it were up to me, I never would've forced you into a world so far away from your own, but I thought it the only way to save our lives.

You need not worry about me, I'm back in my home, and I don't plan on returning to England anytime soon. I hope, no matter what your journey consisted of, that you've found what you're looking for.

If you ever find yourself returning to my land, I hope you'll look me up. If not, may you live out your life in the best luxury and happiness that is known to man.

Your friend,

Tom P.

Josh stared at the letter in awe. He read it three more times just to make sure he wasn't daydreaming, but there was no doubt about its contents or where it came from.

He pocketed the envelope and turned the light off in the bathroom, giving the painting one more glance before closing the door. He walked through the sitting room to the entrance of the flat and smiled to himself before leaving.

After Josh returned to Salisbury that night, thoughts of Lumenaria were always at the forefront of his mind. He wondered what became of the friends he made, of the people he'd helped save, and of Thomas, who was responsible for getting him there in the first place. He decided that someday he'd have to find a way back, if for no other reason than to find Tom and thank him for the adventure.

And as it turned out, the wish that Josh had expressed to Arya came true.

After his return, his parents rarely fought. Whether it was because they'd nearly lost their only child, or because they realized they all needed each other, or because the small figurine of a horse that Arya had given him—which was infused with a power that could do great and wonderful things—was sitting on his desk, Josh never found out. He finally had the family he'd always wanted, and nothing else mattered.

It didn't, however, stop him from gazing up into the sky at night every once in a while with a smile, wondering if any of the tiny specks of light in the heavens was the one he'd remember for the rest of his life.

CPSIA information can be obtained
at www.ICGtesting.com
Printed in the USA
BVHW031411240719
554260BV00001B/22/P

9 781467 956604